**Praise for**

# carly

"Fast-paced and fabulously fun, Carly Phillips entertains with witty dialogue and delightful characters."
—*New York Times* bestselling author Rachel Gibson

"In this launch of a new trilogy, Phillips does what she does best: deliver stories that are light but not silly, with believable characters and plots that flow into satisfying stories. Fans will be stalking stores to get all three of these."
—*Romantic Times BOOKreviews*, 4 1/2 stars, on *Lucky Charm*

"*Lucky Charm* kicks off Carly Phillips' new series with pizzazz. The protagonists are attractive, the romance is h-o-t, and the fantastic supporting characters make the pages seem to turn by themselves."
—Betty Cox, *ReaderToReader.com*

"*Cross My Heart* engages readers with a light and perky story that will absorb you from start to finish.... You'll be smiling while you read the book, and grinning when you finish."
—Lezlie Patterson, *MCT News Service*

"Phillips has penned a charming, fast-paced contemporary romp."
—*Booklist* on *Hot Item*

"A great summer read that should not be missed."
—*BookReporter.com* on *Hot Item*

"A sassy treat full of titillating twists sure to ring your (wedding) bell."
—*Playgirl* on *The Bachelor*

"A titillating read...on a scale of one to five: a high five for fun, ease of reading and sex—actually I would've given it a six for sex if I could have."
—Kelly Ripa on *The Bachelor*

# carly
# phillips

lucky*break*

**HQN**™

Recycling programs
for this product may
not exist in your area.

ISBN-13: 978-0-373-77401-2

LUCKY BREAK

www.HQNBooks.com

**Printed in U.S.A.**

Dear Reader,

I am so excited for you to read *Lucky Break,* the final installment in my trilogy about the sexy, charismatic Corwin cousins, modern men who are dogged by a centuries-old family curse. According to legend, any Corwin man who falls in love is destined to lose his love and his fortune. Now it's Jason Corwin's turn!

Jason knows he should resist his attraction to Lauren Perkins, but they have a past—and after a reunion that includes one night of mind-blowing passion, he can't bring himself to stay away. How will the curse, placed by one of Lauren's ancestors, affect this couple?

I can't wait for you to find out! If you missed the other books in this series, Derek's story, *Lucky Charm,* and Mike's story, *Lucky Streak,* are in stores now.

Visit www.carlyphillips.com for release dates and so much more. You can write to me at: P.O. Box 483, Purchase, NY 10577 or e-mail carly@carlyphillips.com.

As always, thank you for buying my books, and happy reading!

Best wishes,

Carly Phillips

To my friends—each and every one of you serve a different purpose in my life, but I love you all!

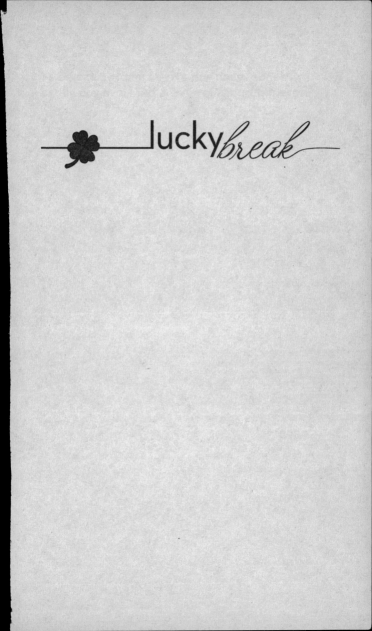

# INTRODUCTION

In the late nineteenth century, in the small village of Stewart, Massachusetts, 1.5 miles west of Salem, site of the now infamous Witch Trials, fear of curses and witchcraft ran rampant. During this time, William Corwin fell in love and eloped with a woman who was already betrothed to another. The man William wronged, Martin Perkins, was the oldest son of the wealthy Perkins family from the neighboring village of the same name. To William Corwin's misfortune, Martin's mother, Mary Perkins, was a witch.

She immediately sought revenge on her son's behalf with this curse: Any Corwin male who falls in love will be destined to lose his love and his fortune.

No male Corwin since has walked away unscathed....

# CHAPTER ONE

LAUREN PERKINS'S red Porsche looked as out of place in the parking lot of the Bricksville Correctional Institution's psychiatric ward as it did in Perkins, Massachusetts, the small town her family had founded. She pulled into a spot that might as well have had her name on it, she was here so often. She waved to the guard and walked to the old building where her sister was being held, bypassing the construction site of a new wing. After six months, she recognized some of the men in hard hats, and as usual, a select few eyed Lauren and her car with a sleazy combination of envy and lust. The only thing missing was catcalls, but since the actual prison was only a few hundred yards away, she assumed it kept them on their best behavior.

Lauren stopped short of flipping the men the bird. She had held her own in Third World countries and in the Garment Center of Manhattan. Not much could make her uneasy, but this place did, and she hated like hell having to be here.

Thanks to her sister Mary Beth and her antics, Lauren had no choice. She consoled herself with the promise that her visit to the prison would be like her trip to her grandmother's home.

Short and to the point.

Paris was waiting and nothing was going to keep her from being there in person when her dress designs debuted under the Galliano label. She'd sold the designs, so now she was free for the few weeks she needed to restore her grandmother's old Victorian into salable condition. Then she would fly to Paris and watch the fashion show in person. And pray her designs succeeded beyond her wildest dreams.

Haute Couture Fashion Week in Paris was every designer's goal and Lauren had been gearing herself up for this for the past five years. After taking fashion classes in the city, working odd jobs to pay for them, and designing at night, she'd earned this chance. Though she was torn between her good fortune and her sister's situation, there wasn't anything else she could do for Beth that she wasn't already doing.

She'd had to uproot herself in order to focus on her grandmother's house because, as usual, her parents felt their humanitarian efforts were more important than Lauren's *materialistic pursuits*. Never mind that those pursuits had amounted to a successful career.

Her parents had never understood why Lauren and Beth hadn't shared their calling. Not even Beth's breakdown had caused them to put their work helping others on hold. They'd only visited their daughter, diagnosed as "unresponsive" by her doctors, once since she'd been incarcerated for arson, among other charges.

Lauren still couldn't understand her sister's actions. For reasons trapped in Beth's mind, she'd attempted to burn down a building full of innocent people about a year ago. According to Beth's own hysterical explanation, the police claimed that she'd been attempting to hang on to the Perkins family's declining power. Since many townspeople had come forward with tales of how her now deceased grandmother, the longtime mayor, had consolidated her power using blackmail and other forms of fear and manipulation, it wasn't a stretch to think Beth, her grandmother's loyal assistant, had followed in her footsteps.

Lauren had had no idea how mentally ill her sister had become and felt guilty that she'd been too busy with her own life to notice. As for her grandmother's mental state prior to her death, Lauren didn't have a clue. Except for occasional visits to her sister, Lauren hadn't had a relationship with the older woman in years.

Lauren did know firsthand about her grandmother's ability to control and manipulate. But Mary Perkins was gone, having passed away in the aftermath of Beth's arson attempt. She'd had a fatal heart attack while awaiting trial for her own crimes. And Beth continued to stare at the walls here in Psych Central.

Lauren visited her sister at least once a month, more often when she could. Revolving her life around Beth's wasn't much different from their childhood. Lauren had always taken care of her younger sister. Older by five years, she had been Beth's mother, father and authority figure as they grew up, because their parents had no time for them. Though the sisters were close back then, Beth had still been a handful. Even at twenty-seven years old, Lauren was still cleaning up her sister's messes.

She quickly crossed the parking lot and proceeded to the first checkpoint. Lauren hated the prison grounds. Even though Beth was in a separate building from the prison itself, Lauren detested the depressing psychiatric ward. But she hoped that by visiting Beth and keeping her aware of the outside world, her sister would recover faster.

Today Beth sat upright instead of lying in bed, but nothing else had changed. Before her breakdown, Beth had been a stickler for perfection, if not fashion—that was Lauren's forte and orange had always been her favorite color. But after seeing her sister in the fluorescent prison hue back when she'd originally been processed, Lauren had pulled the color from her portfolio. Beth now wore institutional gray with bold writing on the back, an outfit that would have horrified their grandmother. Something Lauren never mentioned to Beth.

Why upset her sister, who'd eagerly earned Mary Perkins's approval in a way Lauren never had. While Beth had pleased Mary, Lauren's one teenage *indiscretion* had isolated her from her grandmother. Lauren didn't care. That summer with Jason Corwin had been worth risking her grandmother's wrath.

Since Beth remained docile, she was never handcuffed for their visits, although guards patrolled the hall outside the room and a nurse regularly checked in.

"Hi, Beth. How are you today?" Lauren asked in a cheery voice.

No reply, not that Lauren had expected one.

Beth stared straight ahead, her hair hanging in

her face. The once perfect, if conservative, bob had grown out, leaving her looking unkempt. The gray outfit didn't help her pale skin. Sometimes Lauren wondered if holding a mirror to her sister's face would shock her out of her unresponsive state.

Lauren cleared her throat. Trying not to fidget, she placed her hands in her lap. "Remember last week I told you I'd be staying at Grandma's house? Well, I've been in for a couple of days and I'll stay there until closing on December first."

Beth's eyelashes fluttered up and down.

Lauren had no way of knowing what her sister heard or understood. The prison psychiatrist encouraged Lauren to talk to Beth about the familiar and about Lauren's life. As if Beth were fine. So she chattered away, feeling like an idiot talking to herself but doing it anyway.

"As long as I get the house into what the buyers consider move-in condition, the closing will go off without a hitch." Afterward, she'd have two weeks to return to New York and get herself packed and ready for Paris.

Assuming she closed. The offer she had was conditional and the deadline was only four short weeks away. The renovation wouldn't be as easy a task as she'd first hoped. The house had been empty for the past year, held up in probate. On

Lauren's arrival she'd discovered it was in worse condition than she'd anticipated. It seemed her grandmother had been more concerned with outward appearances, putting money into superficial aesthetics without fixing the structural problems that came with age. Between the general dilapidated condition, the holes in the walls from vandals or pranksters, and the old pipes and plumbing, Lauren's limited budget would be stretched. She hoped to find a contractor who was hurting enough to take on her project at a reasonable price.

She drew a deep breath and forged on. "The broker said the potential buyers are a nice family. They're moving from overseas and have no time to do the renovating themselves. In this market, I'm lucky to have them interested. I have to finish the repairs in the next month or they won't take possession and then what are the chances I'll ever find another buyer?"

A feeling of déjà vu overtook her and Lauren suspected she'd told Beth the same thing last week. But who knew? Beth loved her grandmother's old house. If there had been money left in the estate after the debts and her grandmother's lawyer bills, Lauren knew Beth would have wanted to keep the place, but that wasn't possible. There was no alternative now but to sell. By keeping Beth aware of the situation, Lauren hoped to trigger something inside her sister's mind.

Suddenly, the sound of hammering and sawing came from right outside Beth's window and Lauren tensed.

"Not again." For the last six months, Lauren's visits had been disturbed by construction of the new wing.

Beth's eyes flashed and a tick seemed to pull at one side of her mouth.

She was obviously upset and Lauren didn't blame her. The noise level was hard to take and Lauren didn't see how patients could heal in this environment, let alone hear themselves think.

She patted her sister's hand. "Let's try to ignore the noise," she said, pointing to the barred window and the construction beyond. No sooner had she spoken than drilling suddenly accompanied the hammering. Beth, who already seemed agitated, flushed and her eyes widened. Even Lauren was getting a headache.

"Excuse me," Lauren said to the nurse who had come in earlier, shuffling papers and making notations on her chart. "Isn't there anything you can do about the noise? It's upsetting my sister."

The young woman shook her head. "I'm sorry, but until they finish there's nothing we can do."

Lauren frowned. "I know. They aren't patients in a private facility. They're prisoners living on the state's dollar and taxpayers' dime, so let them suffer."

The nurse placed a comforting hand on Lauren's shoulder. "If it's any consolation, she normally doesn't seem to mind the noise."

"I suppose I ought to be grateful she's reacting at all." At the thought, Lauren rose from her chair. "Do you think it's a sign?" she asked, excited at the prospect of seeing some change in her sister's condition.

Again, the nurse shook her head. "This is just a normal reaction. Try not to get your hopes up." Her voice was kind.

Lauren exhaled hard and settled back into her seat.

As she studied her silent sister, she wondered whether even Beth thought that the price of believing in the Corwin Curse to its destructive conclusion had been worth the price she'd paid.

*The Corwin Curse.*

At best, Lauren thought it was a bedtime story her grandmother liked to tell. At worst, she figured it was the Perkins family's way to instill a sense of self-importance in its future generations.

To hear her grandmother tell it, the first Mary Perkins, an ancestor from the Salem Witch Trial days, had placed a curse on William Corwin and all of his male descendants in retribution for eloping with her son's fiancée. All Corwin men who fell in love were doomed to lose their love and their fortune. Whether by coincidence or circumstance, the curse had held true for the male descendants down the Corwin line. Yet she'd heard from her friend Sharon that Jason Corwin's two male cousins were currently married and attempting to buck the curse.

More power to them, Lauren thought.

As for herself, she hadn't believed in the curse at seventeen, when she'd met and fallen for Jason during a summer visit to her grandmother's. But Mary Perkins had, and when she'd read Lauren's diary entries about sneaking out to see Jason, she'd launched into a tirade Lauren would never forget. She'd forbidden Lauren to see that Corwin boy ever again and sent her back to her parents in Sierra Leone as quickly as possible.

Lauren had lost her grandmother's trust and approval from that day on and she'd never gained it back. Not that she'd ever really tried. She'd been too angry at her banishment.

She hadn't given up on Jason. She'd written him more than a few times but she'd never heard back. Once she'd turned eighteen, she'd come back to the States only to find Jason had gone off to follow his dreams of winning gold in Olympic snowboarding.

He hadn't contacted her or even let her know where he'd gone. She'd been devastated as only a teenage girl could be. They'd shared their hopes for a future and she'd believed they would find a way to be together one day. Obviously that summer had meant more to her than to him. He'd forgotten about her, so she'd headed to New York to create some dreams of her own.

Lauren forced her mind away from the past and refocused on her sister. She only had a handful of visits left before leaving for Paris and she wanted to make the most of them.

So she returned to her monologue. "Anyway, as I was saying, Grandma's house is a real mess. The windows are broken—probably some kids with nothing better to do than vandalize the old place for fun." Or payback for Beth's arson escapade, but Lauren kept that notion to herself. "But I'll get it cleaned up in no time."

Beth didn't reply, of course.

Lauren glanced around and suddenly felt claustrophobic. A pang of guilt followed at the realization that Beth was incarcerated here without the option to leave.

"Don't worry, Beth. Even when I'm in Paris, I'll be in touch with your lawyer. I'm still trying to get you out of here."

The lawyer was working hard to ensure Beth's case was appealed. Beth had spent the first months after her arrest in a regular hospital being evaluated by both state and her own defense psychiatrists. She'd been declared unfit to stand trial and placed in this prison psych ward for the criminally insane until such time as she was deemed fit.

Beth's lawyer was appealing her placement here, trying to have her moved to a mental hospital where she could get better treatment and eventually be released. To whom and to what, Lauren didn't want to imagine. In truth, the lawyer had said the entire scenario was a long shot but Lauren wasn't giving up hope.

Paying the lawyer's fees had put a strain on Lauren's once comfortable savings. She'd bought the pre-owned Porsche before Beth's arrest with the money she'd obtained from selling her designs to Galliano. The Porsche was proof that dreams did come true. That hard work, pounding the pavement, believing in herself paid off.

Sure she could sell it, but she'd worked hard for the convertible and she loved it. Loved that every time she drove the car, the rush of the engine reminded her of the euphoria of her first big success. She wasn't willing to sell the car—or that feeling—for Beth or for anyone.

If her runway show in Paris was a hit, her designs would be in demand and money would no longer be an issue. But right now, she had to focus on the renovation. Another blow to her savings.

She glanced at her sister, the cause of this mess. Trying not to show her dueling anger and frustration, Lauren covered Beth's hand with her own.

"I have to go, but I'll be back soon." She rose and kissed her sister's cheek.

As she walked out, Lauren had the weird sensation her sister's gaze was following her, watching her as she headed for her life outside the prison walls.

THE PORSCHE BOXSTER, engine revving, zoomed past the open field in a flash of fire and blinding speed. The convertible—top down, unusual for this time of year—dazzled for an instant before disappearing in a screeching cloud of dust. The vibrant red sports car caused a commotion in Stewart, Massachusetts, a sedate New England town consumed with getting ready for tonight's Annual Fall Festival, always held the weekend before Halloween.

Jason Corwin glanced toward the heavy thrumming sound. His heart rate picked up speed, much as it had before a snowboarding race, until he deliberately clamped down on the unwanted reminder of his previous life. A life where he'd had the more expensive Carrera. A life of excitement and a constant rush of adrenaline through his veins. A life that was over, he harshly reminded himself before turning back to the more mundane task of building a tarot card booth for tonight's big event.

"I wonder who could be so determined to make an entrance," Clara Deveaux pondered aloud.

"Couldn't tell you." Jason hammered the last nail into the sign for Clara's booth.

But considering the brightly colored exterior of the car and the deliberate way the engine had been revved up full throttle, the driver had definitely wanted people to notice.

"I'm sure we'll find out soon enough," Clara said. "So are you almost finished?"

He nodded. "As a matter of fact, I am." He'd agreed to help with setup for the festival, but since Clara was a friend of the family, Jason had also helped to build and decorate her booth and bring over supplies.

As owner of Crescent Moon, a New Age Wiccan gift shop she'd recently relocated to Stewart, Clara was sure to be a success, her booth filled with people who wanted their future told. After all, this town believed in spells and curses. As a Corwin male, direct descendant of William Corwin and, some might say, recipient of the infamous Corwin Curse, Jason wanted nothing to do with witchcraft.

But Clara insisted on doing a tarot reading for him as thanks for all his hard work. And Clara didn't take no for an answer.

"Great!" She seated herself in front of him and pulled out an oversize deck of cards. "Shuffle." Her bangle bracelets clinked against one another as she handed him the deck.

With a feigned groan, he did as she asked, shuffling under her watchful eye.

After four months in a relationship with his uncle Edward that no one in the family could define, Clara was obviously here to stay. Jason liked the woman. It was her do-gooder tendencies that drove him nuts. Clara, like Gabrielle and Amber, his cousins' wives, pushed and prodded him to get out of his present funk.

He could understand they were sick of his attitude. He was pretty sick of it himself, which was why he'd humor her and let her read his cards.

He handed the deck back to her.

"This deck is my personal favorite," she said as she turned over one card. "Knight of Pentacles reversed. You're a hard worker and can take care of yourself, but something recently happened to turn your world upside down."

Jason held back a snort. The whole town knew his goal of winning Snowboarding gold in the winter Olympics had gone south after he'd tested positive for steroids at the World Championships. He'd never touched an illegal substance in his life, but the IOC had banned him from competition for two years. His appeals had been denied, leaving him out of the upcoming 2010 Olympics. With no sponsors to support him, he'd lost the income that enabled him to practice and compete.

Unable to prove his innocence and the fact that he'd been drugged, Jason had no choice but to concede defeat. He'd maintain his innocence forever, but snowboarding was in his past. The winter Olympics this February in Vancouver would take place without him.

"I see that skepticism," Clara chided. She waved her arm and the sleeve of her colorful caftan created a breeze of its own.

"You have to admit, you're not telling me anything you don't already know."

With a smile, Clara turned over another card. "Crossing card is what is affecting you. Three of Cups, a betrayal of the heart."

Jason's thoughts immediately turned to Kristina Marino, the woman who'd set him up for the fall.

He'd met her six months before his failed doping test and they'd become inseparable. Jason, who usually had a hard time sustaining a relationship because few women understood or respected his dedication to the sport, had finally found someone who didn't resent the time his training required. Or so he'd thought. In reality, she'd been in love with his main competitor, Rusty Small, but she'd hidden the connection and seduced Jason, gradually adding a banned ingredient into the power shakes he consumed daily.

Kristina had confirmed Jason's hunch in person after Rusty dumped her for someone else. She'd arrived on his doorstep last month to clear her conscience. Too little, too late, and she was still completely unwilling to clear his name by confessing. Jason was left with being seen as yet another athlete proclaiming his innocence to a disbelieving world.

"You're going to have to do better, Clara." Jason teased her, but she wasn't deterred.

"Bottom card." She turned it over.

Jason didn't pay much attention as she spoke about his past and what had brought him to this point in life.

"To the left." She revealed another card. "Your

recent past. Knight of Cups upright. You need to find your meaning again. Your holy grail, if you will. You are committed to seeking what you need for yourself," she said.

"Care to elaborate?" he asked.

Clara smoothed her jet-black hair. "Of course not. Only you can decide what it is you need."

"Of course."

Ignoring his sarcasm, she moved on. "Card above. What is within your reach. Queen of Wands." Her voice rose in excitement. "She's a passionate woman, impulsive, impish."

Jason let out a chuckle, which sounded rusty even to him. Had it really been that long since he'd had a genuine laugh? "Come on, Clara. Even if I were looking, which I'm not, every woman in town knows to steer clear of a Corwin man."

Not that it mattered. Jason hadn't been interested in any woman since Kristina. She'd soured him on females for a good long while. Although he had to admit celibacy wasn't working for him.

"You don't see me running away from the right Corwin man, do you?" Clara glanced at him through guileless eyes.

"You're different." Clara and Edward had a history. She seemed to be the only one capable of drawing his reclusive uncle out of his shell.

The medications his uncle had been put on a few months ago had finally taken effect, and Edward Corwin, formerly the town recluse, had slowly begun to venture out into the world again. He was wary but trying to rebuild his life. Trying to overcome decades of ingrained fear of the Corwin Curse, which had ravaged his life. But the one thing that hadn't changed was his unwillingness to commit to Clara Deveaux. Edward was scared. Clara refused to give up on the stubborn old coot.

She grinned. "I'm no different than any woman in love. Now let's continue. Card to the near right. High Priestess. Woman of mystery, as you can see by the red mask covering her eyes."

He immediately thought of the red Porsche whizzing through town.

"She represents finding things within yourself instead of looking to the outside world. Interesting we'd get the lady in the mask when tonight's festival is a masked event."

He rolled his eyes. "I haven't celebrated Halloween in years."

Clara eyed him with amusement. "A red rose speaks of a love that awaits passionate expression. Red itself is the color of consummation, raging desire and craving passion."

He felt a heated flush rise to his face. "Come on. You're embarrassing me."

She grinned. "Bottom of the column of four, how others see you." She turned the card. "King of Pentacles. You see yourself as a failure, the outside world sees someone in control, in charge, capable of taking care of others. Next is the card of hope and fear." She revealed the next card. "Ace of Cups reversed. You have no hope of love. You fear being alone forever, viewing the cup as half empty instead of half full." Her words held a hint of sadness and chiding, as if she wanted him to change.

How could he? Jason's stomach constricted at the accurate description. A lifetime of work and dreams had ended with one urine test. He'd lost everything in an instant.

"Third card in this row. Your obstacle. Ten of Pentacles. The card of community fulfillment. In order to get to your outcome, you need to rejoin the community on all levels." She lifted her eyes from the cards set out on the table and met his gaze. "Stop hiding behind your past."

He decided not to argue. There was no point.

"Last card."

He found himself relieved that his torture was almost at an end. Clara meant well but all her hocus-pocus had accomplished was to make him more aware of his failures and how he'd allowed one mistake to control his life for too long. He was tired of being grumpy and miserable all the time.

He'd returned to Stewart and set up a contracting business. It was an obvious choice. To raise money for snowboarding, he'd worked for his father and Uncle Hank's electrical and contracting business, so the work was familiar. But instead of enjoying it, he'd been going through the motions.

Maybe the cards were right, he thought wryly. Maybe it was time to put the past behind him and move on. At the very least he needed to get rid of some pent-up sexual frustration.

"Ready?" Clara asked.

He nodded, wanting this over. "What the hell. Show it to me."

She revealed the final card. "Ten of Cups." A large smile spread over Clara's face. "Do you see the white picket fence?" She splayed her hands in front of her. "This goes perfectly with the red mask, the ultimate expression of romantic and abiding love." She sighed on the last word. "Do you know what this means?"

"No, but I'm sure you're going to tell me."

"The cards show you have the potential for happily ever after, Jason." She smiled.

Those words conjured up another time.

Another place.

Another woman.

He'd been eighteen years old, working and trying to save money to fund his snowboarding. She'd been seventeen and visiting for the summer. He was a Corwin. She was a Perkins. She'd had some starry-eyed notion of them running off together. He'd had selfish dreams of Olympic gold that didn't have room for anyone else.

Even if he sometimes wished they had.

He often wondered what would have happened if her grandmother hadn't sent her packing. If he'd gone looking for her once he'd had enough cash. But he hadn't. He'd used the money to build a name for himself. Hire a coach. Chase a dream that wasn't meant to be.

"What are you thinking about?" Clara asked, interrupting his thoughts.

"About how you should give me a break." He'd humored her up until now, but she was bordering on delusional if she thought she could convince him he was headed for a fairy-tale ending.

He hadn't thought about Lauren in years. When her family had fallen apart a year ago, he'd been far from home, immersed in practice, and she hadn't been around since he'd come back. The rumor mill had her in New York City, far from the Perkins family mess. He couldn't blame her there.

"I don't need to give you anything." Clara's voice broke into his thoughts. "The cards say it all." She began sweeping the deck together, unfazed by his skepticism.

"Next thing you'll be telling me is that the woman I'll meet will be wearing a red mask."

Clara tapped the cards to even them out. "You said it, I didn't."

He didn't want to insult her so he remained silent, but the facts remained. If a man's last name was Corwin, it wasn't easy getting laid in Jason's hometown, never mind finding someone to settle down with.

He bent to pick up his extra equipment and tossed the items into his tool chest.

"You weren't always so cynical," Clara said.

Jason raised an eyebrow. "How can you be so sure?" Although he liked and respected her, he couldn't help challenging her so-called intuition. And he knew from previous exchanges, she enjoyed a challenge.

Clara merely shook her head. "I just know you were different before. Just like you'll be different after."

He knew he'd regret asking, but he did anyway. "After what?"

"After *she* rocks your world."

DESPITE THE COOL FALL temperatures, Lauren drove back to her grandmother's house from the prison with the convertible top down. After being in the small room with her sister, she needed the fresh air, open spaces and wind blowing on her face.

As she always did after one of these visits, she searched for something to focus on that didn't involve her sister, grandmother, the jail, or the damn Corwin Curse. Paris and her upcoming show consumed her thoughts for the better part of an hour until she came to the outskirts of town and saw the sign for the fall festival.

An annual event, the masquerade ball was always held in time for Halloween. The party sounded like fun. She remembered hearing about the festival from Jason. Back then he'd wished she could stick around long enough to go with him. Well, it looked like she was going to get her chance. Years too late. And she wouldn't exactly be attending *with* him.

But he might be there, a small voice in her head whispered. She'd heard he was back in town from her one friend here. Lauren and Sharon Merchant, now Sharon Stern, wife of the current mayor of Perkins, had met during Lauren's summer visits to her grandmother's, and they'd kept in touch over the years.

Sharon was the only person she'd confided in

about her relationship with Jason Corwin. She hadn't trusted her sister, knowing Beth would run off to tell their grandmother that Lauren was consorting with the enemy. Sharon had been understanding then and she'd been understanding years later. Lauren's grandmother and sister had blackmailed Sharon in order to try to prevent her husband, Richard, from becoming mayor, so Lauren considered herself lucky her friend didn't extend a grudge toward Lauren by default.

Sharon would be there tonight and Lauren could surprise her by showing up. Behind a mask, of course. She'd rather observe without outing herself. The executor of her grandmother's will told her the townspeople wouldn't welcome her with open arms. Lauren could handle their disdain with her head held high. *She* hadn't hurt anyone and she didn't approve of her family's behavior. Still, remaining anonymous while she took the temperature of the town, so to speak, appealed to her.

Especially if she ran into Jason. Her stomach curled deliciously and with nervous anticipation at the thought of seeing him again. Ten years was a long time and he probably wouldn't recognize her behind a mask. She remembered him telling her no self-respecting man would wear a mask, so she'd have the opportunity to watch and observe him with anonymity.

Yes, she thought, a night out was exactly what she needed to put the depressing prison visit behind her.

Once back at the house, she searched through an old trunk in her grandmother's attic, picking through feathers, lace and masks. She discarded the orange mask for obvious reasons and bypassed the boring blue one in search of the perfect color.

Suddenly, she found what she was looking for. The mask that called to her. The boldest color. The one destined to make an impact.

A red mask to match her red car.

## CHAPTER TWO

JASON MILLED around the festival grounds, a stretch of farmland that had been donated to the town and dedicated as a park. Although this was an event he'd enjoyed as a kid, tonight he was uncharacteristically on edge and Clara's prediction was to blame.

Not that he believed in tarot readings.

Yet, as he smiled at people without stopping to make conversation, the uneasy feeling remained. The fact that most wore masks didn't help. Nor did the sheer volume of people. Almost the entire town had turned out for the evening.

"Jason, no mask? I'm disappointed." Gabrielle, his cousin Derek's wife, zeroed in on him, pink feathers covering her face.

If her long chestnut hair wasn't a giveaway to her identity, her trademark stiletto heels were. His cousin was one lucky son of a bitch, but he deserved good fortune. Derek had suffered plenty before finally reclaiming his high school sweet-heart and the love and family he was meant to have. As the oldest of the Corwin cousins, Derek had set a stoic example for Jason and Mike to follow. Each had held out on relationships for a long time before succumbing. As for Mike, despite a rocky start, he and his wife Amber seemed to be going strong.

Jason, on the other hand, was finished with women for anything but sex—and that was something he hadn't had in too damn long. Five months to be exact. But now he was open to the possibility. He wasn't desperate, never had been, and not even a self-imposed dry spell would change that. He just knew better than to expect to find someone from around here. Predictions be damned, he was a Corwin and therefore a realist.

"Jason?" Gabrielle repeated. "I asked you what happened to your mask?"

He refocused his attention on his cousin's wife. "No self-respecting man would wear one of those things."

"He's got a point," Derek said, joining them. He wasn't sporting a mask, either.

"You two are just no fun." Gabrielle let out a long-suffering sigh and placed her hand over her rounded stomach.

"What's wrong? Are you okay?" Derek asked, covering her hand with his.

"I breathed loudly," she said, exasperated. "I didn't moan in pain!"

Jason laughed at his cousin's reaction.

Ever since their announcement of Gabrielle's pregnancy, Derek had been wired. Jason didn't blame him. Their first try had ended in miscarriage and the damn Corwin Curse hung over their heads.

Still, Jason couldn't help but lighten the mood. "Derek, it's going to be a long nine months if you keep this up."

"Only five more to go," he said, before glancing at his wife. "I'm sorry, but—"

She shook her head. "Don't apologize. I understand. I just wish you'd relax and enjoy this as much as I am. The doctor swore the last time was a fluke, and I'm determined to believe him."

Derek wrapped his arm around her waist and kissed her on the lips.

Jason tried not to roll his eyes. It was time he made himself scarce. "Excuse me. I think I'm going to refill my beer. This one's getting warm." Leaving his cousin alone with his wife, he turned and started across the field.

Catching sight of his father, Thomas, Jason

headed his way. "Hi, Dad." Another Corwin man without a mask.

"I'm so glad you decided to join the party," Thomas said.

"I could say the same to you." Jason eyed his father warily.

Wearing dark pressed chinos and a white buttoned shirt, he was perfectly dressed. Typical Thomas, showing the outside world all was well, no matter what turmoil was going on inside. "Is Uncle Edward here?" Jason asked.

"He's supposed to be." Thomas glanced over his son's shoulder. "I haven't seen him yet."

"He's coming with Clara, isn't he? That's who you're looking around for."

Thomas had been attracted to Clara from the moment they'd met, and thanks to Corwin history, Jason was worried his father would somehow end up with his uncle Edward's woman.

Thomas shook his head. "No. I promised I'd steer clear and let those two make their way back to each other," he said, sounding sincere.

"Or not?" Jason guessed. "Come on, Dad. Are you waiting for Uncle Edward to blow it so you can step in and sweep Clara off her feet?"

"No. That would be too close to history repeating itself."

"You said you never took Mom away from Uncle Edward. She chose you." He watched his father carefully.

Thomas nodded. "It's true. But your uncle's psychological problems obviously go way back. He blamed me, blamed the curse. His life was a mess. So whatever happens between your uncle and Clara begins and ends with them. I'm out of it." He raised both hands and took a step back.

Jason nodded, satisfied his father wouldn't make a move on Clara. The older Corwin men had just begun to repair their fractured relationship. The slightest look in Clara's direction could conceivably send Edward over the edge. "I'm proud of you, Dad. Putting Uncle Edward's needs before your own."

Thomas shook his head. "You're mistaken. I'm being selfish. I need my brother, too. We both missed out on too much."

Jason gave his father a brief hug. "The Corwins are making progress," he said, forcing a laugh.

"Oh! There's Hank. I think I'll go hang with my other brother," he said. "You go find someone your own age." Thomas slapped Jason on the back and strode away.

Chuckling at his father, Jason headed for the beer tent, not surprised to find a line ahead of him since all beverages were being served in the same place. Settling in to wait, he leaned against the stacked bales of hay and glanced around.

That's when he saw her.

She captured his attention immediately and not just because she was wearing a red mask, though he had to admit Clara's tarot reading had predisposed him toward noticing her.

This woman would have rocked his world anyway.

*Rocked his world.*

Not his usual way with words. They were Clara's. But they were true.

She made her way closer and he couldn't tear his gaze off her long, lean legs encased in hip-hugging, slimming black denim, black suede boots, and a black long-sleeved shirt. Her long, beautiful hair, light brown with blond streaks, hung down to the middle of her back, while breezy bangs fluttered over her forehead. But it was her red mask that stood out, covering most of her face, curving seductively lower on one side. She'd wrapped a matching red scarf around her neck.

As she walked toward him in the moonlight, a strange sense of déjà vu enveloped him but he couldn't say why. The band played "That Old Black Magic," winding a seductive spell around him—if he believed in such things.

But even as he told himself he didn't, he was drawn to her.

Her gaze never left his as she came up behind him. She looked him over and he did the same to her. Silky hair draped her shoulders, and though the mask covered her face, her matching lipstick drew his attention to her red mouth. She ran her tongue over her lips in a clearly unconscious gesture and every rational thought fled his brain.

"Is this the line for hot cider?" she asked through those lush lips, full, ripe and begging for him to taste.

That voice, also familiar, nudged at the back of his mind even as his thoughts were already churning with the unbelievable notion that Clara's prediction had come true. And he couldn't do more than nod in response.

"What's wrong? Cat got your tongue?" she asked in a teasing tone.

A wry smile pulled at his lips. "You wouldn't believe me if I told you."

She raised her eyebrows warily over the top of the mask. "Try me."

He shrugged. Why not? "This is going to sound corny as hell but a fortune-teller told me I was going to meet you tonight."

She tilted her head back and laughed, a full,

throaty sound that knotted his stomach and sent desire rushing through his body at breakneck speed. No woman before had ever made such an impact.

Only one had come close and he'd been too young to appreciate her.

"Tell me about that fortune-teller," she urged.

He shook his head. "I'd rather not."

She sidled up to him. "Then tell me about you." Her green eyes sparkled with interest.

"I'm just a local." He eyed her curiously, still wondering why that déjà-vu feeling hadn't subsided.

"You're not *just* anything," she assured him flirtatiously.

That's when he knew.

He immediately flashed back to their first meeting. "I'm just a skier," he'd said in an attempt at false modesty. He'd wanted her to appreciate him, not the medals he'd won.

"You're not *just* anything," she'd said, those inquisitive yet knowing eyes boring into his.

The connection had been made, their bond solid from that moment on.

Jason swallowed hard and studied her now, attempting to see beyond the mask she wore to the intervening years they'd been apart. The same green eyes, those lips he'd kissed, the body he'd known as well as his own.

Blood rushed from his head to other demanding body parts as reality hit him. The woman behind the mask was Lauren Perkins and she apparently had no intention of admitting it.

Jason was curious as well as intrigued. She certainly had to recognize him.

Always up for a challenge, he decided to play along and pretend they were indeed strangers. "I appreciate the compliment," he said, stepping closer, invading her personal space. "Despite the fact that you probably think the fortune-teller story is a corny pickup line."

She grinned. "It's not just a corny line, it's the worst I've ever heard."

A light burst of cold wind whipped around them and he inhaled her warm, seductive scent, increasing his interest as well as his desire.

He wondered what she wanted. And when she'd reveal herself.

"What if I told you I can do better?" he asked, still playing along.

"I'd tell you to go for it." Lauren barely recognized her own deep, husky voice.

She'd made her way over here on trembling legs, determined to check him out up close. Foolishly believing she could handle him. She'd thought that whatever impact he'd had on her in the past would have died. She'd been wrong. The man he'd become packed more of a punch than the boy he'd been. He blew her away and she needed time to process her reaction. Flirting with him was fun and safe behind the anonymity of the mask.

"So what's a gorgeous woman like you doing at this small-town festival?" he asked as they moved up in the line.

She swallowed hard. "I'm just passing through," she said, keeping her explanation deliberately vague.

"Lucky me." The words rumbled from deep inside his chest, reaching down to her soul.

They'd made out, they'd kissed, and he'd taken her virginity. He'd been her first and she'd never forgotten him, not even when she'd tried to convince herself she had. She'd also never forgotten the pain of coming back here and finding him gone.

He extended his hand just as the band switched to Cher's "Dark Lady." "Dance with me."

He didn't ask.

He commanded, in a gruff tone that had seduction written all over it and had her experiencing the same tremors of excitement and anticipation she'd felt when she used to sneak from her grandmother's house to meet him late at night.

And he spoke with the certainty she remembered when he talked about heading to Vail to show his skills to Bud Keene, his dream coach. Jason Corwin was a man who went after what he wanted with blind determination.

He held his hand out and waited.

It was one dance, she thought, and a chance to have his arms around her again.

She placed her hand in his.

He led her to the makeshift dance floor in the center of the field and swept her into his arms, gliding rhythmically to the soulful beat of the music.

His fingers intertwined with hers and his hard body did crazy things to her insides as he pulled her against his chest. Warmth seeped through her, heightening her senses. She tried to keep her emotions in the past and concentrate on the delicious sensations he created inside her.

Couples moved around them in a blurry haze but he was all she could see. And feel. They might as well have been in a world of their own. This spiraling need and sense of euphoria had been missing from her life. She'd come alive again, the yearning for him overwhelming.

The day she'd discovered Jason was gone, she'd sworn she'd never fall under any man's spell. She ran through life at breakneck speed, never slowing down long enough to get to know anyone—man or woman—well, and she liked it that way. She didn't need a shrink to tell her why. What was the point of letting another human being in when all they'd do was find her lacking the way her family had, or leave her behind when something more important beckoned. Men came and went from her life when she had time for sex or a short relationship.

Yet here was Jason again, bewitching and entrancing her. Erasing the memories of her sister and her family problems, overpowering her dislike of this town and her reasons for being here.

She hadn't sought him out for this. She'd just wanted a glimpse of him. To see how he'd changed. But they'd locked gazes across the field and she hadn't been in control of her emotions or her actions since.

"Tell me about yourself," he said, bringing her back to earth as he swept her around, her feet barely brushing the dirt on the ground.

She tensed at his question. Too much. Too personal.

But his intent, curious eyes never left hers as he waited for her to answer.

"I'm just visiting. You?" she asked.

"I live here." Without warning, he spun her around with the combination of grace and strength that had made him a successful athlete.

His strong thighs brushed against hers, hard and demanding, awakening needs only he'd ever aroused.

"I like your mask," he said, his eyes focused on hers.

"Thank you. I like that you aren't wearing one. It lets me see your face." She wanted to trace the strong lines of his jaw, explore the stubble on his cheeks.

"I like what I can see of yours," he said, his voice huskier than before. "What made you choose that color?" He touched the edge of her mask with his finger.

"It called to me."

His eyes darkened at her response. "Any chance you drive a red Porsche?"

She grinned. "It just so happens I do. How did you know?"

"It suits you for one thing. But there's also the fact that this is a small town with few new people or cars. Yours stood out." He paused, then added, "And so do you."

He inclined his head until his forehead touched hers and the dance continued. The night was truly magical and she was forced to admit she wanted more than this one dance.

She wanted *him,* and the throbbing erection against her stomach told her he desired her, too.

The music suddenly picked up tempo, interrupting their slow, intimate seductive dance. They paused and she met his gaze.

"I'm hot," she murmured.

His eyes darkened with a heat she recognized. "Then let's get out of here." He never broke eye contact, just waited for her to decide.

Life had very few pivotal moments, but Lauren sensed this was one. She needed this night.

"It's up to you."

She swallowed hard, knowing her decision was already made. "Lead the way."

He smiled, his expression one of surprise and relief. Before she could blink, he dipped his head for a kiss. A tantalizing, too brief brush of his mouth on hers that left her lips tingling, her senses soaring and her mind reeling.

Now all she had to do was keep the mask on and Jason too satisfied to notice or care.

JASON WAS ENJOYING this stranger game Lauren was playing and wondered how far he could push her. He held her hand and led her toward the empty barn in a secluded corner of the field. They'd hung out together in various spots like this in the past, including this old barn. Did she remember?

"My cousin and I used to sneak beer here when

we were kids," he said, pointing to the building he hoped would be empty.

"So you were trouble back then?" she asked.

"For a while." He squeezed her hand and held on tighter. "Until I found my focus."

Jason remembered confiding in her about his past. She knew all too well that he'd been happy to be a troublemaking Corwin in high school until he'd discovered snowboarding at sixteen. More exciting than skiing, the daredevil sport had changed his life, given him his real passion and focus, and he'd been set on Olympic gold ever since.

"Yet you're being bad again now. With me. Does that mean you've lost that focus?" she asked softly. Quietly, and far too perceptively.

She obviously knew about the scandal and was hoping he'd confide in her now. He swallowed the explanation she sought. No matter how much he wanted to reveal his pain, knowing she'd understand, he couldn't. Not until she'd revealed herself to him.

He pushed open the barn door and she followed him inside. The heavy wooden door banged shut behind them and he turned on the lights, hitting the switch on the wall. "Don't you worry. I'm extremely focused," he assured her, pulling her into his arms. "Focused on you."

He aligned his hips with hers, knowing damn

well his erection would be obvious, reminding her of why they were here.

Her eyes darkened at the intimate contact. "That's what I was hoping you'd say."

Her husky voice turned Jason on even more than dancing with her already had. As much as he remembered the past, the good times and the summer that had been too short, he was totally in the present now. She smelled so damn good and fit in his arms even more perfectly now.

She'd filled out. Her breasts were fuller and plumper and he wanted to see her without the barrier of clothes. But first he needed to taste her more fully. With a low growl, he slid his tongue inside her mouth, taking possession and control. He ran his tongue through the damp recesses, soaking up the moisture, reveling in her sweetness. His body burned and throbbed more from this one kiss than any other sexual experience in his lifetime.

Merely kissing her did something to him that defied logic, and though he was primed and ready to glide into her hot body and feel her slick walls tighten around him, he couldn't stop devouring her mouth. Her tongue dueled and tangled with his, matching him, teasing him. She grabbed the back of his head with her hand, grasping onto his hair and holding him tight, arousing him beyond thought and reason. Until finally the throbbing in his groin couldn't be denied.

He released her slowly, keeping one hand around her waist. When he met her hazy eyes, he wasn't surprised to see her adjusting the red mask.

He somehow withheld a grin. Though he wanted to rip off the covering and see her face, for whatever reason, she sought the anonymity. He needed her too much to break the spell by removing the mask. Besides, he had to admit the aura of mystery, and playing strangers heightened his desire.

"Come with me," he said, heading across the room to the stairs leading to the loft. On the way, he spotted a blanket that had been left on a hook on the wall, grabbed it and gestured for her to go first.

Once in the loft, together they spread the blanket over the floor. Lauren was grateful for the few seconds to regain her composure. She was here again, with Jason. She shook her head in disbelief.

"Is this where you used to drink with the guys?" she asked as they settled onto the blanket. "Or is this where you used to bring the girls back when you were trouble?" She found she couldn't meet his gaze.

She'd thought she was special. After he'd left town, she often wondered if she'd misread that summer and that she'd been one of many. All these years later, she still needed to know.

He lifted her chin with his hand. "There's only one girl I used to bring here," he murmured.

Her mouth ran dry and an unwanted lump formed in her throat, the emotions so overwhelming.

"But let's not talk about her now," he said, and dodged further explanation by easing her onto the floor.

Lauren was finished talking, too. She slipped her hands inside his shirt and placed her palms against his chest, feeling his hair-roughened skin, savoring the warmth and inhaling his masculine scent.

She let her hands drift over his nipples, pausing to savor the hard puckering against her skin. He let out a satisfied groan, allowing her to grow bolder. He'd been a boy and now he was all man, kissing her thoroughly as she continued to explore. From the hard planes of his chest, she roamed lower to his tight stomach, then to the waistband of his jeans. Her breasts tightened and moisture dampened her panties, desire growing ever stronger.

He did his own share of exploration, too, pulling her tight top upward and cupping her covered breasts in his hands. Her nipples puckered against his palms and she writhed and moaned beneath him.

"You are so responsive, so sweet," he murmured, bending his head and pulling one nipple into his mouth.

She arched her back and moaned aloud.

"God." He unhooked the button on her black jeans and eased them down her legs, getting caught halfway.

Laughing, she shimmied her hips to help him, ending up wearing only her skimpy black lace panties.

His dark gaze settled on her *there*.

"Gorgeous." He sounded almost reverent as he spoke.

"Thank—" He placed his palm over her mound, cutting off any thought.

Her hips jerked upward, demanding relief, and he seemed to sense what she needed and slowly rotated his hand. Waves sprang to life inside her, building as he continued the torment, teasing her with one finger, filling her until she moaned aloud.

"Hang on." He paused long enough to shed his jeans and underwear, grab a condom from his wallet.

She eyed the packet with relief and a stab of… jealousy? "You're prepared."

"The men in my family always are."

She didn't want to get into a conversation about the curse and its havoc. Not now. "I wish you'd hurry," she said, reaching for him. Distracting him.

"Now, that I can do."

With practiced ease, he slipped on protection while she quickly did her part, undressing— panties off, legs parted. So when he rejoined her, she was ready.

He slid over her, his thighs aligned with hers, his erection pulsing against her stomach. Still, he paused to brush her bangs off her forehead. A tender gesture that reminded her of the past and made this moment all the more special.

"I want you," she said, needing him to hear the words. Parting her thighs, she invited him in.

His throbbing head nudged her open further as he slowly eased himself into her, his eyes never leaving hers. "Good?" he asked.

She'd dreamed of him, of this. Her throat was almost too full to speak but she needed to lighten the mood so she looked at him and smiled. "It's a start."

He grinned. Then he thrust deep. His thighs crushed hers, their bodies joined tight, and he pulsed inside her, thick and alive.

Lauren gasped but she accepted all of him at once. Full to bursting, she felt the pleasure rever- berate inside her, in every cell of her being. She could barely think, she felt so good.

Suddenly he pulled out, leaving her empty, making her want to beg, but just as quickly he thrust back in again, filling her, pleasuring her, taking her higher. He was thick, hard, and she felt every velvet ridge inside her as he ground his hips into hers. He teased her as he picked up rhythm. Out…in…out…in…until the first wave took hold, washing over her and taking her breath away. And he continued to plunge into her hard and fast, over and over, even as he let out a groan of intense pleasure that served to increase her own until he finally collapsed on top of her.

Accepting his weight, she hooked one foot around his and laid her head back on the blanket, gasping for air, her body still tingling.

He breathed heavily in her ear as she struggled to come back to herself. As she did, she realized she had to tell him.

But he spoke first. "We're better with age, aren't we?" he asked, his voice rumbling against her chest.

Lauren gasped. *He knew?*

Before she could reply, the barn door creaked open, then slammed, and a voice called out from downstairs. "Hello, is anyone in here?"

"Oh my God." Lauren took in his equally stunned expression.

She had no desire to get caught up here with her pants off in a small town that thrived on gossip. Gossip about the Perkins gossip. And she was the only Perkins around.

"Get up!" Panicked, she shoved at his shoulders.

They both scrambled to their feet and rushed to find their jeans.

Lauren dressed in record time, but like a man, he was faster.

"Hello? The light's on so come on down and show yourself!" the female voice called.

Sharon.

Lauren narrowed her gaze. Face her friend or have a heart-to-heart with Jason. Neither choice appealed. Heart pounding in her chest, she wanted nothing more than to get away from them both. Once she gathered her thoughts and feelings, she could deal with what happened much better. She buttoned her black jeans and did the best she could to smooth wrinkles, pick off stray pieces of dirt on her clothes and look as if she hadn't been having sex on the floor.

She had pride and she had more than a little bit of modesty and she didn't want to embarrass herself.

She brushed her bangs and hoped her mask wasn't sideways as she headed for the ladder.

"Wait!" He reached for her arm.

"Not now."

He shot her an amused glance. "Later, then?"

She scowled at him before starting down the stairs from the loft. As she peeked across the cavernous barn, she saw Sharon standing by the door they'd entered.

Without risking another look in her friend's direction, Lauren raced for the door at the opposite end of the barn, headed for fresh air and freedom.

She didn't even pause at the sound of her name.

# CHAPTER THREE

"LAUREN! COME BACK!"

Jason recognized the woman who'd interrupted his and Lauren's reunion.

He climbed down from the loft and faced the mayor's wife. "Hey, Sharon. What are you doing here?"

Of all people to catch him, Sharon wasn't the worst choice. At least she wasn't a nosy relative and she did know how to be discreet.

"Jason!" Her voice rose in surprise, her attention darting from him to the door Lauren had bolted through minutes before. "Richard asked me to pick up his jacket. He thought he left it here this afternoon." She studied him without saying a word.

She obviously knew what he'd been doing in the loft. Did she expect him to apologize? She was one of the only people who knew about his past relationship with Lauren and she'd never judged. But she looked about to do so now, hands on her hips, frown on her face.

Sharon finally groaned. "Jason, what's going on? Lauren's only back in town for a few weeks, until she gets her grandmother's house ready to sell. If you hurt her again, I swear to God, I'll kill you myself."

Women and their damn loyalty to each other, he thought, and then her words registered. "What do you mean hurt *her?* Her grandmother sent her away. End of story."

And the tough guy he'd thought he was had hurt more than he'd wanted to admit. He'd thrown himself into his Olympic dreams with everything he had, so he wouldn't have to think or feel.

Sharon waved her hands in front of her. "Oh, no. It's not my story to tell," she said.

A chill shook Jason to his core. "Fine."

"What does that mean?"

"It means I'll find out myself." Because seeing Lauren again had given him a lift he hadn't felt in a long time.

*She* had done that for him. Not even his family had been able to shake his depression and sense of loss over his career. If there was something more to her departure all those years ago, he wanted to know. He also wanted to see her again.

"Fine. I'll grab the jacket and let's get out of here."

They walked back to the festival in silence. Sharon no doubt was consumed with concern for her friend, while Jason was consumed with thoughts of the same person, but for very different reasons.

Suddenly he heard their names being called and Derek and Gabrielle and Amber, his cousin Mike's wife, descended.

"There you are!" Gabrielle said, pulling her husband along with her. "I've been looking for you!"

"And I told you he was perfectly fine," Derek muttered. He sent Jason an apologetic glance. "Sorry. She forgets you're a grown man."

Gabrielle frowned, realizing she might have overstepped her bounds. "I just wanted to make sure you hadn't gone home early to sit around and watch TV when you could still be with us having fun."

"And we definitely didn't want you to be all alone," Amber said, backing up Gabrielle.

"He wasn't alone," Clara objected, joining the circle.

"What do you mean he wasn't alone?" Amber and Gabrielle asked in unison.

Jason rolled his eyes. This was the way of things every time his family got together. Good-natured meddling. "How would you know I wasn't alone?" he asked Clara.

"It was a hunch. But thank you for confirming it," she said, smiling. "I'm glad to know my reading was correct." She folded her arms across her chest, pleased with herself.

Jason groaned. "Why aren't you in the booth I spent hours constructing?"

"Because I needed a break," she explained. "I had a lineup for the last few hours."

"Well, I'm happy for you," he muttered.

"Who is she?" Gabrielle asked. "Who were you with?"

"What was the prediction?" Amber added.

Derek grabbed his wife's arm and started to pull her away. "We're leaving," he promised Jason. "And Amber's coming with us."

"Not until we hear everything!" the women said in unison.

Jason gritted his teeth.

Beside him, Sharon remained silent. Of all the women, she was the most discreet.

"Sharon?" Gabrielle asked her best friend. "Did you happen to see?"

Jason sighed, resigned to his fate. "Go on," he said to Sharon. "Tell them."

Clara leaned in closer so she could hear, too.

"What? Your cards didn't tell you her name?" He couldn't help but tease her.

Sharon shrugged. "If you're sure you want them to know."

He nodded. They wouldn't give him peace otherwise.

"He was with Lauren Perkins," Sharon said.

Gabrielle and Amber stared, shocked.

"Shit, Jason. You do know how to pick them," Derek said, one corner of his mouth lifting in an amused grin.

Jason speared his cousin with an annoyed glance. "I thought you were taking your wife and leaving."

Clara stared at him in silence. Unaware of his and Lauren's past, she was clearly processing the implications of a Corwin man hooking up with a Perkins woman. As far as Jason knew, that hadn't happened since the eighteen hundreds and the affair had resulted in the infamous Corwin Curse that had haunted the men in his family for generations. He didn't much give a damn, but knew there were some in his family who would.

"Ooh, wait until the uncles hear about this," Amber said, ending her comment with a long whistle.

"I'd rather they didn't," Jason said pointedly. No sense putting them into an uproar the likes of which his family probably hadn't seen since the curse was invoked.

The news might put Uncle Edward back in the hospital, Uncle Hank would run for his shotgun— not that he'd ever used it—and Jason's father might end up starching his underwear in order to keep that facade of perfection for the outside world.

He stared at his cousin's wives until they both nodded in understanding.

Derek and Clara knew all too well what would happen if Hank and Edward, especially, discovered this secret.

Satisfied, Jason let out a long breath. "Where's your husband?" he asked Amber, turning the subject away from himself.

"The town hired him as extra security for tonight, remember?" Amber asked. Mike Corwin was a cop.

After his reunion with Lauren and their short mind-blowing time in the barn, Jason barely recalled his own name.

LIKE CINDERELLA running from the prince after the ball, Lauren entered her grandmother's house at the stroke of midnight. For someone who didn't believe in fairy tales any more than she believed in curses, that was a huge analogy for her to make. She should have stayed and faced Jason, but once she realized he'd known it was her all along, she'd panicked at the thought of having some kind of deep conversation.

Childish, immature, but completely rational, she thought, her heart still racing in her chest. She'd just slept with Jason. How on earth did she deal with that after all these years?

With coffee, that's how. As she headed to the kitchen, a cool draft hit her cheek. She glanced at the window—one she didn't recall opening earlier—and frowned.

She pushed it down but couldn't lock it. "Damn."

Had someone broken in while she was gone? She shook off the thought. This house was just falling apart. The lock was probably faulty, and she must have left the window open. Another thing to tack on to her To Do list.

She walked to the refrigerator and pulled out a container, pouring the last of the cream into a bowl for the cat that had come with the house. She'd been living here for over a week, and until now, she'd only fed him cat food, but she'd run out and had forgotten to buy more on the way home from visiting Beth. So all she had now was cream for the cat. The black cat.

Given her family history, she couldn't afford to be superstitious, which was a good thing. Lauren wasn't a cat person by nature and she didn't know the first thing about having one, but this animal didn't seem to care. He hung out by the front door despite Lauren's attempts to shoo him away. From his hefty build, he wasn't starving. The empty bowls on the porch had led Lauren to conclude that the neighborhood kids must have been feeding him prior to her arrival. The same kids who'd vandalized the windows and walls had a soft spot for a stray?

Stranger things had happened, she thought. Like the cat finding its way inside the house, making himself at home and eating and drinking enough for three.

Said cat now sat at her feet and meowed endlessly.

She glanced at the furry feline. "Fine!" She set the bowl on the floor, realizing there was no cream left for her coffee, but at least now there was blessed silence. The cat happily lapped up the liquid.

"Looks like I'm going to have to make another trip to town tomorrow," she said to the cat she hadn't yet named.

He didn't have a collar. Lauren could put up signs in town advertising a lost cat. And if no one claimed him? She wondered if she could include him with the house. Since there was no way she could take him to Paris, she'd just have to make sure she found him a good home before she left.

He finished the remainder of the cream, looking

as satisfied as Lauren had felt after having sex with Jason earlier tonight.

Flushing at the memory, her body still tingling, she rinsed the bowl and headed for the downstairs bedroom. Lauren sat down on the bed and the cat jumped beside her and snuggled onto her pillow.

Right in the middle.

She sighed and stretched out beside her furry friend, wishing the warm body beside her was Jason. A dangerous thought and another reason she knew she had to leave town fast. He'd hurt her once but that was before she'd had her dreams to follow. Maybe that was how he'd felt all those years ago. She had been a potential distraction from his Olympic dreams and her leaving had been for the best. If so, she understood him that much better now.

At least she'd had tonight with him.

Tomorrow she'd head to town and ask around about hiring a contractor to work on the house. The sooner she completed the repairs, the sooner she could close on the sale and be finished with this town.

And with Jason Corwin.

"CATS SHOULD COME with a manual," Lauren muttered as she picked up items she needed for herself and her pet in the grocery store.

First stop was the cat food aisle. No more cream for this kitty. On awakening, she'd discovered that the midnight snack had resulted in a mess she didn't want to think about or face ever again.

When she'd called a friend in New York who owned a cat, Liza had burst out laughing. "Didn't you buy him a litter box?" she'd asked.

No, she hadn't. Because Lauren had thought the outdoor cat would do its thing in the great outdoors.

She paid for the groceries and a litter box with cash, placed the bags in her car and headed for the hardware store.

When she was younger, the creaking sounds in her grandmother's old house had frightened her and she'd always slept with a flashlight by her bed. After the scare with the window last night, she'd gone looking for a flashlight only to find it didn't work. New batteries hadn't helped, so she needed to buy a new one.

She rounded the aisle and headed for the register.

There was one person in front of her and she waited for him to put his change away and step aside before she walked forward and placed her purchase on the counter.

The middle-aged clerk stared at her "You're Mary Perkins's granddaughter, aren't you?"

The few times she'd come to town to do her shopping, she'd had mixed reactions, from silent acceptance to overtly rude whispers.

"Yes, I'm Mary's granddaughter." She didn't recognize the clerk, but he must have seen her on one of her visits to Beth.

He braced his hands on the counter. "I heard you were in town."

She nodded. "You heard right." She pushed the flashlight forward, hoping to urge things along.

"Whatcha doing back here? It's not like you got any relatives left to visit."

Apparently manners weren't his strong suit. She straightened her shoulders and looked at him head-on. "I'm here to fix up the family home so I can sell it and move on. Which reminds me, do you happen to know the name of a contractor I can hire?"

He frowned. "Not off the top of my head, but if I think of one, I'll let you know." He wouldn't meet her eyes.

He was lying. There was no way a hardware store clerk in a small town didn't know a contractor.

Gritting her teeth, she pulled her wallet from her purse and slid a credit card across the counter.

He glanced down at it. "Can't use a credit card for something less than ten dollars."

She narrowed her gaze. "Well, I just spent the last of my cash at the grocery store."

"Then I guess you're out of luck." He folded his arms over his chest.

"Guess Perkins credit is no good here?" she asked sarcastically, shoving her card back into her wallet. "Tell you what. I'll just take my business somewhere else."

"Put it on my account," a distinctive male voice said.

Jason materialized beside her. She wondered how much he'd overheard and her stomach cramped in embarrassment. "Thanks but that's not necessary. I can pick up a flashlight at another store."

"Hey, Corwin, you know who that is?" the clerk asked.

"What I know is that's no way to treat a lady, Burt." Jason stared at the man, a frown on his handsome face.

Burt scratched his bald head. "That's not a lady, that's a—"

"I said put it on my tab." Jason grabbed the flashlight in one hand, her elbow in another, and led her out of the store.

Once on the sidewalk she looked him over in broad daylight. He appeared even more handsome than last night. He wore faded jeans and a black turtleneck. Razor stubble covered his cheeks, giving him a scruffy, sexy appearance, and her stomach fluttered in excitement.

"I looked all over for you last night." He studied her just as intently.

"I left."

"Places to go, people to see?" he asked wryly. "Or were you just avoiding me?"

He'd hit a nerve and she straightened her shoulders. "Avoiding a conversation we didn't need to have."

"You should know that I intend to have that talk sometime."

Not here, where anyone could see them. "You really didn't have to put the flashlight on your tab," she said, changing the subject. "But I appreciate it."

He inclined his head, accepting her thanks. "There was no call for Burt to treat you that way," he said gruffly.

She shrugged, unconcerned with the other man's rudeness. "Maybe he had his reasons. I wasn't about to ask what my grandmother or sister did to piss him off. But don't worry, I'll pay you back."

He rolled his eyes. He didn't care about the money. "Flashlight's on me." He held it out for her.

She took it, avoiding his touch. "Thanks."

But he stepped closer, his body looming over

her. "So how much longer are we going to do this dance?"

"What dance?" She knew playing dumb wasn't the answer but the words slipped out.

"The one where you avoid telling me why you didn't just admit who you were last night?"

She had no rational reply. Last night, it had made a kind of crazy sense. She'd wanted to watch from afar, see him again and walk away. In the light of day it seemed plain silly.

"Why didn't you just tell me you recognized me?" she asked instead.

He shrugged. "You seemed to need the anonymity. And frankly, pretending to have sex with a stranger kind of turned me on." The corners of his mouth pulled up in a wicked, sexy grin.

His words set her entire body aflame, much the way his hands had last night.

"You look good," he said, his voice thick.

"Thank you. So do you." His dark hair was still as thick, his eyes still as blue and his body as hard and—

"I heard you ask Burt for the name of a contractor?"

She nodded, grateful he'd interrupted her thoughts before they could get X-rated. "Do you know of one?"

"As a matter of fact, I do. Jason Corwin, contractor, at your service." He swept his hand through the air and executed a mock bow.

Now that was a life change and she couldn't let it go unspoken. "Listen, I heard about what happened—"

He quickly dismissed the subject. "Forget it. It's in the past."

She understood and respected the fact he wouldn't want to discuss it. "I just wanted to tell you…I believe you're innocent. Jason, you couldn't have changed who you are in here." Unable to help herself, she reached over and placed her hand on his heart. "I just thought you should know."

At the unexpected touch, his nostrils flared, his pupils dilated and his heart rate kicked up beneath her palm.

Lauren slowly lowered her hand. "So you're a contractor?" she asked, severing the physical connection.

"It's what I know best."

Next to snowboarding.

Years ago he'd told her how he'd gotten into the sport. Once he'd discovered the alternative to skiing, he'd started a snowboarding club at school, arranging trips to Wachusett Mountain an hour away. He raised money for equipment and practice time by working for his uncles in construction. A means to an end, not a passion. If anyone took fashion design away from her, she'd be adrift and miserable. She couldn't imagine how Jason was getting by.

But he wouldn't want her pity.

"I'm free to handle your job," he said, interrupting her thoughts.

But she couldn't handle the temptation of working side by side with him, day after day for the next few weeks. Heat rushed through her at the thought, which was exactly the reason she couldn't hire him.

Lauren drew a deep breath. "Don't take this the wrong way, but we can't work together."

He'd be a distraction that would keep her from focusing on the house. And if that weren't enough of a problem, she didn't want to spend time with him, get to know him again, grow more attached and face the pain she'd lived through once before. She didn't want to fall in love with him all over again.

And she certainly didn't want ties to this town after she was gone.

He raised an eyebrow and shot her a knowing look.

She ignored him. "Can you recommend anyone else?" she asked instead.

"I can." He shoved his hands into his pockets and shrugged. "But none as good as me."

She already knew that firsthand. Fire burned her cheeks and she hoped a blush didn't give her away.

He paused for a good, long time. So long she wondered if he was going to even answer. Finally, he said, "Got a pen and paper?"

She dug through her purse and handed him what he asked for.

He scribbled names and numbers on her small notepad. "There are two other local contractors, one in Perkins, the other one here in Stewart. We refer each other when we're overbooked."

"Thanks."

"Good luck."

She nodded and reluctantly turned away, surprised and strangely disappointed he'd given in so easily.

# CHAPTER FOUR

WHEN LAUREN REJECTED him, Jason's fighting, competitive spirit returned. When he wanted something, he went after it, and he wanted Lauren Perkins. The woman and the job. She wanted the same thing. He'd seen the disappointment in her eyes when he'd given her those other contractors' names. She was just too shocked to admit that their chemistry was as strong as ever. Jason intended to make sure they both got what they wanted.

Taking a page from his past, he decided the best way to accomplish his goal was to eliminate the competition. Growing up in a small town had its advantages. So did having uncles still working in subcontracting. Jason had enough contacts and friends in town to call in favors and even return a few to get what he wanted.

His first stop after Burt's Hardware was a building site where he could find Greg Charlton, head of Charlton Construction, one of the names he'd given to Lauren. Jason had recently outbid Charlton on a job to renovate a large estate home on the edge of town. Their estimates had been close and the client would do well with either company. Though Jason could always use the money the job would bring, some things were more important. A brief meeting, confirmation with the client and a handshake later, and Charlton had taken over the estate home project from Jason's company, and the other man had agreed to tell Lauren Perkins he was too busy to take on her renovation in the time frame she needed.

Jason returned to his home and office, the reno-vated barn behind Uncle Hank's house. The place was perfect for Jason except for the added attrac-tion of Fred, his uncle's basset hound. The fat, lumbering old dog had gotten used to staying at the barn when Derek lived there with his daughter, Holly. Hank's one condition for letting Jason move in was that he take over the care and feeding of The Fat Man, as Jason had started calling Fred.

It seemed a small price to pay and Jason had agreed. Then he learned how Fred made his presence known. He'd peed on Jason's new work boots. And that had been the beginning of their relationship.

Jason settled into the chair behind his desk. He

kicked his feet up on top as Fred flopped down beneath, and called contractor number two, Mark Miller. Jason had known Mark since high school and they were now friendly competitors who occasionally had a beer together after work.

Jason caught Mark on his cell phone and explained he'd be getting a request from a woman who'd need renovations in a short period of time.

"No problem, I can fit her in," Mark assured him.

"No, you can't. You're too busy."

"Okay, I'll bite. Why?"

"Because I want the job."

"Then why didn't she just hire you?" Mark asked.

Jason pinched the bridge of his nose and leaned back in his swivel chair. Mark was like a damn girl. He wouldn't do a favor without knowing the reasons behind it.

"Let's say we have a history and she'd rather not deal with me again," Jason said.

He recalled Lauren's expression when she'd realized *he* was the answer to her renovation dilemma and held back a laugh. The attraction between them was so strong it was a live, tangible thing and it obviously frightened her. But she was leaving town in a little over a month. Why not indulge while she was here?

"I'll be damned, Corwin. You're finally interested in women again. I was beginning to wonder if you'd taken a vow of celibacy."

"You're a laugh riot, Miller. So you'll do it?"

"Why not. What did you say her name was again?"

"Lauren Perkins."

"Damn, you know how to pick 'em," Mark said, laughing. "Aren't you afraid the curse is going to bite you in the ass?"

Jason rolled his eyes. Everybody thought they were a comedian. "Thanks. I owe you one," he said, ignoring the gibe. Satisfied the other man would turn down the job, Jason hung up the phone.

Still leaning back in his chair, he glanced at the ceiling and thought of Mark's question. Did it bother him that Lauren was a Perkins?

Now, as back then, the answer was the same. Not at all. He wasn't foolish enough to think that a centuries-old spell had been responsible for Kristina and Rusty's actions, even if he had lost the woman and his fortune.

Recalling how he'd felt when he'd discovered their betrayal, Jason felt a twinge of guilt at manipulating Lauren's situation to fit his needs. But this wasn't the same thing. He wasn't looking to hurt her. He was giving her what she really wanted.

What they both wanted.

He might have to maneuver things to fall into place but he wouldn't lie to her. She'd figure out what he'd done and eventually she'd thank him for it. Of that he was certain.

He knew her intimately. He understood what she wanted. And that changed the rules.

WHAT WERE the chances of both contractors being too busy to take on Lauren's renovation project? And what was she going to do about it?

She walked through the house, making an inventory of the obvious damages, and there were many. From broken windows to funky noises coming from the boiler, she had problems. She'd called both contractors back and begged them to fit her grandmother's house into their busy schedules— to no avail. But each man had highly recommended Jason Corwin.

If she was going to hire Jason, she needed a glass of wine and a long talk with an old friend first, so she'd invited Sharon over for a drink.

Lauren set out the wine in the den. Unlike the office with bookshelves full of legal tomes, old volumes and framed pictures of Mary Perkins in various official capacities, this room had no overt reminders of Lauren's grandmother and her term as mayor, and Lauren thought Sharon would be more comfortable in here.

Sharon arrived at eight o'clock. Lauren poured two glasses of wine, handed one to her friend and settled down beside her. "Thanks for coming over." Lauren took a sip of the Chardonnay she'd found in her grandmother's wine rack and hoped the alcohol would go to her head quickly.

She was so uptight about hiring Jason, afraid of how easily she could fall for him again, she needed a buzz to take the edge off.

Sharon took a long sip, too. "I have to admit, your grandmother had good taste in wine."

Any compliment to Lauren's family was huge coming from Sharon, and Lauren smiled in appreciation. "Thank you. And thanks for coming. I know it can't be easy hanging out in this house."

Sharon waved away the sentiment. "The company is more important than the setting."

Lauren nodded. "I agree. I wish I could say this was purely a social invitation, but I need to talk."

"About Jason." Sharon's eyes gleamed, but being Sharon, she didn't mention the fact that she'd caught them—or that Lauren had run away.

Lauren nodded.

"Ask away," Sharon said. "I kept you up-to-date on his big news because I figured you might hear about the steroids in the papers or on television. But since you'd moved on, I never filled you in on the little things going on with him. I didn't want to stir up old memories that you didn't want stirred."

Lauren exhaled hard, then took another sip of wine. Sharon's perceptiveness had enabled them to remain friends. The other woman had an innate sense of caring that Lauren appreciated and valued.

"Did you ever hear how he tested positive?" Lauren asked. That question had nagged at her since the start.

Sharon shook her head. "As far as I know, he's never told anyone what happened. He's just maintained his innocence, and frankly, I believe him." She lifted her wine and took a long sip.

"No argument here." Jason might be competitive and dedicated, but he was honest.

Sharon laughed as she drained her glass.

"More wine?" Lauren lifted the bottle.

Sharon nodded and Lauren topped off their glasses.

She stared into the golden liquid as she explained her problem. "He's the only contractor available to work on this house."

"I'm assuming from the look on your face when you talk about him, he's still good with his hands?" Sharon rose and stretched her arms into the air, unsteady on her feet thanks to the alcohol she'd consumed too quickly. Thank God.

"Too good for me to get any real work done and that's the problem."

"And you want me to tell you it's going to be okay, right?" Sharon flopped back onto the couch and stared at the ceiling. "It's a good thing Richard is picking me up after his meeting because there's no way I can drive."

"I know what you mean." Lauren's head spun from the wine and her stomach swirled at the thought of hiring the one man she didn't trust herself to be around. "And you're right. I want you to tell me I can work side by side with him and not fall in love."

"You can do it." Sharon sounded like a cheerleader, obviously too buzzed to think clearly.

Which was fine. Lauren didn't really need her friend to tell her anything. She already knew the score. Her nerves tingled at the thought of him. Her body still craved him. And her heart was already softening toward him.

Deep down, Lauren knew it didn't matter what Sharon said. Working with Jason was a risk. A risk she had no choice but to take.

WORKING WITH HIS HANDS used to provide Jason with a means to pay for his snowboarding and

Olympic dreams. After being forced to give up the sport professionally, he'd fallen back on what he knew in order to make a living. But painting and fixing things didn't provide the creative challenge that snowboarding had, nor did it give him a goal to work toward.

Since he'd moved back here, his life had become stagnant, but Lauren's return had given him new purpose and a new goal—winning the Perkins job. He'd even cleared his schedule in anticipation of working at Lauren's house, but she hadn't called.

Three days and not a word, although he knew she'd been in touch with Mark and Greg, and they'd both turned her down. He was tempted to stop by the house later today and check on her, but she'd been so resistant to them working together, he thought it would go better if she came to him.

To kill time, he turned to working on his own living space. He hadn't had a chance to put his mark on the place yet, so he'd spent the past few days priming the walls in the lower section of the loft so he could paint over the gray his uncle had chosen. The sun didn't shine in the windows until late in the afternoon and he needed a brighter color to perk up the place.

His sisters, Ruthie and Allison, lived close to each other in New York with their husbands and kids and had opened up an interior design business together. They'd both offered their advice, suggesting navy or hunter-green walls with white trim and had sent him photos of offices in their portfolio to back up their advice. Since this was the first permanent place Jason had lived in, as opposed to hotel rooms and short-term rentals, he'd chosen stark white instead. Like snow. He'd be surrounded by proof he was no longer hiding from his past. So here he was, standing on a ladder painting his new home, and waiting for a girl to call.

A few more broad strokes of the brush and he decided to take a break.

He stepped down, but instead of the floor, his foot hit something soft. Jason jumped back as Fred the basset hound yelped, trying to make his escape. But as slow as Fred moved, Jason tripped on the dog. He lost his balance and reached for the ladder to stop his fall, causing the paint tray to topple to the floor, splattering him with white paint along the way.

He landed on his ass, beside Fred, who looked up at him with those big, sad eyes. "Yeah, I know. You're sorry."

Jason pushed himself to a standing position and glanced at his paint-splattered shirt. "Another one bites the dust," he muttered, and stripped off the gray tee. He was going to have to do laundry soon or else he'd have to go shopping. Neither prospect held much appeal.

He was headed to the loft stairs so he could get a clean shirt when the doorbell rang. "Come on in," he called, assuming his father or uncle had stopped by.

Lauren walked in instead.

"Hi." She strode in with purpose, wearing those high black boots he'd noticed the first night they'd met, dark jeans and a black-and-white-striped shirt with some funky vest on top. The neckline of the shirt was rounded and covered her assets. So did the vest. But he could still see the slight swell and curve of her breasts, enough for him to be distracted by the sight.

And the way she was staring at him, she was equally off-kilter.

"What can I do for you?" he asked.

"I was hoping we could talk."

He nodded. "I'm glad you're here. Let me go upstairs and grab a shirt."

He hoped she didn't bolt before he got back.

## CHAPTER FIVE

JASON DISAPPEARED up the loft stairs, leaving Lauren with one thought. Thank God he'd gone to put on a shirt, because his bare chest was a distraction she didn't need or want. She'd taken in his muscled forearms and the dark sprinkling of hair that tapered into the waistband of his jeans and her mouth had grown dry. She knew what lay below those jeans.

Now she had a chance to shore up her defenses. Business first. Last. Only.

She glanced around the room, noticing the fallen ladder, paint tray and a sullen-looking dog with floppy ears who lay beside both. "Hey there, what's your name?" she asked as she knelt down beside him and patted his head.

The telephone on Jason's desk rang and the answering machine picked up on the second ring. "Corwin Contractors, leave a message and I'll get back to you as soon as possible," Jason's deep voice said, followed by a long beep.

"Hey, it's Greg. I can't thank you enough for trading me the Dunning house for turning down the Perkins job."

Lauren heard her last name and rose to her feet, paying close attention to the rest of the message.

"I'm hoping to bag some of the landmark restorations due around here and this job ought to help. I owe you one." He paused and Lauren thought he'd hang up, but there was more. "Good luck with your lady," he added before disconnecting the call.

Jason had sabotaged her opportunity to hire Greg Charlton, Lauren thought, and her blood pressure spiked. She now had no doubt he'd done the same thing with Mark Miller. No wonder both men had been unable to take on her small project.

Of all the nerve.

Footsteps sounded as Jason came down the stairs.

He'd pulled on a long-sleeved navy sweatshirt, but his feet were bare, which she found ridiculously sexy.

He hit the bottom step and came to a halt. "I take it you heard that?" He pointed to the answering machine on the desk.

"Rhetorical question. I'm not deaf." She clasped her hands in front of her, squeezing them tight, feeling the blood flow nearly stop.

She took one look at his handsome face, and the words just toppled off her tongue. "Just tell me why. Why do you want to work beside me so badly? Ten years ago you left without so much as a word, and now after one night you're manipulating people to get this job?" She whirled away, frustrated and embarrassed she'd admitted so much.

He came up behind her and wrapped his arms around her, pulling her back against his chest until his body heated her from the outside in. She struggled not to melt back into him and enjoy the sensations, but she sensed a losing battle. Just as she'd known it would be.

"How?" Jason asked her.

"How what?"

"How did you expect me to get in touch with you?" he asked, his breath warm in her ear. "Your grandmother found out about us, packed you up and sent you away. One day you were just gone. It wasn't like you left a forwarding address."

"How did you find out I was gone?" Lauren asked.

"Your grandmother came by and took great pleasure in letting me know I'd never see you again."

Lauren's stomach cramped at that. "I'm sorry," she whispered.

He shrugged, leaning his chin against her head.

"It's not your fault. Now answer my question. How did you expect me to find you?"

She turned. "From the letters I wrote you…" Her voice trailed off as she caught the stunned expression on his face. "You didn't get any letters, did you?"

He shook his head, the regret in his expression as obvious as the pain she'd been through all those years ago.

"I'd lay odds my grandmother intercepted your mail at the post office." Her reach had been that far, her deviousness that deep. Lauren drew a calming breath. "It doesn't matter now anyway."

Even if he'd received her letters, she had no way of knowing whether he'd have waited for her. If his feelings had been as serious as hers.

She was wrong, Jason thought. It mattered. He just didn't know how much. What would he have done differently if he'd known where to find her? If he'd known she still wanted him and he hadn't been just a brief summer fling she'd forgotten about as soon as she'd been sent home?

He shook his head at the unanswered questions, knowing too well how futile it was to try to change the past.

He was better off focusing on the future. "If that's true, if it doesn't matter, then you should have no problem hiring me for your construction project." He brushed her hair off her shoulder, sliding his fingers down the long strands.

The silky sensation shot through his body as if he were stroking her bare skin.

"If we're going to work together, we need to have boundaries." Her voice shook, telling him his touch affected her, too. "You shouldn't have manipulated me to get this job."

"I tried asking you outright," he reminded her. "You turned me down." He shot her a sheepish, apologetic grin.

"That doesn't excuse your underhanded dealings," she said, trying to sound stern.

And failing. A cute smile pulled at her lips.

Jason knew how to push to get what he wanted. His persistence had paved the way for him to win successive snowboarding championships until he'd been derailed. He knew Lauren had come here because she was out of options, but he didn't want to force her. He wanted to make her acquiescence as easy as possible.

"Look, if it's any consolation I was going to tell you eventually. I'm not big on secrets. I just wanted an in, something you weren't about to give me. So can't we just move on from here? What do you say?"

She finally shrugged. "I say we get to work." She extended her hand and he grasped it.

On contact, white-hot darts of desire licked at his veins.

"Not so fast," she said, throwing the equivalent of cold water over him.

She attempted to slide her hand out of his grasp, but he held on tight.

"What is it?" he asked.

"You have to agree to my rules."

"And what would those be?" he asked, amused.

"All work and no play. So do we have an agreement?"

He burst out laughing. Did she honestly believe they could work together and not act on their crazy attraction?

"Something funny?" she asked.

He shook his head, sobering fast. "There's nothing remotely amusing about that rule," he said.

"I agree. So?"

He swallowed a groan.

What choice did he have if he wanted entry into her life? He also wanted entry into her body again, but he was a long way from that particular goal. Unless he could figure out a way around her stipulation, he was destined for cold showers for the next few weeks.

Her hand remained inside his. He caressed her palm with his thumb and she inhaled a barely audible sigh. It was low but he heard it and his body reacted, hardening in an instant.

That's when he realized he had a solution. "We have a deal," he said, adding one qualification. "As long as I have the right to try and change your mind."

Since he'd effectively cornered her into hiring him, his addendum wasn't fair and he knew it. But she obviously wanted him, too, which to his way of thinking put them on equal footing.

Her eyes were glazed with desire, narrowed in thought.

But in his mind it was a win-win situation. They'd get to know each other again in the time she had left. That she was leaving soon helped ease his mind about getting involved with a woman who had always affected him so strongly. So did her reticence.

He'd been recently burned by a hot and heavy romance with Kristina, but this one with Lauren had a beginning, middle and predestined end.

Surely she was smart enough to realize the same thing.

"Well?" he asked, staring pointedly at their intertwined hands.

She drew a deep breath and looked him in the eye. "Jason?"

"Yes?" He held his breath.

"Tomorrow morning, my house. Game on." She pulled her hand from his and straightened her spine, swinging her hair over her shoulder in a sassy display of attitude surely meant to cover her uncertainty.

No way was she sure of victory. Not the way she'd been nearly panting from just holding his hand. Damned if he wasn't rock hard and ready to go, too.

She turned and started for the door.

"See you then…sweetheart."

She missed a step, righted herself and kept on going.

Satisfied, more than satisfied really, Jason folded his arms across his chest and glanced down at Fred. "Game on, Fat Man," he said to the dog.

Tomorrow morning at nine, their battle of wills would begin. As a competitor of the fiercest kind, Jason looked forward to the challenge.

PROGRESS WAS a thing of beauty, Clara Deveaux thought as she dusted the old treasures in Edward's house. Things he'd accumulated over the years. Some might call them clutter, but she respected them because they had meaning to the man she loved. She'd always been a believer in good Wiccan magic, never a believer in bad.

She emulated her Jamaican grandmother's ways

and lived by the saying, first do no harm. It had worked well for her until that fateful day her father had arrived from Jamaica, determined to marry Clara off to a man he'd chosen. She'd already met and fallen in love with the gruff, eccentric Edward Corwin by then, but she hadn't wanted to disappoint her father. Never mind that she was already forty years old, the situation had been a tricky one since she was raised to respect and honor her parents.

She'd been planning to tell her father the truth, but her two worlds collided; the tall Jamaican with the flowers, her father moving fast and discussing wedding plans, and the wounded man she loved. Edward had walked into the shop and correctly interpreted the men's intent. He hadn't trusted in Clara's feelings and had stormed out.

After explaining to her father and suitor that she had no intention of agreeing to an arranged marriage, she'd gone in search of Edward. She'd tried to reach him but he'd wanted nothing to do with her. That had been the last she'd seen of him for seven years, until Amber Rose Corwin had walked into her shop to buy a gift for her new father-in-law, Edward Corwin. That had been Clara's sign.

She'd returned to Edward's life, determined to wait as long as it took for him to heal so they could have a future. After his hospitalization last year, the doctor put him on antianxiety medication. Mike, Edward's son, had asked her to move in, make sure he took his pills and keep his appointments. Clara knew the Goddess was looking out for her then.

It had only been about four months, but there was light. Edward talked to her at dinner. Not rambled, disjointed thoughts but real conversation. He'd ask about her day, her business. He had begun reaching out to her at last. Baby steps, but she was so grateful.

She replaced old candles around the house with fresh, new ones, wanting the scent to permeate by the time she returned home from work. Ever since she'd reopened her shop, Crescent Moon, here in Stewart, her New Age gift business was better than ever.

Her home life was harmonious and she was at peace. Maybe tonight she'd kiss Edward on the cheek before going to bed. It would be their first physical sign of affection but Clara felt certain Edward was ready.

JASON ARRIVED at the Perkins mansion at nine on the dot. Clipboard in hand to take notes on the project, he walked up the front porch to find the door ajar. As he stepped inside, a flash of fur whizzed past him, brushing his pant leg as it made a mad break for freedom.

"Hello? Lauren?" he called out.

"I'll be right there!" Her voice sounded from deep inside the house.

Shoving his hands into his jeans pockets, he paced the outer hallway of the large house. He'd never been inside before and, based on his history with this family, he expected old ghosts to reach out and touch him. Instead, all he sensed was an old home with peeling paint, a mildewed smell and dilapidated flooring.

"Sorry, but you won't believe the morning I've had," Lauren said, out of breath.

She came toward him, closing the last button on her light pink man-styled shirt. Her feet bare, her long hair swinging as she moved, no makeup on her face, she was a breath of fresh air in this stuffy house.

"What's wrong?" he asked.

"What isn't? I woke up late, stepped into water all over the bedroom floor. The cat still has an upset stomach—and that's putting it mildly." She pulled her hair back into a ponytail with her hands, securing it with a covered elastic. "All of that and it's just nine a.m."

"It could be worse."

She raised an eyebrow, hands perched on her hips. "Care to tell me how?"

"You could still be without a contractor instead

of having the best at your beck and call." He couldn't help but tease her.

"Good point." She shot him a wry smile.

"What kind of flood?" he asked, concerned that the old pipes were giving her trouble.

"The kind that isn't going anywhere," she said, turning and walking away. "I need caffeine," she called over her shoulder. "Want some coffee?"

He blinked in surprise at her change of subject and, given no choice, he followed her. "Black would be great," he said to her back.

Once in the kitchen, which appeared to have been renovated in the last decade at least, he sat at the table, placing his clipboard down.

Lauren worked quickly. She poured them both cups of coffee that had already brewed and handed him a steaming mug.

"Thanks," he said.

She nodded, lifted the cup and finished her caffeine fix in short order.

"So where's the fire?" he asked, taking a sip of the hot coffee.

She placed her mug in the sink and ran water inside it. "We have work to do."

He wasn't sure if she wanted to keep things moving quickly to avoid any serious conversation or because she really did want to get started on the job.

Regardless, he took the hint. Steeling himself, he downed his coffee and placed the cup in the sink, rinsing it as she'd done with hers.

"Let's start with the flood." Picking up his clipboard, he gestured for her to lead the way.

After surveying the water in the large bedroom on the main floor, he realized things didn't look good. "Where's the water heater?"

"There's a laundry room over here." She led him out of the bedroom, which he appreciated since the bed hadn't been made and the rumpled sheets only served to remind him of what he'd rather be doing.

What she'd prohibited him from doing, unless he could convince her otherwise. But he was a professional and he knew she needed to sell this house, so he focused on the job first.

"The laundry room backs up to the bedroom," he said, reaching for the door. He opened it carefully and, just as he'd feared, found the old water heater surrounded by a huge puddle.

"Is it bad?" Lauren asked, hovering over his shoulder, so close her scent surrounded him.

"Seems that way. Considering how old and corroded the water heater looks, I'd guess it needs replacing, which means a big expense. Plus labor." He turned to see her shocked expression.

"Well, that'll put another huge hole in my

bank account, but I don't have a choice. When will you know?"

"Contrary to popular belief, I'm not an expert at everything."

She propped one shoulder against the wall. "Really? What a disappointment." Despite the situation, her eyes sparkled with amusement.

He laughed. "Plumbing's not my thing, unfortunately. I'm going to have to subcontract the job. I'll make a few calls and see what I can do."

The first plumber who came to mind was Uncle Edward, but the notion of asking him to work on the old Perkins house seemed wrong. Jason didn't want to jeopardize his uncle's recovery by pushing him too far.

"Let me start with JR Plumbing." He called and the owner answered on the first ring.

Jason explained the situation, the emergency nature of the flood and the need to inspect the rest of the pipes in the old house as soon as possible.

"I understand and thanks." Jason hung up. "All his guys are busy working at the elementary school. One of the pipes burst and they're getting it fixed."

Lauren gnawed on her lower lip. "What next?"

"He has a new guy who he just interviewed but hasn't officially hired yet. He says he's eager. Keeps checking in to find out if J.R.'s got room to hire him. He's going to give the guy a call and send him over."

She exhaled hard. "Okay, that's one down. Ready to see the rest of the house?"

Half an hour later, he had a basic list, certain he'd be adding more as he started to work. Lauren would be in charge of cleaning and removing her grandmother's clutter and deciding what large items needed to go. The buyers were coming from a small apartment and had agreed to take most of the existing furniture.

"We need to test the appliances and see if any require repair or replacement, check the overhead fixtures for the same thing, repaint the walls, refinish the floors, check the windows and doors, and that's just off the top of my head."

She nodded, appearing pale and overwhelmed.

"Before we go further, what's with all the holes in the walls?" he asked. "It looks like someone deliberately broke through the Sheetrock."

She shrugged. "Your guess is as good as mine. They weren't here the last time I visited my grandmother."

"What about the alarm system?" he asked.

"Broken."

He made a note of that and realized Lauren had clenched her hands into tight fists.

"Listen, the next step is for us to talk budget," he said.

Lauren drew a visibly shaky breath. "Let's sit," she suggested, leading him to the den, where he sat beside her on the couch.

"What's wrong?" he asked, reading the worry in her expression.

"It's the budget. There's just so much more to do than I originally expected."

He nodded in understanding. "I assumed as much."

"Look, I make a great living. That's not bragging, it's fact."

"Based on the Porsche in the driveway, I figured as much," he said, grinning.

"It's preowned but it's my baby."

He caught the satisfaction in her voice and understood. "I bought the Carrera after I nailed my first sponsor. And I sold it after the scandal." It wasn't easy to reveal his biggest humiliation, but he wanted her to know he truly understood her. Better than she might think.

She moved her hand, covering his, squeezing tight. "I'm sorry. That must have been awful."

"By then there'd been so many degrees of awful, it didn't matter all that much."

"Liar," she said softly.

His mouth pulled upward into a smile. Leave it to Lauren to call him on it. "Let's focus on you, okay?"

"For now," she said, giving him fair warning she wasn't finished with him yet. "Anyway, after the first of the year, my dresses are debuting for a huge label in Paris. If it's successful..." Her eyes widened, filled with excitement and anticipation. "It would be the answer to my dreams."

"Then I have no doubt you'll succeed." He placed his hand over hers.

"Really?" She tilted her head to one side as she looked for his reassurance.

"Really. You have the drive, you have the talent and you've already been discovered. Now you just need for the world to see it, too." He smiled, his pride in her growing as he spoke.

"But it doesn't matter how much money I earn after the show. I don't have a lot now. Whatever my grandmother had in her estate went to creditors I didn't know anything about until she died, and the bulk of my savings has gone to keeping my sister's lawyer working on her case." She curled one leg beneath her, shifting positions, not looking at him as she spoke.

He didn't much care what happened to her arsonist, Corwin-hating sister, but he didn't blame

Lauren for her family's sins. He'd had enough of being blamed for his own, and he was innocent.

It galled him, though, that the price of fixing her family's mistakes fell on her shoulders. "Are your parents still building toilets and roads for the poor?"

She grinned. "Yes, they're still out of the country doing humanitarian work."

He hesitated about asking his next question then decided what the hell. He wanted to get to know her again, to understand what drove her and why. "That explains why they aren't here to help now, but what about financial help for your sister's attorney or for this house? Didn't they write some huge self-help book?"

She pursed her lips. "They co-wrote a parenting book, and between sales, television appearances and new editions every few years, they earned themselves a huge amount of money. They promptly took their earnings, kept a modest sum to live on and donated the proceeds to charity, something they continue to do yearly. There's nothing left to help me. And frankly even if there was, I don't think they'd find my issues outweighed those of the poor."

He shook his head. "I wouldn't have thought giving to charity could be a bad thing." And at the expense of their children, he thought, disgusted.

Lauren shook her head and laughed, a low, dry, humorless sound. "Tell me about it. They believe their money is going for a good cause, whereas my income, earned through a materialistic lifestyle, is expendable. Hence Beth and this house have become my responsibility." She swept her arm through the air.

He was speechless. She'd stepped up to take care of responsibilities that should rightly belong to her parents. He admired the adult she'd become in light of the obstacles she faced.

"I have enough to cover these repairs, even with the water heater, but it'll be tight," she said at last.

"I understand. And I promise to do this as quickly and efficiently as possible." He'd fix as much as he could himself to save her outside costs, and he'd do it without letting her know. He had plenty of time to spare.

"Thank you for that. And for not judging." Her smile lit up the room as well as his heart.

It was the first time they'd had a genuine conversation and a swell of emotion filled his chest. He met her gaze and wanted to kiss her. To reassure her that she could rely on him in a way she so obviously couldn't on anyone else in her life.

He leaned in closer.

She didn't back away.

And the doorbell rang, breaking the connection between them.

She pulled back, eyeing him warily before heading to answer. Leaving him to dissect the complicated, protective feelings she aroused.

"Where's my nephew?" a familiar voice bellowed.

Uh-oh.

Uncle Edward was here. Jason didn't know how he'd found him or why he'd shown up now, but it couldn't be good news and he didn't want Lauren greeting the older man alone.

Jason ran to catch up and the three of them converged in the marble entryway.

One look at his uncle and Jason knew something had set him off.

"Hi, Uncle Edward. How'd you get inside?" Jason asked.

"The door was already open, so I let myself in. If she didn't want visitors, she should've locked her door. I always lock mine."

Jason swallowed hard. The rambling was a sign of his agitation. "Well, I'm surprised to see you here. I'd like you to meet Lauren," he said, deliberately omitting her last name.

Edward looked her up and down. "She's a

Perkins, isn't that right?" he asked, running a hand through his hair and making it a mess.

"Well yes, and this is her house you barged into," Jason reminded his uncle, hoping he'd take the hint and be polite.

"It's nice to meet you, Mr. Corwin," Lauren said, extending her hand.

Edward jumped back as if she were poised to attack. "How could you take a job working for a Perkins?" he asked his nephew.

Jason stiffened, mortified on Lauren's behalf as well as his own. "How did you find out?"

"I was at JR's Plumbing Supply House when you called, that's how! You can't work here. Not without invoking curses and trouble. Curses. They're the cause of all the problems we've had and it's her family's fault." Edward began to gesture at Lauren, clearly upset.

Jason shot Lauren an apologetic glance. "Let me get him home and settled and I'll be right back, okay?"

She nodded, her eyes wide, a combination of sadness and regret in them.

"Uncle Edward, let me take you home to Clara." Jason wrapped his arm around the older man.

Edward shook his head. "Clara's gonna put one of her spells on me, too."

Jason let out a groan and directed his uncle toward his car. Edward had walked here, as he did to most places in town. But right now, Jason needed to get him home as soon as possible.

He dreaded Clara seeing Edward in this state. His uncle had only recently begun to soften toward Clara, but now it seemed he'd reverted to his old fears and behavior.

All because a Perkins and a Corwin were working together. Imagine what would happen if Edward knew they were sleeping together?

## CHAPTER SIX

LAUREN FOLLOWED Jason and Edward Corwin out to Jason's car with Edward mumbling the entire way. It didn't help that the cat was settled on Jason's hood like a king.

"It's another sign, I tell you," Edward muttered, pointing to the black ornament.

"Is it yours?" Jason asked Lauren.

"In a manner of speaking. He came with the house."

Jason glanced over his shoulder at her. "Can you get him off?"

Lauren shrugged. She wondered if a cat would come when called. Of course, it didn't matter since she didn't know his name.

"Come on, Cat!"

The feline didn't budge.

What she didn't know about cats could fill volumes. She'd already given the cat diarrhea. What next? "I'm sure he'll jump off when you start the car."

"Don't want that thing near me any more than I want a dang Perkins near me," Edward said. "Should have brought Stinky Pete with me, I tell you."

"Who's Stinky Pete?" she asked Jason, all the while reminding herself not to take a demented man's ravings seriously.

"The pet skunk he uses to keep people away," Jason said, shooting her a look that clearly said, *Don't ask.*

After settling his uncle in the passenger seat, Jason turned back and walked over to Lauren and squeezed her hand. "I'm sorry," he said, tilting his head toward the car.

She shook her head. "It's not your fault. Go take care of him. He obviously needs you."

And she needed to forget the sight of Jason leading his uncle to the car, taking charge and caring for the older man. She'd come too close to kissing him moments earlier. Noticing his warm, caring nature wouldn't allow her to keep a safe emotional distance.

Luckily, as soon as Jason started the engine, the cat raised its head—haughtily, in Lauren's opinion— and jumped off the hood, clearly annoyed.

Lauren tried not to laugh. She'd never realized a feline could have such an uppity disposition.

The car backed out of the driveway, slowing

down as Jason opened the window. "I'll be back soon," he promised.

She nodded.

"Are you sure you can handle the plumber?"

"Of course." She waved him on his way.

She hadn't even walked up the porch steps when an old, battered pickup pulled into the driveway.

A young guy stepped out of the truck. As he approached, Lauren had the distinct feeling she'd seen him somewhere before but found herself unable to place his face. He was tall and lean, wearing dark jeans and a solid gray T-shirt. He wasn't half bad looking, although she was already spoken for. Lauren stopped short in her tracks, unsure of where that thought had come from.

"Is this the Perkins house?" the man asked as he strode up the walkway.

She nodded. "Can I help you?" She assumed he was the plumber but couldn't be certain.

"I'm looking for Jason Corwin?"

"He was called away but he'll be back soon. Can I help you?"

He nodded and extended his hand. "Brody Pittman. JR Plumbing sent me over."

Lauren shook his hand, which was roughened from work, and he stared down at her, his eyes boring into hers. Once again she had the feeling she'd seen him somewhere before. "Do I know you?" she asked.

He looked her over, head to toe, before answering. "Nope. I think I'd remember if we'd met before."

"You just look familiar," she murmured.

He glanced over her shoulder. "I must have one of those familiar-looking faces. Ready to get started?" he asked.

"Sure." She gestured for him to follow her inside. "I woke up and stepped into a flood. I think it's the hot water heater," she explained.

"It's an old house, so it wouldn't surprise me."

"Actually I need you to give all the pipes a once-over. I'm planning to sell the house soon and the prospective buyers will be doing an inspection prior to closing. I need to know of any potential issues ahead of time."

"That shouldn't be a problem."

"Good." They'd reached the bedroom. "Flood's in here and the water heater is around the corner." She pointed down the hall to a closed door on the left.

"Okay. Let me take a look and see what we're dealing with. I'll get back to you before I start any work."

"Thanks. I'll be in the kitchen if you need me." She left him and retreated to the kitchen for another cup of coffee.

Half an hour later, Jason returned, looking more tired than he had before. Clearly the episode with his uncle had taken a toll on him.

She barely had time to say hello, when the plumber joined them.

Introductions went quickly and Lauren got to the point. "How bad is it?" she asked the plumber.

"You're going to need a new heater, for starters." He wiped his dirty hands on a rag. "As for the rest of the house, things are hit and miss. The plumbing's old, no question about that. There have been some recent replacements, but there are a lot of pipes that need replacing, as well."

Jason nodded. "I figured as much. How long until you get the heater?"

The other man shrugged. "I'm new so I'm not sure. Let me call my boss and see what's in stock, but it's a standard unit, so with a little luck I can pick it up today."

"Great. Do that and get me an estimate on the rest of the house. We'll go from there."

The other man shifted from foot to foot. "I need to write down everything, but I gotta tell you, some of it needs to be done ASAP or else you're looking at bigger problems down the road."

"I understand. Then get me an estimate quickly, Mr. Pittman."

"It's Brody, and sure thing." He turned and headed back to work.

"I'm just looking out for your budget and bottom line," Jason said to Lauren as soon as the plumber had gone.

"I appreciate that." Lauren smiled. "How's your uncle?" She'd been trying to put his disparaging remarks about her being a Perkins into perspective, but they still bothered her.

Lauren had returned to town telling herself she didn't care what other people thought of her, yet when it came to Jason's family, she realized their opinion of her mattered.

"It's just frustrating." A muscle twitched in Jason's jaw. "He was doing so well, but when it comes to the curse, he isn't rational. Anything Perkins-related sets him off." Jason glanced out the window over the kitchen sink, staring into the wooded area beyond.

"I'm sorry." She stepped up behind him, placing her hand on his shoulder. "We seem to find ourselves saying that a lot."

He turned and they were close. Nose-to-nose close. "Then let's stop. None of this Corwin Perkins stuff is either one of our fault."

She shrugged. "I know that, and yet—"

He cut her off, placing his finger over her lips. "Your last name doesn't define you. It never has."

Unable to help herself, she looped her arms around his neck. "You're still a nice guy, Jason Corwin." Smiling, she leaned in close for a kiss.

Just one. Because he didn't blame her for her family's sins and because he was kind, compassionate and sexy.

She touched her lips to his. He immediately cinched his arm around her waist, pulling her close and sealing his lips against hers. His tongue swept into her mouth, creating dizzying sensations that had her clenching the fabric of his shirt and kissing him back as if she were starving.

He rocked his hips against hers, teasing her with possibilities as he kissed her thoroughly, deeply, and oh so erotically. Her skin tingled. Her nerve endings were on fire. She never wanted the moment to end.

Yet incredibly, he pulled back, staring into her eyes with his mesmerizing gaze.

"What's the matter?" she asked, her hands still gripping his shirt.

"Don't get me wrong, I could do this all day but you'd only use it against me later on, when we don't get any work done."

Reality came swarming back fast. "Oh." She licked her damp lips.

The man had a point.

"But I do need you to remember one thing for after work hours." An amused smile pulled at his lips.

"What's that?" she asked warily.

"I'm not the one who broke the all-work-no-play rule, sweetheart. And I didn't even have to try." He placed a warm kiss on her cheek and headed out of the kitchen, back to work.

CLARA LOVED the women she'd befriended since moving to town. She cherished the loyalty and she needed their support. But since she'd gone from joy and optimism to true concern for her Edward, she wasn't in the mood for Ladies' Night.

Once a month, she, Amber, Gabrielle and sometimes Sharon met at The Wave. Since she'd become pregnant, Gabrielle drank a blend of Clara's favorite tea that the restaurant now stocked and Clara usually joined her, while Amber and Sharon nursed white wine. They shared their joys and their problems and Clara loved having these close female friends in her life.

Ever since Jason had brought Edward home, mumbling and upset, she had been thrown by the change in his personality. She'd thought they'd made progress, yet now at the merest mention of Lauren Perkins working with his nephew, Edward had suddenly regressed. Clara had left him in the boathouse near the lake, hammering and muttering and basically not dealing with the world, including her.

She'd called his psychiatrist, and Dr. Shelby said he'd fit Edward in tomorrow. In the meantime, Mike promised to look in on Edward, while Clara headed to The Wave.

Thanks to the townspeople pitching in with donations of money and time, The Wave had been rebuilt in the year since Beth Perkins had set the place on fire. The restaurant was once again a hub in the community where people gathered at night and met up for lunch during the day.

The aqua-blue of The Wave's logo welcomed Clara as she stepped inside and looked for her friends. She found them already seated and laughing around a table in the rear.

"Hello, ladies," Clara said as she hung her jacket on the back of her chair and settled in.

"Clara, we're so glad you could make it," Amber said. "I know you'd rather be home with Edward, but it'll do you good to get out." She placed her hand over Clara's. "How is he?"

"Puttering out back." She knew that statement would explain it all.

Gabrielle shook her head. "I'm so sorry."

"I know. Let's talk about other things tonight. You

cut your hair again!" Clara said, taking in Gabrielle's angled bob. "I always loved that look on you."

"Thanks. I had it cut this morning. I used to keep it this way because it was in style. Now it's just easier because I'm so tired all the time," she admitted, flushing as she spoke.

Clara smiled. "You fought hard for this pregnancy, so enjoy every moment."

"I can't wait to be Aunt Amber!" Amber said.

Gabrielle leaned her elbows on the table. "How about becoming mommy? I need someone to go through this with and the baby will need a playmate! You, too, Sharon."

Clara studied Amber and Sharon intently, sensing their answers before they replied.

"What's that knowing look?" Amber asked, her focus on Clara.

Folding her hands in her lap, Clara replied, "I have my feelings, that's all."

Sharon, cheeks pink, asked, "Care to share them?"

Clara was happy to oblige. "You'll be giving Gabrielle's daughter a playmate soon," she said, pointing to Sharon. "And you, not for a while." Clara inclined her head toward Amber.

Clara didn't know if she had second sight or just the deep intuition that ran in her family, but Sharon had a glow about her that told Clara the other woman would be pregnant soon, while Amber was too busy enjoying her new husband, her move east from Vegas and her recent job as a concierge in a hotel chain new to downtown Boston.

"Am I right?" Clara asked.

Both women glanced away, neither eager to reveal their personal feelings.

Clara merely smiled. "Time will tell," she mused.

"Drinks on the house," the waitress said, stopping by with a tray full of their usual orders. They'd been having these Ladies' Nights for the past four months and their choices were pretty standard.

"Thank Seth and George for us," Gabrielle said, referring to the father and son owners.

"Yes, and also remind them that if they don't stop doing this soon, they won't have any profits," Amber said in full business mode.

But they all knew that after nearly losing their business, George and Seth Saybrook were doing all they could to repay people for their kindness during the rebuilding.

"Will do," the brunette said, laughing. "Let me know if you need anything else."

Another half hour passed as they filled one another in on their lives, then the subject turned to Jason. Clara was surprised they hadn't focused on him earlier. These women were so happily settled down they wanted everyone around them to be the same way.

Two Corwin cousins down. One more to go.

"Sharon, you're the one who found Jason with Lauren Perkins at the festival, and we all know Uncle Edward heard he's working on restoring her grandmother's house," Gabrielle said, eyes gleaming. "So do you know what's going on?"

"Wait, how does Sharon know Lauren?" Amber asked.

"Lauren used to spend summers with her grandmother and we were friends," Sharon said.

"Then didn't you know her, too, Gabrielle?" Clara asked. Sharon and Gabrielle had been childhood pals.

Gabrielle shook her head. "Most summers my family visited relatives in Paris. I really never met Lauren until right before the fire."

"This is getting complicated," Amber said, laughing. "But back to Jason and Lauren. What's going on with them?"

"I know there's mutual interest," Sharon replied with her usual caution. "But I also know Lauren's fixing up the house so she can sell it to waiting buyers. So if you're aiming to matchmake, I think you're out of luck. She's leaving for Paris at the end of the year."

"Paris? What's in Paris?" Gabrielle asked.

"Haute Couture Fashion Week. I'd think you would have that on your radar, considering how much you love clothes and shoes," Sharon said, laughing. "Lauren Perkins is an up-and-coming dress designer."

Clara saw Gabrielle's astute mind start to work. The woman loved fashion and anything related to style. "I don't recognize the name Lauren Perkins... Wait!" She snapped her fingers. "LP Designs, right? She's with Galliano now."

Sharon looked thoughtful for a moment. "I think that's the name of her company. I'm not sure."

"How could you not know? Oh, never mind." Gabrielle rolled her eyes at her friend. "I'll have to get over to the house and reintroduce myself."

"So you don't hold it against her?" Sharon asked, obviously relieved. "That her sister and grandmother tried to destroy your husband's family? That they perpetuated the curse?"

"No, why would I?" Gabrielle said. "She didn't have anything to do with it."

Clara smiled, so pleased at the friends she'd made, their wisdom and openmindedness.

"So if she and Jason got together, a Corwin and a Perkins," Sharon pushed, spelling things out, "you really wouldn't care?"

"If she made Jason happy, I'd be all for it!" Gabrielle announced.

Sharon nodded. "Good, because I really want her to be accepted while she's here. I didn't want anyone to hold what her family did against her."

"Well, she won't get that kind of treatment from us," Gabrielle promised.

"I agree," Amber said. "Of all people, I know what it's like to try and outrun past mistakes."

Clara smiled. Yes, Amber would understand. She'd met Mike Corwin in Vegas, married him on a whim and abandoned him before he even woke up the next day. She'd had her reasons, but she'd spent a long time making up for her choices and still hadn't forgiven herself completely, even though her husband had.

"As long as Jason is happy, that's all we care about," Amber said. "So does she make him happy?"

Clara, who'd been content to let the other women speak, decided it was time she added her two cents. "She makes him more than happy. I think she's his destiny." Finally she'd admitted aloud what she'd been keeping inside since the day of the tarot reading.

"Now that's a mouthful," Amber said, her eyes wide.

"Tell me about it." Clara's biggest problem was

that Jason's chance for happiness reinforced Edward's greatest fear.

"What do you mean you think she's his destiny?" Gabrielle asked.

Clara didn't want to push for this relationship when it would only hurt the man she loved. It wasn't that Clara was worried about whether or not Edward would eventually accept her love. If they were meant to be, then they'd have a future together. But she knew that revealing her sense of inevitability regarding Lauren and Jason might trigger something in Edward that would lead to further regression or even breakdown.

Still, Clara believed in following the clues of the tarot to wherever they led. She couldn't keep this to herself. Not if the family could help.

"I did a reading for Jason before the festival and I saw her," Clara said.

"Saw who? Lauren?" Sharon asked.

Clara nodded. "In a sense. I saw a woman of mystery wearing a red mask—the ultimate expression of undying love."

She'd also seen the white picket fence and the potential for happily ever after. "A Corwin and a Perkins union would undo the past," Clara said softly.

"I love it!" Amber said, her blond curls bouncing around her face as she practically jumped up in her seat.

Clara had expected Amber's enthusiastic reaction, but she glanced warily at Gabrielle. An author who debunked the paranormal, Gabrielle had forged a mutual respect with Clara despite their differing beliefs. Gabrielle's last work, written in the months following the fire, refuted the Corwin Curse and put forth other more logical explanations for all the tragedies that had befallen the family over the generations.

What Clara had just suggested was contrary to Gabrielle's commonsense beliefs.

Gabrielle glanced down, then met Clara's gaze. "I love the notion of Jason's happiness even if I don't believe there's a past to undo," she said at last.

Clara smiled. "Fair enough." She admired the other woman greatly. "Sharon?"

She swirled her wine in her glass. "I want Jason to be happy, too, but Lauren's leaving. She has plans and I can't see anything that would make her stay, especially in a place where she would have to face all the problems her family caused day in and day out."

"Women and men do strange things in the name of love," Clara mused. "I just think we have to wait and see what the Fates have in store."

"Why wait when we can nudge things in the right direction?" Amber asked.

"As long as things take their natural course," Clara said warily.

Gabrielle cleared her throat. "They're already working together, right? So we just need to keep it that way. What could be more natural than that?"

"Exactly!" Amber's excitement was tangible. "Just a little extra work that will keep Jason in the house more often. Nothing serious or extreme, I promise." She held up one hand.

"See? All natural matchmaking." Gabrielle grinned.

"I like it. Who's in?" Amber asked.

Clara hoped she didn't live to regret this as she joined the other women at the table and raised her hand.

FOUR DAYS INTO Lauren's project, Jason thought he would lose his mind. What had started as a mission to show Lauren he could work on her house like a professional and accomplish everything she needed without distraction—*sexual distraction*—had turned into a form of self-torture. It didn't matter that he had men from his crew milling around or the electrician inspecting the wiring. His focus was solely on her.

He'd been determined to let sex be on her terms. He wanted her to come to him so that she didn't have any regrets afterward, ensuring many a repeat performance. At least until she left town.

But being around her was wearing him down. From the tight jeans she wore, to the way she hummed off-key to the music she played on her iPod, to the sexy sway of her hips as she cleaned and scrubbed each room from top to bottom, she slowly, systematically was driving him insane. He didn't think he could wait for her to give in first.

As a successful athlete, he'd always attracted women easily. Whether it was the ski bunny groupies who hung around the lodge where he worked and practiced, or the women who wanted to say they'd scored with the world champion. Judging by the chemistry between them, which was stronger now than in the past, Lauren wasn't more than a kiss away from being in his bed again.

Yet for one of the first times in his life, he wasn't eager to take what he wanted just because the woman in question could be easily swayed. He didn't know if it was the bruising his ego had taken in the past year, or if it had just been too long since a woman had wanted Jason Corwin the man, not the athlete. He feared it was more about the woman herself. And she was doing her best to remain elusive.

But he needed Lauren to come to him and admit she wanted him.

Now that work was finished for the day, he headed to check in with his lady boss. He couldn't locate Lauren, which surprised him since they'd fallen into a routine. He arrived at the house at eight in the morning, before his small crew, and he worked later than his men, until Lauren called a halt. She enticed him away from patching holes in the walls with the lure of dinner, always some kind of take-out food.

She didn't cook and didn't apologize for it. He wasn't great around the kitchen either, which normally left him eating at the diner in town or mooching some of Clara's home cooking, which was delicious. But since he'd started working at the Perkins house, he was back to eating takeout.

He didn't mind one bit. He preferred sitting across the table from Lauren each night. Learning more, with every meal, about the woman she'd become.

He finally found her in a far room, one he knew she was putting off fixing until last. She was on her knees, her head half inserted into one of the holes in the wall, her delectable rear end sticking out for him to see.

The woman had amazing curves and soft skin. He knew that firsthand, but seeing her in such a provocative position took him off guard and his mouth went dry at the sight. His groin hardened, throbbing against the zipper of his jeans. Visions of stripping off his clothes and taking her in that position, his entire body wrapped around hers as he thrust into her over and over again, filled his mind.

He let out a groan, knowing no way in hell was he going to be able to wait for her to come to him.

THE CAT HAD BEEN crying pitifully from somewhere inside the house. Lauren had done a systematic room-to-room check, listening for the sound to grow louder, but no luck. She'd worked her way from the bedroom, where the cat stayed with her at night, to the far end of the house when finally the meows had grown more distinct and she realized the cat had crawled into one of the many ridiculously large holes punched in the drywall and gotten stuck there.

She'd lowered herself to her hands and knees, gingerly easing her head into the wide space, and peeked inside. Pitch-black, she couldn't see a thing.

"Now that's a nice sight." Jason followed up his words with an appreciative whistle.

Startled, Lauren jumped up, banged her head and fell back onto her butt, her head aching from where she'd smacked it on the wall.

She braced her hands on either side of her hips and glared up at him. "Didn't anyone ever tell you not to sneak up on a person?" she asked as she rubbed her sore head.

"Sorry." She noticed he was trying not to laugh but the corners of his mouth kept tugging up. "You okay?"

"Nothing bruised but my head—and my ego," she muttered.

This time he allowed the grin. "Mind if I ask what you were looking for?"

"The cat's stuck inside. He's been crying on and off."

"And here I thought his favorite place was the hood of my truck."

"Try to control your jealousy," Lauren said. "He's there more often than not." As long as the hood of Jason's car was warm from use, the cat tended to sit on his throne and survey his kingdom.

"I knew I shouldn't have left those holes uncovered," he muttered. "Well, I can't possibly patch them all in one day, but I'll cover them so he can't get stuck again. Let's get him out of here first."

"Sounds like a plan."

"Tell you what," he said as he held his hand out for her. "You get a treat to help coax him out and I'll go find a flashlight."

"The one you paid for is in the drawer near the dishwasher. I'll get it." She placed her palm in his and he pulled her up. Electricity shot up her arm and settled in her chest.

Light-headed from the sensation, she held on to his grasp and she couldn't stop staring at his mouth. Suddenly aroused, she wanted those lips on hers, wanted him to pull her into his arms and not let her go until she agreed to let him make love to her here and now.

Not that it would take any persuasion at all. And from the way he stared at her, his expression taut, his gaze hungry, she knew he felt the same way.

How had this happened? She'd been telling herself she didn't want to get involved with him any more than she already was, yet every evening she'd ordered enough dinner for two and invited him to stay. Each night, she'd shared just enough information about herself to keep conversation going, convincing herself she was maintaining a reasonable distance. Pretending the sexual deprivation and longing weren't killing her.

But now she knew there was no such thing as distance.

And if she didn't feel his hot touch on her body, she was going to explode. "Jason…"

Without warning, a loud, disgruntled *meow* reminded them of their priorities.

With a regretful glance at Jason, she started to head for the kitchen but he held on to her hand.

"What were you going to say?" he asked, his voice rough. "I need you to tell me."

She licked her lips. "No more games. I know I said all work, no play, but I can't do this anymore." Her voice cracked at the confession, but she'd finally admitted her feelings out loud.

"Thank God." His relief was clear.

But once again, she had to make sure he understood her intentions. "As long as you know I'm leaving in a few weeks, we can pick up where we left off in the barn."

Unable to stop herself, she ran her thumb over his stubble-roughened cheek, inhaling his scent, waiting for his reply.

He kissed her hard and fast, sealing the deal.

## CHAPTER SEVEN

BEFORE LAUREN HAD a chance to think about what she'd just agreed to, Jason sent her to the kitchen, and by the time she returned, he'd enlarged the hole. With the treat, they finally rescued the troublesome feline.

Jason had scratches and claw marks on his hands, but the smile on Lauren's face made up for them.

"I'll get the holes patched first thing in the morning," he promised. There were too damn many to fix them all tonight. "I'll seal this big one shut now, though. I wouldn't want Trouble here to climb back in."

The cat, grateful to have been rescued, curled up in Lauren's lap on the couch in the family room and refused to budge. "Do you hear that? Jason's worried about you," Lauren said as she stroked the cat's head in a calming, rhythmic motion. "His little heart is still beating so fast," she murmured.

So was Jason's.

He settled into the seat beside her, his eyes never leaving hers. Now that they'd agreed on what was to come, the energy around them kicked up a notch and anticipation filled the air.

"Don't you think it's time to name him?"

She grinned. "I think you just did, right, Trouble?" Lauren laughed.

Trouble suddenly sprang off her lap, apparently deciding he'd had enough affection for the night.

Jason was just beginning. He slid his arm around her shoulders and pulled her close.

"What are you doing?" she asked, a husky murmur in her voice.

"Picking up where we left off in the barn," he said, sealing his lips hard on hers.

With a groan, she gave in to their mutual desire, threading her hands through his hair and kissing him back just as greedily. But kissing wasn't enough and didn't last long. She reached for the bottom of his shirt and pulled it off, burying her face in the crook of his neck.

She inhaled deeply and let out a low moan. "You smell good."

Everything inside him reacted to her words, including the part of him that needed to join with Lauren now. He wasn't surprised at the urgency between them. They'd been pushing this aside for too long. So although he'd like to take her into the bedroom and make love to her slowly on a comfortable mattress, he knew this wouldn't be the time. At least the couch was better than a scratchy blanket on a hard barn floor.

She shed her shirt next, then removed her bra, baring her breasts for his hungry view. He dipped his head and covered one breast with his lips, pulling the rosy nipple into his mouth. She tasted so hot and sweet, he wanted more. He grazed the tight bud with his teeth, then soothed the gentle bite with long laps of his tongue.

She arched her back in response, thrusting her chest forward and her breast deeper into his mouth. Her wanton, eager response excited him, making him want her pleasure far more than his own.

With his free hand, he covered her other breast, treating her to a thorough massage before focusing his attention on the waiting nipple. Too soon, she was writhing beside him, squirming in need, her soft sighs causing his groin to tighten with building pressure he didn't know how long he could control.

He didn't need to worry.

Lauren's urgency matched his. She stood and quickly unzipped her jeans. He did the same. He turned, naked, ready to reach for her, but she placed her hands on his shoulders and lowered him to a sitting position on the couch.

"What are you doing?" he asked.

"Taking control." She swung her legs over his and lowered herself onto his lap, not yet joining their bodies but teasing him with the possibility.

He wrapped his arms around her and placed his hands over her soft buttocks, caressing both cheeks until she began to rock her body over his. "Don't think I don't know what you're doing," she said, her voice low.

"What would that be?"

"You don't like me being in charge, but tough." She leaned forward and bit his earlobe, his most sensitive spot.

She'd remembered, he thought, shuddering as she continued to nibble on his ear. He laid his head back and groaned aloud. "I'm all yours."

Her wicked laughter inflamed his senses as her tight nipples brushed against his chest, setting him on fire. She licked and kissed her way down his neck, his chest, his stomach, her tongue dancing over his skin, lower and lower until her lips settled *there*.

He groaned raggedly, but she didn't hesitate as she pulled the entire length of him into her warm, wet mouth. He thought he'd died and gone to heaven. She made him her sole focus, drawing her lips up his shaft, then back down, creating intense friction that increased both sensation and pleasure. He threaded his hands through her hair, cradling her head, while she brought him closer and closer to climax. His body tightened and his hips bucked upward, but she didn't seem to mind. She hit just the right spots, used exactly the right pressure, until finally his body exploded in the most intense, satisfying pleasure he'd ever had.

When his head cleared, he pulled her toward him for a long kiss.

"I take it you liked it?" she asked, pleased with herself.

He grinned. "Honey, you can take charge like that anytime. As long as you know when to submit."

Her eyes darkened and she immediately slid to the far end of the couch, stretching out her long, lean body.

"How's this?" she asked, eyes gleaming as she extended her arm and crooked her finger toward him, beckoning him to come to her.

"Works for me," he said, attempting not to show his surprise at the changes he was discovering in her.

She hadn't been as bold when they were younger, and most things they'd done had been firsts for her. Now she seemed more at ease with herself and her sexuality. He hoped that time had brought the change and not experience. He didn't want to think about Lauren and other men. On the heels of that thought came another. He needed to make certain *he* was the only man she remembered.

Starting now. He reached for his jeans and pulled out the condom he'd replaced after the festival.

All single Corwin men were taught by their fathers to use protection, to avoid being tied to any woman and risk falling in love and invoking the curse. He'd always thought the assumption that pregnancy would lead to marriage and then love was absurd. Either the feeling existed or it didn't. Jason was pragmatic that way.

But he'd taken the lesson to heart for other obvious reasons, and he never went without a spare. With Lauren in town, he always intended to be prepared.

He slipped on the condom, then slid over her. Gazing into her eyes, he brushed his thumb across her damp lips, leaned forward and kissed her, sliding his tongue into her mouth.

She shuddered and wound her arms around his neck, pulling him close. His hips nestled into hers, and that quickly he was ready to go again.

"Jason?" she asked, her breath warm against his neck.

"Hmm?"

Her fingers tunneled through his hair. "I want you," she murmured.

As if he needed more than her words to convince him, she rolled her hips against his. Warm, dewy moisture trickled between her thighs and he was lost.

He spread her legs, staring into her green eyes as he parted her with his aching member and thrust inside.

Lauren accepted him with a soft moan of pleasure. Nestled deep inside her body, knowing she'd already taken him in her mouth and given him that gift, Jason felt as if he'd come home.

The thought unnerved him before she rocked her hips and he couldn't think at all. He started to shift and realized the couch wasn't going to work well.

"We need to change positions," he said.

She looked into his eyes and smiled. "Okay, let's do it."

He grabbed her hips and maneuvered them so he was sitting, and she sat on his lap, her thighs on either side of his, completely impaled on his throbbing erection.

Gripping his shoulders, she rocked back and forth, her body joined tightly with his, the movement sending shocks of sensation through his groin and spreading outward. Thoroughly in control, she rode him, gliding up and down, taking him into her body. All the while, he couldn't tear his gaze from her face. She'd squeezed her eyes shut in the throes of passion, the most incredible sight he'd ever seen. And when her orgasm took hold, she pressed him tighter between her slick walls, bringing him up and over the edge along with her.

After a long, shared shower involving wet hands and soapy bodies and, on Lauren's part, a distinct refusal to allow herself to delve too deeply into her feelings, her stomach grumbled. One hunger satisfied, another demanding attention.

"I'm starving," Lauren said as she ran a brush through her hair.

"I worked up an appetite myself." His eyes gleamed with a predatory satisfaction. "I think we've run through every place that delivers in both neighboring towns, so what did you have in mind?" He pulled his T-shirt back over his muscular chest.

"I don't mind picking up burgers from The Diner. I'll get a turkey burger. Cheeseburger and fries for you?" she asked, attempting to act as if her body still wasn't quaking from his touch.

"Perfect. In the meantime, I'll get started on that big hole in the wall." He paused. "How about I call in the order ahead of time?"

"Thanks. That would be great."

He reached for his phone and she noticed he was listening to voice mail first. He deleted the message, then turned to her. "What would you say to dinner with my father and uncle instead?"

She narrowed her eyes. "I'm pretty sure they invited you, not us."

He shook his head. "The message was clear. They're having a late dinner at Uncle Hank's and would like *us* to join them. Gabrielle and Derek are going, too."

Lauren raised an eyebrow, surprised. Wary. And a little nervous. "Why?"

"They didn't say, but I can promise you they won't treat you badly."

"Gabrielle was nice the one and only time we met, but that was before…" She trailed off. Why go into the details of her family's actions. "Do *you* want to go?"

He studied her then nodded. "I do. You?"

"I just don't want to give your family the wrong idea about us, that's all."

"What wrong idea would that be?" he asked, sounding more curious than upset.

Lauren turned to face him. "We're working together."

"And sleeping together," he said with a grin.

"They don't need to know the details. I just

don't want them thinking we're seriously involved." She sat stiffly on the edge of the bed.

"You mean you don't want *me* to think that."

"I'm just being honest, up-front."

"Point made. I'll call my father and let them know we'll be there." That muscle jerked in his jaw, but otherwise she couldn't read his expression.

Which she figured was just as well. She couldn't bear to know she'd hurt him as much as his words had hurt her. But her designs were debuting in Paris and she had a plan for her future. She'd been hurt badly once before. She couldn't handle it again. Keeping an emotional distance this time around was the safest route for them both.

AMBER SAT in the parking lot of Petco in Salem, holding her cell phone closer to her ear. "Are you sure Jason and Lauren are going to Hank's for dinner?" she asked Gabrielle.

"I'm sure. Thomas asked Jason and Lauren, and Hank invited Derek and me. So nobody will be in Lauren's house at eight. Did you pick up the mice?"

"I just left Petco. They're disgusting," Amber said, shuddering as she glanced at the three baby mice sitting in the cage on the passenger seat.

"Oh come on, don't be a wuss."

"Easy for you to say. You're not the one sitting

with Algernon times three staring at you," Amber hissed. "I can't believe people keep these things as pets. Are you sure this is going to work?"

Amber and Gabrielle had come up with their first idea to keep Jason at Lauren's side, but now that Amber had the animals in her possession, she was getting cold feet.

"If you saw a tiny mouse in your house, would you let Mike leave?" Gabrielle asked.

"Good point. Still, this is crazy, you know that, right? Crazy as in 'Mike and Derek will kill us if they find out we've been meddling in Jason's life' crazy."

"It's only meddling if something bad happens as a result. The doorbell's ringing. They're here and I've got to go. So you do your thing." Gabrielle disconnected the phone, leaving Amber to let herself into Lauren's house and leave the furry creatures behind.

JASON LIKED having his family gathered around Hank and Thomas's rectangular dining room table with Lauren by his side. The brothers weren't any better cooks than Jason, so the meal of choice was from The Diner, the same as he and Lauren would have eaten anyway. He wasn't sure what the men's agenda was in having this dinner, but if it meant making Lauren comfortable with the Corwins, he was all for it.

Even if she wasn't.

*I just don't want them thinking we're seriously involved.* Her words sliced through him, but what had he expected? He'd known she wasn't interested in anything long-term or permanent. And if he was honest with himself, neither was he.

He just didn't like her dismissing their relationship as if it meant nothing.

"We're so glad you could make it," Thomas said, interrupting his thoughts.

Jason held Lauren's chair as she settled into her seat before he sat down beside her.

"I appreciate the invitation," Lauren said, her voice neutral.

Careful.

She obviously didn't trust the reason for this meal, but Jason wasn't worried. Inviting someone over then insulting them wasn't the Corwin way.

Which led to his own curiosity. "So to what do we owe the pleasure?" Jason asked.

Derek, seated next to Gabrielle, stretched his arm over the back of her chair. "Good question. I was wondering the same thing myself."

"Thomas has an announcement." Hank's eyes gleamed at the prospect of his brother's news.

"Uh-oh," Gabrielle said, placing her napkin in her lap.

Though everyone already had food on their plates, no one was interested in their meal.

All eyes were on Thomas.

"I have a plan to get Clara and Edward together for good," Jason's father said, explaining the reason for this gathering.

"They're already living in the same house," Derek said. "I'm not sure we're ever going to see much more than that. I think we should be grateful Uncle Edward's made such big strides in such a short time and not mess with his head."

Jason shot his cousin a grateful glance. "I agree."

"Nonsense," Hank said, running a hand through his wiry, unkempt hair. "Tell 'em your plan. I bet they'll change their minds."

"I doubt it," Jason muttered.

"Don't be such a naysayer, son. I'm going to remind my brother what it's like to feel jealous by showing an interest in Clara. He'll be so determined not to let me near his woman, he'll naturally step up and admit his feelings." Thomas spoke with pride in his voice. "Clara will surely say she never had any interest in me and then I will gallantly step aside, leaving Edward and Clara to live happily ever after."

"Assuming the curse doesn't bite 'em in the ass," Hank said. "But you two seem to be doing all right." He gestured toward Derek and Gabrielle. "And Amber and Mike seem to be holding their own, so I think it's worth a shot for my brother, too." He nodded, then picked up his knife and fork and dug into his food, as if the matter were settled.

Far from it, Jason thought, but before he could say so, he realized Lauren had stiffened at the mention of the curse.

Jason placed a reassuring hand on her thigh beneath the table. Stupid move, he realized, when her body heat shot directly into his palm and through him, settling like a heavy missile in his lap.

He ignored the physical reaction, concentrating instead on his father, uncle and their harebrained scheme. "Has it dawned on either of you that Edward may not be able to handle that kind of pushing?"

"I was going to call it meddling," Derek muttered.

"Of course he can handle it, that's what his medication's for," Hank said, waving his fork as he spoke.

Jason wasn't ready to touch his food. Not until they'd settled this discussion. "I take it no one's told either of you what happened at Lauren's house a few days ago?"

Thomas and Hank looked at each other, clearly confused.

Lauren glanced at her plate, steeling herself. She knew Jason's explanation would only lead to another awkward discussion of the curse and she gripped her napkin in her lap, waiting for this conversation to end.

"Uncle Edward found out I was working for Lauren, fixing up the old Perkins mansion, and he flipped out." As Jason spoke, he reached out once more. This time he grasped Lauren's hand, obviously realizing how uncomfortable she was.

She appreciated the gesture, but it didn't change the fact that she was an intruder here and this discussion only served to remind her of that fact.

"I'm not surprised your choice of jobs is a shock for him." Thomas looked at Lauren. "My brother doesn't deal well with the curse," he explained, suddenly focused on her.

Lauren raised an eyebrow, surprised. "Do you?" she asked Jason's father, curious as to how the rest of the family felt.

He straightened his tie. "I've accepted the curse and its repercussions. I don't let it rule my life, nor do I worry about it much." He let his gaze slide from hers.

Liar, she thought, though she felt no anger at Jason's father. She'd always known about the wedge between the two families. As a teenager, she'd been content to push boundaries and disobey family rules and expectations. As an adult, she saw clearly how other people could be affected by her actions. Corwins and Perkinses were not meant to be together. Another reason to keep her emotions in check with Jason this time around.

"My take is a little different," Gabrielle chimed in. "I think anyone born in the twentieth century has to realize that free choice plays a role in everyone's lives." She tucked a strand of hair behind her ear as she spoke. "There's no doubt this family's had its share of tragedy, but much of it can be traced to poor judgment and the expectation of problems."

Hank let out a groan. "My daughter-in-law likes to think there's no such thing as a curse, just like your grandma used to think the town of Perkins could be ruled by it." He pointed to Lauren with his fork, then continued to eat.

He seemed to be the only one with an appetite. At his words, Lauren lost hers completely.

"Uncle Hank!"

"Dad!"

Jason and Derek yelled at the older man at the same time.

"Relax!" Hank continued to wield his fork as a tool for discussion. "I just want to know what the young lady thinks, that's all." Once again he ran a hand through his already messy hair.

"It's rude," Jason said, his hand squeezing tighter around Lauren's.

Hank frowned. "She asked what we thought. I'm just returning the favor. And considering she's a Perkins, I think it's a legitimate question." He eased back in his seat, annoyed at being reprimanded.

Lauren had rarely experienced family dinners as a child, so this entire situation seemed surreal. Adding the curse to the conversation merely increased her discomfort.

Her own family could define the word *dysfunction,* so she didn't want to judge the Corwins. But that didn't mean she needed to sit here and feel isolated and attacked.

She slowly placed her napkin on the table and looked at Hank Corwin head-on. "I'm not sure why I was included in this family gathering and I'm definitely not comfortable," she said, opting for honesty. "But since you asked, I'll tell you what I think."

Jason pushed his chair back and stood. "No you won't. This isn't an inquisition. You're a guest. We came to hear my father's so-called plan for his brother. We heard it. Now we can leave if this line of conversation is going to continue." He glared at his uncle.

Lauren shook her head, tugging his hand, urging him to sit. "It's fine. I want to clear the air."

If the Corwins couldn't accept her, so be it. It wasn't as though she was staying in this town for long anyway.

Gabrielle pushed her plate forward. "Jason's right. This is ridiculous. You were invited because you're a friend of Jason's and you're new in town. Derek and I thought we'd be welcoming you. *Not* interrogating you," she said pointedly.

Gabrielle was genuine and warm and Lauren relaxed, realizing this generation of Corwins at least didn't hold a grudge. She couldn't say as much for the older one, and though she knew she shouldn't care, she did. Because one of the men still watching her uneasily was Jason's father.

Lauren met Gabrielle's warm gaze, finding it easier to focus on the welcoming members of this family. "I appreciate what you're trying to do. And I understand the curse is something that exists— in theory for some, in reality for others. But as for me, I don't believe in it."

"Well, I suppose everyone's entitled to their opinion," Hank muttered.

"That's very generous of you, Dad," Derek said, scowling. "I'm also glad you're here, Lauren. And I wouldn't worry about Uncle Edward's reaction. If he has a setback, then he hasn't come as far as we'd hoped. But no one is to blame."

"And no one's harebrained scheme is going to push him into Clara's open arms," Jason said.

Thomas stared at his plate, then mumbled something Lauren couldn't hear.

"Excuse me?" Jason asked. Obviously he couldn't understand his father, either.

"I said I'll take Edward's reaction into consideration before I decide what to do."

He'd probably said something more colorful than that, Lauren thought.

"Good. Now can we put these subjects to rest and enjoy our meal?" Jason asked.

"As long as you know I'm going to do everything I can do for my brother," Thomas said, stubborn as ever.

"Does that include picking up the pieces for Clara after Edward retreats so far into himself no one can get him back?" Jason's voice was brittle and angry.

"Low blow, son. That's not at all what I had in mind. I'll do what I need to do." With that pronouncement, Thomas picked up his knife and fork and dug into his food with gusto.

Hank joined him.

Lauren had a hunch neither she nor Jason, Derek or Gabrielle tasted their food. The prospect of how Thomas's actions would affect Edward lay on everyone's mind.

JASON WALKED Lauren to her front door, frustrated and angry at his father and uncle. The evening hadn't gone well and Jason blamed himself. He'd thought that to keep Lauren comfortable, no one would broach the subject of the curse. He'd miscalculated and she'd paid the price.

He leaned his shoulder against the door and looked at her. "I'm sorry about tonight. If I'd known they couldn't behave, I never would have suggested we go there for dinner."

Lauren's cheeks flushed pink. From the cold or embarrassment? She shrugged, her shoulders as stiff as they'd been for most of the meal.

"It's not your fault. I shouldn't have agreed to go. Your father and your uncle are too much a part of my grandmother's generation to accept me with open arms. I really like Derek and Gabrielle though."

He relaxed a little, realizing she was more rational about things than he'd been. "I'm glad. Derek's been through a lot and even he believed in the stupid curse for a while, but he has Gabrielle to set him straight now. He's happy and I'm glad."

She pulled the key from her jacket pocket.

Taking the hint, he stepped away from the door and she inserted the key in the lock. "Well, thank you for a nice evening," she said, her voice neutral.

Her emotional walls were up.

He didn't blame her, but he wasn't about to allow her to keep those barriers high.

"Which part was nice exactly? The part where my uncle grilled you?" he asked, unable to control his sarcasm as he positioned himself in front of her, preventing her from pushing the door open and slipping inside. "Or was it the part when we made love earlier? Was that just *nice?*"

He reached out and grabbed her forearm, intentionally baiting her, wanting to see some reaction beyond that cool facade she'd erected. She obviously intended to leave him at the front door, but he wasn't going without a fight.

From the moment he'd extended an invitation to his father's, she'd drawn a not-so-invisible line meant to remind him they weren't seriously involved.

"I don't know what you want to hear."

He pulled her close and covered her lips with his, kissing her hard until her mouth softened and she willingly let him in. Winding her hands around his neck, she urged him close, telling him with her body everything she'd been unable or unwilling to admit. His pulse pounded and adrenaline surged through his veins, desire and the urge to conquer stronger than anything he'd experienced before, including the rush before or right after a race.

He wanted her to know they weren't through.

To remind her *she* didn't want them to be over just yet. Even if he did intend to respect her need for time alone.

Having made his point, he gently lowered her arms until she faced him, her breath coming in short, uneven gasps.

"Why did you stop?" There was a yearning in her eyes he found difficult to deny.

Reaching out, he traced his finger over her damp lips. "I'll see you in the morning," he said gruffly, surprised he could formulate a coherent thought, given the way his body protested their separation.

He pushed the door open and pressed his hand to her back, guiding her inside. The cat sprang out the door, bolting past them for freedom.

Jason waited until she shut the door behind him and turned the lock before heading to his car, where Trouble perched on the hood. The cat's attention was small consolation to Jason, who had a long sleepless night ahead of him.

THE DOCTORS AND NURSES thought Beth was unresponsive. Near catatonic. And she had been for almost a year. She had selective recall of those months. She'd heard her sister talking to her on sporadic visits in a childlike singsong voice.

Awareness had come to her slowly, over a

period of time. Slowly enough that she'd been able to think and plan. Thanks to Lauren, who liked to reassure Beth that everything was going to be okay and why, Beth had been able to plan accordingly. She wouldn't reveal her recovery until the time was right for *her,* leaving her able to observe everything around her closely and use things to her advantage.

Like Nurse Stupid, as Beth liked to call the woman. She was an easy target. She'd gotten lazy and kept her cell phone in the front pocket of the white labcoat she always wore. Beth knew this and filed the information away, just as she knew the woman called her boyfriend during her half-hour breaks twice a day. Beth knew this because she would sneak out of her bed and watch the staff's routine. It was the only fun she had in this godforsaken joint.

That and seeing her lover.

Another human being without many brains, but at least as a construction worker he had the muscles to compensate. It was Beth who had to figure out that on Tuesdays and Thursdays when the nurses had meetings, the guards were occupied playing poker outside her wing. The construction crew had been working here for the past six months and were allowed in and out during daylight hours. Nobody paid them the least bit of attention anymore.

Picking her lover had been easy. Seducing him easier. And convincing him she wanted to spend the rest of her life with him easier still. The dumb sap. But he was able to come and go from this place at will.

He did her bidding. Like searching her grandmother's house for the hidden diamonds that her ancestors used when they invoked the infamous Corwin Curse.

When Lauren told Beth about her plan to sell the house, Beth had nearly burst a blood vessel in her brain. Playing comatose wasn't as difficult as it was boring. But as long as it kept her in minimum security with a chance of getting out one day, it was worth it. Thanks to her grandmother's trust in her, Beth knew about the diamonds stashed somewhere inside the house.

The Perkins family had founded the town, building their fortune in shipping. The diamonds had come from overseas, adding to their wealth. The jewels could be anywhere. Inside the walls, under floorboards, behind paintings. No one knew where. Because, according to Beth's beloved grandmother, an old diary entry foretold that removing the hidden diamonds would lift the ancient curse. And no Perkins wanted to lose the power that came with it.

But now, with her do-gooder sister selling the house, Beth had no choice but to get her hands on those diamonds before they were gone forever. Her lover had already broken into the house before Lauren had moved in but hadn't found anything. Not that he could check everywhere but he'd done some strategic hacking into the plasterboard with no luck.

He needed prolonged access to the house before Beth's nest egg was gone forever.

## CHAPTER EIGHT

LAUREN WAITED for Jason's car to pull out of the driveway before calling for Trouble to come back inside. As much as she hated to admit it, she liked knowing the cat slept on her bed at night. He snored, which somehow made her feel more secure.

When the furry feline didn't come running, she decided to try the back door off the kitchen and was shocked to find it already ajar. No way had she left the door open. Annoyed and frustrated, Lauren slammed it shut and tried to turn the lock, but it wouldn't budge.

Broken.

"Fine. It'll just have to wait until morning," she muttered.

When Jason returned.

Which brought her to the real reason for her bad mood. She was upset with herself for letting his family bother her. For letting Jason's kiss breach defenses she shouldn't have to raise in the first place. She was a grown woman and she ought to be capable of having sex without commitment or entangled emotions. That was what she wanted and needed in order to leave her heart intact.

She tossed and turned for the better part of the night, wishing she'd made him stay.

She woke up later than usual, exhausted and cranky, which led her to the conclusion that the man who'd caused the tossing and turning was also the solution. She'd just resume their sexual relationship as if that awful dinner at his father's house had never happened. Because clearly she'd feel worse and get less work done if she denied her desire for him.

She'd given Jason a key and could now hear hammering coming from the far end of the house. He and the three men in his crew, Nate, Connor and Ross, always began working farthest from the bedroom, giving her privacy until she joined them.

Since she couldn't do anything about her sexual needs right now, she would settle for coffee to begin her day.

She had taken two steps toward the kitchen when her cell phone rang; she pulled it from her pocket. A glance showed a restricted number.

A shiver raced through her as she hit the send button to take the call. "Hello?"

"Ms. Perkins? This is Dr. Shaw at the penitentiary. I'm your sister's doctor. I thought you should know there was an incident this morning."

She gripped her cell phone tighter, nausea rising in her throat. "What kind of incident?"

"Your sister became unruly this morning. I don't know how else to explain it. She started to scream and yell and we had to sedate her in order to calm her down." The doctor's tone was compassionate.

Lauren swallowed hard. "I don't understand. She's been completely nonresponsive. Staring ahead at nothing for almost a year. Do you know what caused the outburst?"

"No. I'm considering asking that she be sent to the hospital for tests, but that would take a court order, which would take some time."

Lauren stared up at the ceiling and caught sight of a large, ugly crack. Another thing to add to the To Do list.

She refocused on her call. "I'll be there in a little over an hour," she said.

At least a half day of work would be lost, but what choice did she have?

"I wouldn't suggest you come now. She's sedated and sleeping. There's nothing you can do for her at the moment."

Lauren closed her eyes. "I see. Well, I'll call later to see how she's doing."

"That's fine. As soon as I think it's helpful for you to visit, I'll let you know."

Lauren nodded. "Thank you, Doctor." She disconnected the call, feeling more agitated than before.

As much as caffeine wouldn't calm her nerves, she still needed to start her day with the comfort of routine, and that meant coffee.

Wearing an old button-down shirt and soft sweats, her feet bare, she walked into the kitchen and stopped short, frozen in place. Because sitting on the granite counter was a mouse. A light gray, beady-eyed mouse with a long tail.

She blinked.

It wriggled and moved its tail. An old memory of the rat-infested walls in her New York City apartment flashed through her mind. One of *those* rats had jumped from her nightstand onto her bed and raced over her legs.

Lauren let out a loud piercing scream and leaped onto the nearest chair, shaking. She continued to shriek, but the rodent didn't run away.

Jason burst through the kitchen entryway at a run, Nate, Connor and Ross right behind him. Jason caught sight of Lauren standing on a chair and skidded to a halt. "What's wrong?" he asked.

She glanced from him to the counter.

The now empty counter.

She pointed halfheartedly. "It's a mouse." She continued to gesture wildly toward the spot where the animal had been.

He walked over and looked at the counter, then scoured the floor, finding nothing. "It's gone." Walking back to her, he held out his hand. "Let me help you down."

"You got this, boss?" Connor asked.

Lauren ignored him. In her mind, she still saw the moving tail and those beady eyes staring at her, and she shook from head to toe.

"You can all get back to work," Jason said.

He lifted her from the chair and carried her into the den, shutting the door and locking it behind him. He headed over to the couch, settling into the cushion with her on his lap.

Unable to control the tremors racking her body, Lauren plastered herself to him, soaking up his strength and embracing his heat.

"What is it?" he asked, his voice gruff yet soothing. "Seeing a mouse has you this spooked?"

Now that the initial shock and fear had begun to subside, embarrassment flooded her.

As hard as it was for her to revisit the past, he deserved an explanation. "For a minute, it wasn't the mouse I was seeing but a rat in New York. The first apartment I lived in was a hole in the wall above a restaurant. It was all I could afford and the rats used to run inside the walls. I could hear them at night." She shuddered at the memory of the scurrying sounds behind the thin walls.

His palm settled on the center of her back, strong, warm and reassuring.

"Sounds awful." Jason wished she hadn't had to go through that experience alone.

"That's not the worst part. One night I was in bed reading and I heard something. I looked up and there it was on the nightstand. Before I could blink, it ran near me and ended up in my bed." The tremors began again and her entire body shook against him.

He slipped his hand beneath her shirt and ran it up and down her bare, *braless* back, gritting his teeth against the sensation of caressing her skin. "You're safe now." But soothing her couldn't undo the past.

"The mouse was in the kitchen!" She burrowed her face into his neck. Her breath was hot and arousing, though her intent was anything but.

"I'll set some traps, okay?" He didn't know much about mouse traps, but they'd be easy enough to find.

Without lifting her head, she nodded, her fingers

holding on to his shirt in a death grip. "I can't see another one. It just does something to me."

Her revulsion and fear hit him hard. "I can't promise, but I'll do the best I can." He waited but she didn't release him. Didn't move her head from his neck.

He inhaled the fragrant scent of her hair, his body hardening.

He fought against the sensation and shifted, intending to get up and start working on the rodent problem. But she didn't budge.

So he slowly lowered his hand from her back, hoping she'd take the hint and move. Before the comfort he wanted to offer lost out to the desire she so effortlessly ignited. Again, she remained in place, her body aligned with his.

So he waited while her tension gradually eased. Her muscles relaxed and she looked up at him, gratitude in her green eyes.

But when she inched back on his lap, her bottom came into direct contact with his rock-hard erection. Her eyes opened wide in understanding and in an instant her pupils darkened and her cheeks flushed.

"If you want those traps set now, you'd better let me get up," he said, his warning clear.

"You locked the door, right? There are still workmen around?" she asked.

He nodded.

"Then what if I still need more comfort?" She ran her tongue over her bottom lip, dampening the full flesh, seducing him with that simple gesture. She shifted her hips until her thighs bracketed his. "Besides, don't you want to know how I used to ignore the rats and finally fell asleep?"

She rotated her body seductively until she cupped him in his denim-covered sheath. Despite the thick barrier, he could swear he felt her heat.

"How?" he managed to ask.

A smile pulled at her lips, but there was no teasing. Just pure honesty as she said, "I'd think about you. It was the only time I'd let myself go back to the time we spent together." She drew a deep breath. "During the day I was driven to succeed, but at night, when I was afraid, I dreamed about you."

He ran his fingers through her hair, regret swamping him. "I wish I'd known."

It shocked him how much he wished he could have taken care of her.

"You're here now." She reached up and began unbuttoning her shirt, releasing one tantalizing button at a time. She wanted him, yes. But she was clearly using sex to feel better.

And he wasn't content to let her hide her

feelings or run from what had happened between them before dinner last night.

Reaching out, he stilled her movements. "Why are you doing this?" he asked.

"Isn't it obvious?" She wriggled her hips, but he clenched his teeth and held on to his self-control.

"Not when just last night you pushed me away." He wanted nothing more than to rip open her shirt and bury his face between her breasts, suckle on one tight nipple before moving on to the next. But when he did, there would be no misunderstandings between them.

She met his gaze. "*You* went home."

He shook his head. "Because you were playing hot and cold with me. You used that invitation to dinner and then my family's abominable behavior as an excuse to back away."

She opened her mouth, then closed it again.

Obviously she couldn't argue.

"Your point?" she asked at last.

"No more running away. For as long as you're in town, you're mine."

She released a lengthy breath. "I think I can live with that. As long as you promise me one thing?"

"What's that?"

"Don't leave me alone in this house with that mouse. I know from experience, where there's one rodent there's bound to be more." Her entire body trembled again.

"Nights, too?"

Her eyes darkened. "Nights, too."

He nodded, silently thanking the run-down, abandoned house for supplying her with an excuse to ask him to stay.

The next few weeks belonged to them.

And what then, a little voice in his head asked. Her cell phone interrupted his thoughts.

She grabbed for it quickly, glancing at the number.

"Hello?" she asked, her voice tremulous.

He waited, confused by her anxiety.

"I see. And now?" She listened once more. "Just like she's been for the last year. I see. That's too bad. I was hoping that after this morning, maybe she'd come out of it."

Her sister, Jason realized.

"I'll touch base tomorrow morning, Doctor. Thank you." She disconnected the call, exhaled a long hard breath, then inhaled deeply.

For a brief second she appeared hurt and fragile. Then she turned to him and squared her shoulders. "Now where were we?" she asked seductively. But her tone was clearly forced.

He slid his hand from beneath her shirt and grasped her arms, pulling her away from him.

"What's going on? That was a serious call and you're obviously upset. So why pretend you aren't?"

"Because I don't expect you to feel sorry that my sister's having problems."

"How about if I feel sorry that you're having problems?"

She shook her head. "Doesn't accomplish my goal."

"Which is?" he asked warily, knowing he wouldn't like what he heard.

She sighed. "I'd like to keep my sister and her issues separate from us." She gestured between them.

And thereby keep him at arm's length.

Jason suppressed the urge to throttle her. "Didn't we just agree you wouldn't do that anymore?"

She shrugged. "I just figured my sister was different."

"You figured wrong."

Tilting her head to one side, she studied him closely. "So you accept her and what she's done?"

Despite his best intentions, he fidgeted, knowing any answer to that loaded question would land him in Uncle Edward's boathouse.

"Well?" she pressed, a knowing—and disappointed—look on her face.

"I didn't say that. But I care about *you* and the things that hurt *you*. So if something has happened with your sister, I want you to be able to share it with me."

"Even if you can't stand the thought of her?"

This time he knew better than to reply.

"Jason, my sister is a part of me."

He didn't appreciate the reminder. "I know. But how I feel about what she does isn't the same as how I feel about you."

She rose and paced the room, turning to face him. "Okay, fine. You want to know? Here it is. My sister has been nonresponsive for months now. But suddenly this morning, she had an *incident,* the doctor called it. An outburst where she became hysterical and upset. They had to sedate her." She shoved her hands into the pockets of her sweats. "I was hoping when she woke up that maybe she'd be back to her old self."

*Her psychotic self?* Jason knew better than to voice his feelings aloud. "And is she better?" he asked carefully.

Which would mean her sister might attempt to get out of prison on an *I was insane and now I'm fine* plea. The thought made his stomach churn. His entire family would rebel at the notion. Even though Lauren was trying to get her sister transferred, Jason held out hope that the other woman's crimes would keep her behind bars where she belonged. None of which he would admit aloud.

"No. Beth is back to staring at walls." Shoulders slumped, Lauren lowered herself into a chair, clearly defeated.

"And what's the prognosis? Does the fact that she seemed to come out of it mean anything?"

"The doctor doesn't know. And he won't unless she can be moved to a hospital for testing, something that requires court approval. And time. For all I know, getting that approval might cost me money." She ran a hand through her hair, tugging at it in frustration. "Argh!"

He rose and walked to her side, placing a comforting hand on her shoulder. Silence seemed best.

"Happy now that I've confided in you?" she asked, her voice catching.

Actually he felt like a complete shit. She'd had a horrible morning from her sister's incident to the mouse. He hadn't helped her at all.

As he glanced at her tortured expression, he wanted to say something, anything that would make her feel better about confiding in him.

He couldn't.

All his pushing and prodding had done was show him that there wasn't anything about Mary

Beth Perkins he wanted to know or understand. Hard as he'd tried to convince Lauren otherwise, her sister would always be a point of contention between them. He'd just have to see how long he could pretend otherwise.

"Look, there's nothing you can do for your sister right now, so what do you say we get to work? You'll be in a better mood once you see we're making progress on the house, right?"

"Right." She shot him a grateful smile. "You do know me pretty well."

The doorbell rang, ensuring he wouldn't have to discuss the Perkins family any longer, and Lauren jumped to answer. Jason followed her to the door, where the plumber waited on the other side.

"Good morning," Lauren said.

Jason nodded to the other man.

Brody Pittman met them with a wide smile. "Good morning, all! New water heater ready for install." He sounded like a drill sergeant reporting for duty.

The man was just too pleased with himself and something about his demeanor rubbed Jason the wrong way. He couldn't put his finger on what or why.

"That's good news." Lauren stepped to the side, waving the other man inside.

"I have to get the unit out of the truck, but first—" He reached into the back pocket of his jeans and pulled out a folded sheet of paper. "I have your estimate for the rest of the work." He smiled as he shoved the paperwork into her hands.

"Thank you," Lauren murmured. She didn't glance at the numbers, merely folded the paper as she let out a prolonged sigh.

Jason didn't blame her. They both knew the estimate would make her stomach churn, but stalling wouldn't make things any better.

He didn't think she'd appreciate him pointing out that fact.

"Just let me know when you're ready to move forward," Brody said. "I cleared my schedule and I can start immediately." He shifted from foot to foot. "Like today," he said when they didn't immediately reply.

Jason frowned. Something about the man's enthusiasm bugged him. "Just the water heater today. We'll get back to you on the rest." He wanted to check out the numbers, then work a better deal with the man's boss.

"Sure thing." Pittman turned and headed for his truck to retrieve the heater.

"Why don't you let me look at the estimate first," Jason said, once they'd stepped back inside.

"I want to work the numbers myself and see if I can't get J.R. to lower the price."

She turned. "Maybe he was fair."

"And maybe I can get him to be even fairer." Jason knew J.R.'s wife had been bugging him to finish the basement as a playroom for the kids, but with the downturn in the economy, he wasn't about to lay out big bucks for something that was a want, not a need. Jason figured he could work a deal.

Without warning, she stood on her tiptoes and pressed her lips to his in a too brief kiss. "Thank you. You've been beyond generous."

Before he could pull her close, Trouble darted into the entryway, stopping short. His black paws starkly contrasted with the white marble as he slowly began to edge forward. The cat skulked around the perimeter, stealthily tracking what could only be the mouse Lauren had seen earlier.

A quick glance told him she was visibly holding back a reaction. "Trouble, get over here," she ordered.

"He's not about to listen," Jason said. "Not when he's after prey."

She shuddered, unable to hide her revulsion. "Can't you get rid of it?"

"I'll need to take a ride to the hardware store and pick up the traps."

"Let me get my shoes and I'll come with you." She spoke quickly, obviously not wanting to be left alone in the house with the rodent.

Or rodents.

"Eager to visit your good friend Burt?" He gave her a knowing grin. "Don't worry. I won't leave you here to fend for yourself."

She shot him a look of gratitude. "What is it with this house that animals come with it?" she asked as she opened the hall closet and retrieved her warm, furry boots.

"Abandoned houses attract all kinds of visitors," he told her. Stepping beside her, he pulled his jacket off a hanger.

"Speaking of visitors, I need to tell the plumber I'm going out."

He nodded, watching her behind wiggle in her sweats as she headed for the door. A behind he now had permission to snuggle with all night long.

HAVING A TANTRUM was the most activity Beth had had all year. Too bad she hadn't gotten the response she'd been looking for. Where was her sister? She needed her to visit and give her an update on the condition of the house.

So much for crying out for attention. All Beth had gotten was a shot of Ativan and a drug-induced sleep.

Well, she wasn't drugged anymore. She hadn't seen her sister or her so-called boyfriend in too long. He'd been working at the prison weekly, and although their plan called for him to take time off, his absence was making her antsy.

Her little plan had backfired and now she'd be monitored more closely, making it more difficult to get alone time with her boyfriend. If and when he showed up for work.

Maybe he'd found the jewels and bailed on her, a thought that caused her no small amount of worry.

The day nurse walked by, staring at Beth closely as she passed her bed.

Beth swallowed a ripe curse, reminding herself to stay calm. No more tantrums until she needed one.

## CHAPTER NINE

LAUREN FOLLOWED Jason into the hardware store. Burt scowled, his eyes boring a hole through her skull.

She frowned and tapped Jason on the shoulder. "Why does he hate me so much? Other than the obvious reasons, I mean." Lauren knew her family had a poor reputation in town but this man's feelings bordered on fury.

Jason paused. "Burt's last name is Miller. To hear my father tell it, his dad used to own the local pharmacy. A big chain tried to buy them out. They refused to sell. Next thing you know, the landlord invokes a clause in the lease that increased their rent and forced them out of business." He lifted her hand in his. "The big chain went in one month later."

Lauren glanced up at the old, cracked ceiling. "My grandmother was the landlord?" It was the most logical guess.

The most damaging. Thinking about the destruction her grandmother had wreaked around town made Lauren's heart hurt.

Jason nodded. "Let's go pick up the traps." He headed for the back of the store.

"Jason, man, she's a Perkins," Burt called out.

"She's also hot and you're jealous you can't get someone who looks half as good," Jason called over his shoulder, pulling her along with him as he walked.

Ten minutes later, Burt remained embarrassed and silent as he rang up their purchases.

Lauren appreciated Jason's defending her, but even if she didn't deserve Burt's anger, her grandmother did. She paused at the register and met the man's gaze. "I'm sorry for what my grandmother did to your family."

He stared at her strangely, as if he couldn't understand her words. More likely he couldn't comprehend an apology coming from the mouth of a Perkins.

They walked out onto the street. It was sunny, but the wind blew cool air around her. She shivered and Jason pulled her close, wrapping his arm around her.

"Are you sure you want—"

"People to think we're a couple?" he asked, reading her mind. "Yes. Because as long as you're here, that's what we are."

She couldn't deny him. Especially since she wanted the same thing.

"So tell me about your career," he said, passing his car as they walked down the sidewalk.

"Wait. Aren't we going back to the house?"

"In a little while. It's nice out. Let's keep walking."

She shrugged. Why not? The cool air felt good. So did the company. "I always loved fashion magazines."

"I remember. While I read ski magazines, you read *Vogue*."

"Do you miss it?" she asked him. She meant snowboarding.

"Sure I miss it, but the travel part? Not so much. I'm just…" He shook his head. "We already know what happened with me. I'd rather finish talking about you."

She knew he was avoiding discussing himself but she appreciated his interest in her.

"So you loved fashion magazines," he prompted.

She grinned. "I didn't realize you'd paid attention."

"You'd be surprised," he murmured.

"So once I moved to Manhattan—"

"And into that rat-infested apartment."

She inclined her head. "And into that rat infested apartment, I took classes at FIT, which I paid for with student loans and by working at a dress company. I sketched my own designs at night."

"Not much sleep for the determined, hmm?"

"You ought to know."

He grinned. "True. Now go on." He swung her hand back and forth in his, clearly enjoying her story.

"I graduated and took a low-end job. I also hounded all the best designers, hoping to get my work into one of their hands. No luck. One day I brought my portfolio to work on at the dress company during lunch. I ate at my desk, got carried away and forgot to put away my designs. One of Galliano's assistants came by, saw my work and slipped me his card."

"And the rest is history?"

"And a red Porsche," she said, laughing until her cell phone rang, destroying the easy moment. "Hello?"

"Ms. Perkins? This is Franklin Pennington, Esquire."

Lauren's stomach dropped. Her sister's lawyer. "Hello, Mr. Pennington."

"I received notice that your sister's doctors want to have her transferred to a hospital where they can do brain scans and testing."

"They told me that was a possibility. But that's their problem, not yours, right?"

He cleared his throat. "It depends. If they put her through these tests and find something detrimental to our case, that's bad. I'd like to do more research on her condition. Find similar cases and see."

"Okay…" Lauren said, waiting for the punch line.

"But the reserve funds from your sister's retainer are running low."

The gut churning turned to nausea. "Mr. Pennington, this case is depleting my resources."

"I understand. It doesn't help that the court system runs slowly, while the time invested in research and interviewing potential expert witnesses adds up. But time is money."

Jason shot her a curious glance.

She held up one finger, telling him to wait.

"Fine. I'll see what I can do to get a check in the mail."

"Thank you. I assure you, everything I suggest is in your sister's best interest."

"But there are no guarantees," she said at the same time as the lawyer. He always followed up his assurances with qualifications.

Covering his overpaid ass, Lauren thought.

Frustrated, she disconnected the call and tossed the phone into her purse.

"What is it?" Jason asked, placing his hands on her shoulders and turning her to face him.

She swallowed hard. "Nothing you need to worry about."

Despite his earlier reassurance that he wanted to know everything related to her sister, she'd seen the flicker of disgust in his eyes. In her heart she didn't blame him. In her soul, it hurt. She was used to dealing with problems on her own and she didn't want to get into the habit of relying on him.

"Please don't tell me you expect me to accept that answer." He brushed away a tear she hadn't realized had slipped down her cheek.

Lauren drew a deep breath. He'd just be relentless. "Fine. My sister's lawyer is concerned about the tests the doctor wants to run. He needs to do more research and then he'll probably have to file more motions on her case. I know I joked about it earlier but I really didn't expect him to want more money. And that's on top of the plumbing problems in the house."

"I already told you I'm sure I can get J.R. to cut his numbers down some."

She knew "some" wouldn't be enough, but she appreciated his efforts.

"I know and I'm grateful. But what about the other problems? Which reminds me, I forgot to tell you that the back door doesn't lock properly and there are deep ceiling cracks I didn't notice earlier."

He ran a hand over her hair. "I will do everything I can myself, which should bring things within budget."

So much for not relying on him. She ran her tongue over her dry lips and forced a smile. "Thank you."

He inclined his head. "No problem. Now about your sister—"

"Exactly. She's *my* sister." Lauren snapped at him before he could say anything. "Wouldn't you do everything you could for someone in your family no matter what awful things they'd done?"

"Whoa." Jason took a step back. "I don't know what you think I was going to say—"

"You were going to ask if I was sure she's worth it," Lauren said, anticipating the worst.

He braced his hands on her shoulders. "I was going to ask if you're sure the lawyer is billing you legitimately." His voice was quieter, his tone more rational than hers.

"Oh." Embarrassed for jumping to conclusions, she turned away. "I'm sorry. I guess I just don't expect any sympathy from anyone."

"Since when have I been just anyone? Besides, we covered this subject this morning. Now come on. Tell me."

She wished she didn't have to have this conversation, but he'd never give up until she did. "The lawyer is expensive, but so was every attorney I interviewed. He also has experience in this kind of case. And the monthly statements have seemed legitimate. I was just hoping he could make the retainer last longer."

Her savings were dwindling so quickly and the repairs in the house adding up so fast, she was overwhelmed and would have to take drastic measures soon.

Her thoughts went to her beloved convertible in the driveway and her stomach tensed.

"I'm no expert on legal issues, and don't take this the wrong way, but given the circumstances, are you sure he isn't just spinning his wheels at your expense, promising you things he can't deliver?"

She shrugged. "I honestly don't know. But I have to do everything I can for Beth. Just in case he can accomplish miracles. What if she's really mentally ill and wasn't in her right mind when she did those things? Doesn't she deserve good help and a second chance?" Before he could answer, she did. "If that's the case, then the lawyer needs more money."

"Which you'll pay for how?" he asked gently.

She looked away. "I'll figure something out. All I know is she needs better care than she's currently getting." She drew a deep breath, then exhaled, trying to calm her nerves.

A few more weeks until her dresses were shown in Paris. If they were the success everyone anticipated, if stores ordered the numbers everyone hoped, she'd be Galliano's golden girl. She'd be able to afford a new red convertible and her sister's hospital bills.

If not, so be it. She'd pull herself together and move on. Figure something out. What other choice did she have?

"Lauren?" Jason asked.

"Hmm? I still have some savings left."

His dark gaze bored into hers. "I can lend you money to tide you over. And once you hit it big with your dresses, you can pay me back."

She blinked in surprise. "What did you say?"

"I can lend you—"

"No, after that?" Her breath caught in her throat as she waited for his reply.

"I said when you hit it big, you can pay me back."

"You said *when,* not *if.*" Despite all the bad news surrounding her, she smiled. "Thank you for believing in me."

He brushed her hair off her shoulders. "My pleasure. So you'll take the money?"

She shook her head. "Thank you but no. I

can't." Even if Jason and his family didn't despise her sister and grandmother, she still couldn't accept a loan.

"But—"

"But your faith in me means everything." No one in her life had ever believed in her unconditionally.

She wound her hands around his neck and pulled him close for a thank-you kiss.

"Just what do you think you're doing?" a male voice shouted.

Startled, Lauren jumped back.

His uncle Edward glared at them.

Clara stood by his side, shaking her head.

And walking toward them with a determined stride was Jason's father, Thomas.

Jason groaned.

Lauren winced and waited for all hell to break loose on Main Street.

"Well, well, well, I'm so happy to see my family out and about on this beautiful day!" Thomas was dressed to the nines, as he liked to say, his white collared shirt pressed and the top button open. By the determined gleam in his eye, he was clearly a man on a mission.

"Did you see those two going at it like rabbits?" Edward asked, gesturing wildly at Jason and Lauren.

"Eddie, calm down." Clara placed her hand on

his shoulder. "I have the prescription Dr. Shelby just gave you. Let's go on over to the drugstore and fill it. The sooner you take your medicine, the better you'll feel." She waved the prescription papers she held in her other hand.

Jason grasped Lauren's hand to reassure her, hoping he wasn't going to lose her again over his family's insanity. Or their family's shared history.

"Is the medicine going to stop those two from making the mistake of their lives?" Edward asked, wide-eyed.

Jason glanced at Lauren.

She studied Edward with compassion, but she wasn't upset, nor was she pulling away. Apparently the promise she'd made to him earlier meant something. He refused to examine his relief too closely.

Thomas walked up to his brother. "Edward, if you're going to keep a woman as beautiful and smart as Clara, you need to pull it together. Get your new medication filled." His tone was soft and encouraging.

Jason narrowed his gaze, wondering if his father had taken his words to heart the other night. Uncle Edward could not handle anyone pushing him into a relationship or playing the jealousy card. Not now.

"There's nothin' to keep. We're not a couple!"

Edward shouted at his brother. "Couples mean curses and I've already been down that road."

"Really?" Thomas asked, an unholy gleam in his eye.

Uh-oh, Jason thought.

"If you're not a couple, then I'm going to do something I've wanted to do since laying eyes on this lovely woman." Thomas stepped up to Clara and took her free hand in his. "Have dinner with me, beautiful lady?" he asked in his most polished tone.

"I will not!" Clara yanked her hand away immediately.

But Uncle Edward pulled away from her grasp, as well. "I knew it. Old dogs don't learn new tricks. Here you are poaching on my woman again!" he said to his brother.

He physically distanced himself from Clara.

She shot Thomas a deadly stare. "Come on." Grasping Edward's hand, Clara attempted to lead him away before things could degenerate further.

"I'll be in touch," Thomas called out to Clara's retreating back, her long dark hair blowing in the wind.

Edward fought her the entire way to the drugstore on the corner.

Jason inserted himself into his father's space. "What the hell was that all about? I thought I told you your brother isn't up to that kind of pushing."

Thomas blinked, his expression pained. "I want my brother back." He stared in the direction the other couple had disappeared.

"Then stay away from Clara!"

Thomas shook his head. "Did you notice how Edward accused me of poaching *his woman?* After denying they were a couple? I'm on the right track," he insisted.

Jason glanced at Lauren, who clearly was keeping out of a Corwin family argument. "Dad, please."

"I'm a grown man, son. Stay out of it." Thomas straightened his collar.

The determination in his expression, along with the warning in his voice, told Jason the Corwin family was in for a rocky ride.

DESPITE THE DOCTOR'S recommendation otherwise, Lauren needed to see her sister. When she'd told Jason she was taking the afternoon off to drive to the Bricksville prison, he said he'd understood, but his tone and his movements had been cold and brittle. Clearly her sister's criminal actions colored the way Jason viewed her. Something Lauren truly did understand, especially since her relatives had been directly or indirectly responsible for so much of his family's pain.

She knew now that with so much history

between them, there was no way they could ever have more than this short time together. She'd treasure it forever, but this was all there could be. Blood was thicker than water, and he'd support his family while she'd do the same for hers. And in her heart, Lauren believed Beth needed to know someone cared about her despite everything.

So she made the trip to the prison and sat by her sister's bedside. When Lauren arrived, Beth was awake, staring straight ahead.

Lauren brushed her hair off her face, held her hand and talked to her.

"The house is coming along great." Lauren fudged the truth. "I hired a reasonably priced contractor who's patching the holes in the walls and repainting." She forced an enthusiasm and sense of normalcy she didn't feel into her voice as she told her sister things she hoped would soothe her. She deliberately omitted the fact that her contractor and her lover was Jason *Corwin*.

And she didn't mention that Beth's lawyer needed more money or that Lauren was running short on funds. She only told Beth positive things.

"The contractor is also negotiating good prices with the subs, like the electrician and the plumber," she said cheerfully. "The water heater broke but I managed to have it replaced. And my contractor is checking the estimates the plumber gave him before letting him do any more work on the pipes. But we're getting there."

Beth's eyelids fluttered up and down.

Lauren sighed. "What is it, Beth? Do you want to talk to me?" She squeezed her sister's hand.

"Don't upset yourself," the nurse said from the corner of the room.

Lauren had almost forgotten they weren't alone.

"I have to try and reach her," Lauren said. "Someone has to try!" But even as she spoke, she knew the blinking was just a reflexive response, as the nurse constantly reminded her.

"I do have some good news for both of you," the nurse said as she strode to the barred window and looked outside.

"What is it?" Lauren asked.

"The work on the new wing is almost complete. Pretty soon your sister will have the quiet she needs. They're phasing out the construction crews, and as soon as the inspection's finished, no more workers, no more noise."

A low gurgle sounded from the bed.

Lauren glanced over but her sister remained staring into space. Lauren turned back to the nurse. "That is good news," she said. "I'm in the middle of a construction project myself."

"So I hear," she said, smiling.

Lauren thought of her monologues to her sister and nodded.

"How is it going?" the nurse asked.

Lauren walked over to the other woman. "Basically the place needs a ton of work. The electrical is sound but the plumbing is a mess, and there are some structural repairs to make. But I'm determined to get this thing finished and sold on time."

"Good for you. I wish you luck."

"I need it," Lauren said. She glanced at her sister. "*We* need it."

"You're a special person, visiting like this. Not many of the people here have someone who cares."

"Thanks." Lauren hoped her sister knew and appreciated that fact, as well.

JASON HAD NO LUCK catching mice. The traps had been set for over a week but not one mouse had been caught. Lauren didn't want them killed so he hadn't called an exterminator. Besides he wanted to save her money, and all the exterminators would do was set the same humane traps he had. But the little creatures hadn't disappeared. Far from it. And they were smarter than the average trap or cat. Avoidance was their middle name and even Jason was impressed with the little suckers.

They raced through the walls, despite the fact that he had covered all the holes. He'd heard them—there was definitely more than one—and both he and Lauren had caught glimpses. She was so on edge, she thought she saw them everywhere—when she drank her morning coffee, even when she showered. And she claimed she could *feel* them on her skin. They were creeping her out and Jason couldn't do a damn thing about it.

As for the house, things were progressing. He'd assigned Connor to the garage, cleaning and painting the walls. Ross and Nate he'd settled outside, one cleaning leaders and gutters, the other stripping and staining the wood, returning the old Victorian to a clean, New England blue.

He'd hired an electrician to come in and take stock of the wiring in the house, making sure it was ready for inspection and up to code on the day of the closing. Rocco De Martino, a friendly competitor of his father and uncle, assured him all was well.

That left Jason and Lauren working on the main house by day. Thanks to her fear of the rodents, she stayed in whatever room he was in. If he was patching and spackling the walls in the living room, she carted furniture outside and boxed up things for Goodwill.

Nights were even better. He'd lugged Fred over

to his uncle's house so Hank could take care of the dog for as long as Jason was away.

They'd crawl into bed exhausted—but not too tired for sex. He couldn't get enough of her and the feeling was apparently mutual. Afterward, she'd roll over to fall asleep, claiming her space. He didn't know if it was deliberate or force of habit.

The first night, he'd taken her physical withdrawal like a punch in the gut. Ironic for a man who'd spent the last who knows how many years screwing snow bunnies and showing them the door. He'd given Lauren her space, but it had taken him hours to fall asleep. He needn't have worried. Her fear of the mice led her right back into his arms.

Most mornings he woke up with her curled into him, splayed on top of him, or clutching a certain body part in her hand. At which point she more than made up for rolling over to her own side of the bed the night before.

True to his word, Jason had gotten J.R. to take a huge chunk off the plumbing estimate by promising the man he'd do the same when he finished his basement after the first of the year. He wished he could have saved her even more, but she hadn't mentioned being short of cash lately, so he assumed it must have helped. And she was definitely grateful.

Today was master bedroom day. While he

spackled and painted, she emptied drawers and closets, moving items to various piles to keep or give away.

He looked across the room and caught sight of her bending over the bottom drawer of the large chest in the corner. Her shirt rode up, revealing her slender back and fair skin, while her tight jeans dipped low, exposing the edge of what appeared to be black lace panties.

He sucked in a shallow breath and his entire body went into heated overdrive. He'd been aroused all day, watching her breasts rise and fall beneath the tank top she'd changed into after she'd started perspiring. His attempt to keep his mind on work had been downhill for him after that.

A glance at his watch told him it was almost five o'clock. Even a slave driver wouldn't object to him taking a break. He quietly climbed down the ladder and approached her from behind, slipping his hand down the inside of her jeans.

She squealed and jumped up, turning so he immediately caught and pulled her into his arms.

"You're so bad," she said, teasing him, her eyes dancing with delight.

"I couldn't resist another second. Do you know how many times I nearly fell off that damn ladder watching you?"

Lauren wrapped her arms around his neck. "Next time just tell me before you sneak up on me. My body is on constant rodent alert," she chided, but her eyes were already dilating with need.

He slid his hand back into her jeans, letting his first finger dip between the fine crack and settle there.

A soft moan escaped her lips. "We still have work to do." The words didn't come out like much of a complaint.

"We've made remarkable progress this past week." They also made an incredible team, tackling one room at a time.

They'd completed the work faster than he'd anticipated. Probably because he'd known she was waiting for him at the end of each day, soft, willing and ready for him. He wondered if she realized how in sync they were with each other.

"You do have a point." She thrust her fingers through the back of his hair, making him glad he'd been too lazy to go for a haircut.

"I suppose you could convince me to take a break," she said, arching her back so her pelvis rocked directly into his erection.

"Babe, the things you do to me defy description." He nuzzled his lips into the side of her neck, breathing in the scent of her skin and taking in the slight tremors of arousal that shook her as his tongue slid down her neck.

"You don't need words. You're showing me just fine. It's just that—"

"What?"

"I'm all sweaty," she said, glancing down self-consciously.

"Doesn't bother me." He slid the straps of her tank top off one shoulder and planted slow kisses over her skin.

Just then, her stomach growled, reminding him they hadn't eaten since an early lunch hours before. And though he could live on another kind of food, she obviously needed the real thing.

"I guess I'm hungry." Her cheeks flushed pink.

"Then what do you say we go out for dinner?" he asked. The plan he'd been hoping to put in place this weekend suddenly made sense for tonight.

"The pizza place in town?" she asked hopefully. "Because nothing against The Diner's food, but I can't eat from there one more night."

"Amen." His arms encircled her waist. "I was thinking more along the lines of somewhere nice. Away from here. Boston maybe?"

The idea had come to him earlier while he'd watched her take out her clothes to dress. He'd realized he'd only seen her wearing old jeans, tanks and T-shirts to clean the house, while inside the closet he could see at least a couple of dresses, shoes with heels and other female accessories.

The urge to see her dressed up for him took hold along with the desire to take her somewhere she wouldn't easily forget.

"Really?" Her eyes lit up at the idea. "Like I can shower, change and we can go to a real restaurant?" The excitement in her voice, the flush in her cheeks told him he'd been on target.

"Exactly like that. A real date," he said, wanting his meaning clear. "I ask, you say yes, I pay."

"Pay." She pursed her lips and grew silent as she weighed her options.

His paying was the obvious sticking point. She was independent but not stupid, which was why she'd allowed him to do as much free work on the house as her pride would allow, but she'd drawn the line at accepting a loan.

On dinner, he wasn't budging. *His* ego wouldn't allow it. "Well?"

She blew out a long-suffering breath. "As long as when I'm rich and famous, I can repay all this kindness."

He nodded. "You got yourself a deal," he said, placated by the fact that she'd confirmed his hunch about why she was hesitant.

It wasn't just dinner. It was dinner added to everything else. That much he understood.

They still stood close, their bodies aligned, his dick pulsing against his jeans. If they didn't break this up soon, they'd never make it to dinner.

"How did you know I needed the break?" she asked, head tilted, ponytail brushing her shoulders.

He kissed her lips. "Because I needed one just as badly. What made you say yes?" he asked, curious.

She treated him to a sheepish grin. "I want a decent meal and to get out of this house too badly. Not to mention I'd love a chance to wear my good clothing."

"Then go shower and change." He gave her a quick hug and stepped back. "I'll go home, shower and pick you up around seven."

She visibly bit the inside of her cheek. "The mice?"

"Play loud music in the bathroom. They'll leave you alone. I don't have a decent change of clothes here." He'd only brought some jeans and grungy shirts. "Besides, if I stay, I'll shower with you, and if I do that we're never leaving." He brushed her hair off her shoulder. "You'll be fine. Just concentrate on knocking my socks off and don't let your mind wander to *them*." He deliberately didn't use the word *rat, mouse* or *rodent*.

"I guess I can do that."

"Good. I'll call Amber for restaurant suggestions." As a concierge at one of the swankiest Boston hotels, she could work miracles in the reservation department. Or so he'd heard.

"Dress up for me," he said, and headed home for a cold shower in order to make it through dinner before being able to come back here and satisfy his ever-growing desire for this woman.

A woman, he reminded himself, who had every intention of leaving him when this house was sold.

GABRIELLE LAY NAKED in bed, waiting for Derek to return home from work so he could join her. Her pregnancy had merely upped her horniness quotient, something Derek appreciated—when he wasn't worrying about hurting the baby.

The telephone rang and she hoped it wasn't Derek telling her he had to work late. "Hello?"

"Guess what?" Gabrielle recognized Amber's excited voice.

"What?"

"Jason called to ask me to recommend a restaurant downtown. A place where he could take Lauren *tonight*. They'll be out of the house!"

A sinking feeling settled in Gabrielle's stomach. "I am not rushing over there tonight. I have plans!"

She pulled on the sheet, which had begun to slip over her bare breasts.

Just then, she heard the lock turning. "Derek's home," she whispered to Amber.

"Well, find an excuse to run out and cause some benign damage at the house."

"Why? Jason's already sleeping there and he's obviously taking her out for a special evening." She needed her husband in her bed more than Jason and Lauren needed their meddling.

Amber snorted. "You never know what could happen. Uncle Edward could snap, Lauren could get cold feet. We just need Jason to think something's going on at the house and he can't leave Lauren alone."

Gabrielle frowned. "I—"

"Are you waiting for me?" Derek called out.

"Of course I am!" Gabrielle shut her eyes. "I'll see what I can do."

"Did you ever buy the Super Glue?" Amber asked.

"Yes. It's in my trunk. I still think gluing the windows down is a stupid idea."

"Then think of a better one, but do something!"

"But—"

"But nothing. I did the mice and it worked. Jason's been staying over. But trust me, you owe me for handling that one. It's your turn."

"Are you naked?" Derek called out, his footsteps growing closer.

"Gotta go. Bye." Gabrielle replaced the receiver at the same time Derek opened the bedroom door.

He must have been stripping all the way from the front door, because he was naked by the time he stepped into the doorway.

Gabrielle's eyes gleamed as she looked at her husband. They might have been high school sweethearts and he'd been her first lover, but time had only made her love him more.

She raked her gaze over his aroused body. God, he was gorgeous. She slowly, seductively slid the sheets over her now fuller breasts and rounded stomach.

Derek's eyes darkened at the sight. He stepped forward to join her and she thought she was the luckiest woman in the world.

And when his body draped hers, she could no longer think at all.

LIFE WAS all about risks, and Beth had taken a huge one stealing the nurse's cell phone when the nutty patient at the far end of the hall had an honest-to-goodness heart attack. Nurse Stupid, as Beth liked to think of her, had been on the phone when the alarms went off and everyone ran down the hall.

Beth couldn't believe her luck. She'd snuck out to find the nurse had dropped the phone on her desk. She already knew the construction work had been winding down and that would leave her without easy access to her lover, so she had to get her instructions to him any way she could.

She left him a message, telling him exactly what her sister had said about the electrical system being perfect. *A perfect target that no one would ever follow up on,* Beth thought. The perfect thing to sabotage. She instructed him to make sure he caused enough damage that there was no way her sister could close the deal on time. She had to make sure the house remained in her family's possession until she discovered the diamonds. In her message, she warned that if she didn't hear from him soon, she'd break out and come after him herself.

Yes, the call had been a risk, but she had him so wrapped around her finger with the lure of love, sex and money, he'd never turn her in.

She wiped the phone clean of prints and erased all trace of any outgoing calls before replacing it on the desk and climbing back into bed.

## CHAPTER TEN

LAUREN NOW KNEW what it meant to bring a man to his knees. She relished Jason's jaw-dropping reaction to her dress, a modern one-shoulder design with metallic gold body-hugging banding that ended midthigh. She hadn't packed many nice clothes since she'd planned on renovating, not socializing. But she had brought two dresses she'd designed to show to Sharon, and she chose her favorite. She worried she was overdressed until she discovered their destination.

"Amber said the Top of the Hub is the ultimate romantic dining experience," Jason told her on the car ride into Boston. He split his attention between her and the road.

She smiled. "I can't wait."

"I hope it's worth it because I'm not used to wearing a jacket." He shifted in his seat, obviously uncomfortable in his clothes.

She grinned. "It's worth it to me. You look handsome, Jason."

She realized she was seeing him dressed up for the first time ever, in tan khakis, a black sport jacket and a white shirt. A far cry from the boy she'd known or even the man who worked at her house every day.

At the restaurant they ate in comfortable but aware silence. Throughout the meal, their eyes remained locked on each other and not the view of the Boston skyline or the Back Bay fifty-two floors below.

She barely tasted her pan-seared salmon and would lay odds Jason could say the same of his braised short ribs. The fixed-price three-course meal was elaborate, the service attentive and the view spectacular.

But all she could focus on was the man in front of her.

And what a man he'd become. Caring, tender, dedicated. A man who'd lost everything he'd dreamed of and yet still managed to smile.

At her.

To play footsie under the table.

With her.

To whisper in her ear all the sexual, provocative things he wanted to do.

To her.

She barely tasted dessert. Instead she wanted desperately to taste him.

The car ride home was too long. Lauren was tipsy from champagne, antsy with desire, and she couldn't control the need to constantly touch him. She nuzzled his neck and kept her hand on his thigh, just to the right of where touching would probably cause a car accident.

By the time they finally reached town and neared the turn for her grandmother's house, Lauren was surprised the car windows weren't fogged from their heavy breathing. So when she saw smoke coming from the back of the house, she thought she was imagining it.

"Holy shit," Jason muttered, pulling into the driveway and slamming on the brakes.

Panic lodged in Lauren's throat. "Oh my God." A real fire.

"Call nine-one-one," he directed, tossing her his cell phone as if she didn't have one of her own.

She fumbled and started to dial, just as she realized her cat was probably in the house. "Trouble," she muttered.

"I know. So dial. I'll go see how bad it is."

He reached for the door handle but she stopped him with a hand on his shoulder. "No, my cat.

Trouble might be in the house!" She scrambled for the door and this time he stopped her.

"No! I'll go look for the cat, you call nine-one-one. Now—before it spreads." He jumped from the car before she could argue.

Time passed in a blur.

Jason running in through the front door to look for the cat. Smoke at the back of the house turning to flames. Bile and panic racing in her veins while she waited for Jason to come out. And finally the fire engine, sirens blaring, racing down the driveway, the men pulling out the hose.

Lauren had had the presence of mind to back the car into the street to make room for the fire truck and she stood there now, waiting for Jason to come out. She knew he wouldn't go near the fire or put himself in direct danger, but her throat was tight until she finally caught a glimpse of him running out, Trouble in his arms.

Grateful and relieved, she bolted across the lawn to meet him, throwing her arms around him. "Thank you!" she said, peppering kisses on his lips and his cheeks.

"You're welcome. The cat was in the study in the front of the house, looking out the window. Of course it was the last room I checked because it's the room he rarely goes into." Jason sounded out of breath but fine.

"You saved my cat!"

Despite the fire, Jason glanced at her and grinned.

"What? What's so funny?" she asked.

He shook his head. "You said I saved *your* cat. That's quite the change of heart from looking for a new owner for him."

The ungrateful feline obviously didn't like being squished. He purred loudly in protest and jumped out of Jason's arms.

Lauren would never be so stupid.

"Excuse me." A fireman in uniform walked over to them.

"Yes?" Lauren asked.

"Ms. Perkins?"

Lauren nodded.

"Hey, Jason."

"Frank." Jason acknowledged the other man with a nod of his head. "What did you find out?"

"The fire started in the electrical box in the mudroom."

Jason narrowed his gaze.

Lauren knew exactly what he was thinking. "But the electrician signed off on the box. It was one of the few things in the house that wasn't a problem!"

"Well, someone tinkered with it then," Frank said.

"Tinkered with it?" she repeated.

"Sabotage?" Jason asked at the same time.

The other man nodded. "Looks that way, but we'll have a final report in the morning. Another strange thing. Did you know the windows were glued shut? Had to break them to get in. Same with the door, but that's pretty standard. Sorry."

Lauren shook her head, holding up one hand as if to block out the words. When it came to dealing with this disaster of a house, Jason knew she was on the verge of tears. He reached for her hand and squeezed it tight, earning him a look of gratitude.

"In the meantime, I can't let you back into the house until things have cooled off," Frank said to her. "Do you have any place you can stay tonight?"

"I—"

"She'll stay with me," Jason said.

"I'll stay with him," she said, gesturing to Jason.

The fireman grinned. "You still got it, Corwin."

"I need to go into the kitchen so I can leave food and water outside for my cat," Lauren said to the fireman.

Her devotion to the stray was one of the things Jason found so endearing.

Frank nodded in understanding. "As long as we're still here, that's fine. Say hi to your father, Jason."

"Will do."

"We'll file a report tomorrow." The fireman headed to the back of the house again, leaving Jason and Lauren alone.

She turned to face him. "The electrical box? Glued windows? What in the world is going on?" Confusion and exhaustion warred in her expression.

He shrugged. "I don't understand it myself. Look, there's nothing more we can do here tonight. A good night's sleep will help us both figure this thing out."

"I'm not sure sleep will provide answers, but it'll probably make me feel better," she said, her tone bleak.

He placed his hand on the small of her back. "Let's go back to my place." At least there he could comfort her in some small way. "Smile, honey. Things will look better in the morning."

He took in her slumped shoulders and defeated expression and hoped like hell he was right.

FOR THE FIRST TIME, Lauren didn't roll over to sleep alone. Instead, she curled into Jason's arms and conked out until morning. Exhausted, he did the same. He woke up before her. He opened his eyes and glanced at her profile. Relaxed in sleep, she still looked fragile. Last night had taken a toll on her.

Jason couldn't change the past or undo the fire,

but he could figure out who was behind it. So instead of lingering to wait for her to wake up and have sex, something they'd been deprived of last night, he forced himself out of bed.

Once he was seated in the kitchen with coffee and a pad and pen, he began to make a list of people who had access to the house other than himself and Lauren. Someone on his list had the motive and the ability to tamper with the electrical system. Every name he wrote struck him as an unlikely suspect. No one had motive, especially the three men on his crew.

Although Jason hadn't been in business long, his men were members of families he knew well. Nate, Connor and Ross were guys who needed a job and he'd been happy to give one to them. There was also the plumber with the dumb-ass grin. He was annoying but hardly seemed capable of creating an electrical fire.

Jason tapped his pen on the table. What about the electrician who'd walked through and signed off? Could he have "tinkered" with the wiring? It was possible. *Anything* was possible, but the man had been in business for years. What reason would he possibly have to undermine Lauren?

"What's wrong?" Lauren asked as she entered the kitchen.

He glanced up. "I'm just trying to figure out

who'd want to tamper with the electrical box in your grandmother's house." He pointed to the list in front of him, the names staring back mocking his attempt to solve the mystery.

Lauren poured herself a cup of coffee and settled on his lap. She wore nothing but an old white T-shirt she'd pulled from his drawer and her panties, which he already knew were skimpy beyond belief. He had on a pair of sweats and nothing else, making him completely aware of her.

She, on the other hand, hadn't caught up. Her mind was where his had been for the past half hour as she studied the paper.

"People with access." She read his words from the pad. "But the motive column is empty."

He brushed her hair off her neck and nuzzled his lips against her skin, something he'd gotten used to doing each morning when he woke up with her sprawled on top of him.

He forced himself to concentrate on their problem. "Is there a remote chance you can fill in a possible motive for any of these guys? Is there someone your grandmother…"

Her body immediately stiffened and he let his sentence trail off.

"Go on," she finally said, her words holding no anger, only resignation.

"I was going to ask if there were any names on the list you might recognize. Anyone who could hold a grudge against your family?" He struggled to find a palatable way of phrasing it.

She held up the list in front of her. "I wouldn't know," she said at last. "But I'm sure it's possible."

He braced his hand against her back, feeling a sudden need to protect her against the repercussions of her grandmother and sister's actions. The only way to do so was to help her finish the house without further incident and allow her to leave town as planned.

The thought hit him like a blow in his midsection, hurting more than Kristina's betrayal. And she had ruined his life's aspiration.

Lauren meant more to him than Kristina ever had.

"We need to know what exactly the fire department found last night," Lauren said, oblivious to his train of thought.

He pushed the revelation from his mind, at least for now. "I agree," he said, focusing on the fire instead. "There's something else you need to find out. Do you have insurance on the house?" he asked, hoping maybe she could collect money in the long run.

"Of course." That had been another hit to her pocketbook. She expelled a long breath. "But so what? By the time the police and fire department complete their arson investigation and clear me, the closing will have come and gone. I need to move forward with the renovations regardless of filing the claim."

"We still have to get the insurance adjuster in as soon as possible."

Lauren nodded. "I'll go through my papers and call them today."

"I had another thought," he said. "Maybe you could also look through your grandmother's papers to see if any names from this list jump out at you," he suggested.

"Good idea. I think the police confiscated a lot of her files before she died but I can see what's left." Lauren leaned back into him, relaxing as he wrapped his arms around her waist.

Together they sat in silence, each with their own thoughts. He was completely comfortable with her. He'd never before experienced this sense of rightness with another human being. A knot formed in his throat at the thought of becoming so attached to Lauren.

"Okay, enough of me being lazy. There's work to do." She jumped off his lap and turned to face him. "I'm going to shower so we can get back to the house. I want to look through my grandmother's papers like you suggested." She grabbed the mug from the table and took another sip of her coffee, then put the ceramic cup into the sink and rinsed it.

He stared at the long legs that stretched beneath his shirt and caught a glimpse of her almost bare cheek. He wanted to sneak up behind her, lift the shirt and make love to her right there in the kitchen.

"In the meantime, can you call the police and the fire department and catch up?" she asked, turning back to him.

Damn, he resented work right now. He swallowed hard. "Sure thing."

She walked over and entwined her arms around his waist, pulling him in for a long kiss. "Did I ever say thank you for helping me with all this? I know it's a lot more than you signed up for. Good thing for you there's an end in sight," she said lightly.

As if he needed the reminder that she was gone after the house sold in a few short weeks. After all, she'd never indicated she wanted anything more than a brief affair. And the Corwin Curse continually reminded him he should know better than to think beyond the moment. He'd never been a big believer in the curse, but he had to admit he'd never had reason to feel threatened by it before. There'd never been a woman with this much potential—and a Perkins to boot.

His stomach churned at the thought of losing her. Son of a bitch, he thought, accepting the truth he'd been trying to push away all morning. What had begun as a fun affair and a revisiting of the past had become much more.

At least for him.

He met her gaze, her expression curious as she waited for a reply.

"Don't thank me," he said gruffly. He hadn't signed up for the work. He'd signed up for her.

But he wasn't about to ruin their easy relationship by telling her as much. Instead he leaned forward and captured her lips in a kiss that wasn't soft or easy. He devoured her mouth, tasting, feeling, and giving back to her in return.

With a soft sigh, she molded herself against him, her breasts pushing through the soft cotton of her shirt, her hard nipples grazing his chest. God, he wanted her. Wanted to be inside her, feel her heat contracting around him.

But he also knew her priorities and he'd respect them even if it killed him.

Pulling back, he looked at her, pleased with what he saw. Her eyes were still fogged with desire, her lips damp, her head tilted in a way that told him she remained in that dreamy, desire-filled state.

Although he could have her now, his thoughts returned to the rules she'd set. "Work first," he reminded her. "You'd better go shower or we'll never get out of here."

She closed her eyes and a rumble of disappointment escaped her throat. "You're right. We've got to get back to the house."

"But I'll make it up to you tonight," he promised.

A sexy smile pulled at her lips. "I'll hold you to that," she said, before she turned and ran for the shower, leaving him alone.

Aroused.

And while he cleaned the coffeepot, his thoughts returned to the two of them. And why *they* could never be. The biggest obstacle was Lauren herself. Her career path was set. Paris was waiting, along with a glamorous life he had no part in. She'd made it clear she was leaving this town and its memories as soon as her grandmother's house was sold.

He didn't miss the irony. Last time they'd been together he'd been the one who'd had a goal and no time or inclination to change course for anyone else. Now he'd be the one left behind.

He envied Lauren her goals.

He missed waking up every day with something driving him beyond the nine-to-five routine. He missed the adrenaline. Since Lauren's return to town, he'd managed to convince himself that pursuing her substituted for other goals. But he knew now he'd been deceiving himself. He needed more.

For now he had the deadline of finishing her house and solving the mystery of who'd deliberately set the fire.

But then what?

LAUREN STEELED herself as they returned to her grandmother's house. She wasn't ready to see the fire damage, but she had no choice. The sooner she viewed the house, the sooner she'd be able to deal with reality.

Jason turned the corner and pulled into the driveway right behind a car she didn't recognize. "Who is that?"

Jason shook his head and groaned. "No rest for the weary," he muttered. "It's my father and Uncle Hank. Are you up to dealing with them?"

The older men had exited the vehicle.

Lauren glanced down. She wore a pair of Jason's drawstring sweatpants and a baggy sweatshirt. It had been borrow or wear last night's dress. As it was, she had on a pair of stiletto heels. Yet she surprised herself by not feeling the least bit uncomfortable.

She faced Jason and shrugged. "I'm rested, I'm showered. I can take on the world."

Or at least Jason's part of it.

The worst had already happened. Between the fire and the general state of the house, she doubted it would sell on time. But that didn't mean she wouldn't give it her all anyway.

Jason leaned over and kissed her cheek. "You're amazing."

His words warmed her all over. "You're pretty amazing yourself."

He'd stepped up and taken on her problems as if they were his own. He gave her a shoulder to lean on and he'd become her personal body warmer at night. In a short time, she'd grown accustomed to his strength and it scared her.

A knock on the windows jarred her and she jumped.

"You all coming out or do I have to come in after you?" Hank asked through the glass.

Jason rolled his eyes. "We're coming!"

They climbed out of the car and met the men on the driveway.

Before Jason could say a word, Hank launched into a monologue first. "The one night I fall asleep early and don't listen to my police scanner before bed, there's a big fire. Here, of all places. And nobody called us!"

"You have a police scanner?" Lauren asked.

"From my days as a volunteer fireman," Hank said proudly.

Thomas stepped forward. "His *day* as a volunteer fireman. Don't let the old fool kid you."

"Just one day? What happened?" Lauren asked, genuinely curious.

"Nothin'. A small difference of opinion, that's all." Hank flushed red in the face and glared at his brother.

Jason grinned. "Uncle Hank has a problem following orders, which happens to be a serious issue in the fire department."

"Whatever," Hank muttered. "Anyways, I still have my scanner—"

"He refused to give it back and nobody wanted to show up at the door and ask for it, not when he tends to greet unwanted strangers with an old shotgun," Thomas explained.

"Unloaded shotgun, you ass," Hank yelled at his brother. "I'd never hurt anyone." He drew a deep breath and jerked around to face Jason. "When I listened this morning, they recapped last night's fire and we came at once!"

"We're fine," Lauren assured the two men who, despite their bluster, looked genuinely concerned.

She couldn't help but feel sorry for them. "Why don't you both come inside? I'll make some coffee and we'll tell you what happened." She waved toward the house. "The fire was in the back, so I'm sure the kitchen is fine."

At her invitation, Jason shot her a grateful look.

But Hank stared at the old Victorian, trepidation in his eyes. "No offense, honey, but I can't go into the old Perkins place."

Thomas adjusted his collar and smoothed non-existent wrinkles in his pressed khaki pants. "I'm with my brother on this one. It's not that we don't appreciate the offer," he said, almost bowing before Lauren in apology.

She swallowed over the unexpected lump in her throat.

Jason protectively grabbed her elbow. "As you can see, we're perfectly fine. We have work to do, so you two can go home." His voice was laden with disappointment.

After the two men left, Lauren walked into the house, planning to go straight to her grandmother's office and sift through her papers. Instead, the first thing she noticed other than the smoky smell was the mouse caught in Jason's trap.

Before she could react, he came up behind her, grabbing her arms and steering her past it.

"I've got this. You go check out the bedroom, open the windows to air it out—if they aren't Super Glued sheet. Same with the rest of the house."

She didn't mind taking orders if it meant he was protecting her from rodents. "What are you going to do with it?"

"I thought I'd take it for a ride and let it go somewhere far away. Okay with you?" he asked.

She nodded, feeling silly. "Thanks."

She left the room without looking back. For the next few hours, she holed up in her grandmother's study, poring over business papers for names. Some Lauren recognized, others she didn't. None were related to the workers who'd been in the house since she'd begun renovations and her frustration grew.

She called the insurance company and asked how to file a claim. They promised to get an adjuster in touch with her in a few days. She explained she didn't have the time to spare, that she needed to get started on fixing what had been ruined in the fire, but they insisted she leave things until the inspection.

She lowered her head to her hands and fought back tears of anger and frustration. If she didn't get this house sold, it wouldn't be the end of the world, but it would mean she'd have 2500 square feet still on her shoulders—her responsibility and depleting her bank account.

Lauren knew she still had the chest in her grandmother's closet to look through, something she'd been putting off because she sensed the drawers contained more personal items and papers. Considering their rocky relationship, Lauren felt like an intruder, looking through Mary Perkins's private things. The fire gave her the excuse and push she needed.

She rose, stretching her legs, but before she could head to her grandmother's room, Lauren heard voices coming from down the hall. Jason had his crew here, not just for work but to question them about the fire, but the voices Lauren heard didn't belong to the men. She'd grown used to the low timbre of their conversation.

She stepped into the hall and saw Amber and Gabrielle, as well as Jason's cousin Derek and a man she didn't recognize.

"Hi," she said warily.

"Hi," both men said.

"I'm Mike Corwin," the good-looking, dark-haired stranger said.

Lauren nodded, noting the family resemblance. "Lauren Perkins."

He shook her hand. "Nice to meet you."

"Same here." She had no idea what they wanted. "What's going on?" Lauren asked.

Jason strode to her side. "Derek was just about to tell us."

"We were," Derek said. "But I think it's best if you hear it from Gabrielle."

"And Amber—" Mike added.

"Both have something to tell you," Derek said.

And from the serious look in everyone's eyes, Lauren suspected they wouldn't like what they were about to hear.

## CHAPTER ELEVEN

JASON PROPPED one shoulder against the wall and glanced at Gabrielle and Amber as they walked down the hallway. Even to Lauren's untrained eye, the two women looked guilty, looking everywhere but at Lauren or Jason.

"Tell them," Mike instructed, staring at his wife.

"We…umm…we did a few things to the house," Gabrielle said. She glanced down at her colorful Emilio Pucci rain boots, which Lauren loved.

But now wasn't the time to discuss fashion. Lauren's stomach churned as she asked, "You did *what* to the house?"

"And why?" Alert and wary, Jason straightened and stared at the women in confusion.

Amber stepped forward. "It's like this. We were having a Ladies' Night at The Wave. It's something we do once a month, Gabrielle, myself, Sharon and sometimes Clara."

"And we'd very much like you to join us next time." Gabrielle treated Lauren to a wide smile.

Derek rolled his eyes. "Quit stalling."

"And trying to soften her up," Mike said. "Just tell her."

Amber sighed. "I'm getting there. Anyway, it was right after the fall festival and we already knew you two had sort of hooked up."

Lauren's cheeks flared hot but she forced herself not to touch her face and call attention to her embarrassment.

"We immediately saw the potential for the two of you," Gabrielle continued. "It was obvious how different Jason seemed after that night. So we figured we'd just help Cupid along, so to speak."

Jason narrowed his gaze. "Help *how?*"

Gabrielle swallowed hard. "Well, we didn't want to do any harm. We just wanted to keep you two together. So—"

"We bought pet mice at Petco and snuck inside— did you know the locks are pretty flimsy? Easily picked." Amber's words rushed together quickly.

"Then we let the mice loose in the house." Gabrielle stared at a point over her husband's shoulder, unwilling to meet anyone's gaze.

"Actually *I* let the mice loose," Amber admitted.

Mike muttered a curse.

Derek said something about stupidity and meddling women.

Jason's jaw merely hung open.

And Lauren couldn't believe what she was hearing. "The mice are *pets?* As in people actually want to own them?"

Gabrielle nodded. "They spend hard-earned money on them."

"Hold on!" Derek said. "That's what's bothering you about all this? Aren't you upset that they broke in and meddled in your life?"

"Hey!" Amber said, sounding affronted. "That's a really negative spin on things. We were just trying to help!" She placed her hands on her hips and glared at her husband's cousin.

Gabrielle walked over to Derek and calmly stroked his arm. "We just wanted to give Jason a reason to have to stick close to Lauren. Most normal women who see a mouse would freak and not want to be alone."

"It worked," Lauren admitted, shaking her head in disbelief.

"But she's petrified of rats and mice!" Jason exploded. "And for good reason, not that it's any of your business! Do you have any idea how stupid your plan was?"

The women winced and neither male Corwin

cousin stepped in to protect his wife from Jason's anger. They obviously agreed with his assessment. And though Lauren should as well, she just couldn't manage to get upset with them. All she could think about was that, unlike Jason's father and uncles, these women didn't mind her relationship with Jason. She wasn't sure where his cousins fell on the Perkins scale, but they seemed more upset with their wives' behavior than Jason and Lauren.

"Jason, they meant well," Lauren said, standing up for Amber and Gabrielle. "And they apologized. That ought to count for something."

Jason frowned, clearly unwilling to forgive and forget just yet. "Why are you confessing now?" he asked, shooting his cousins a look of pity for having to deal with these two women.

Amber groaned. "Because I was in town and I heard the fire was deliberately set—which means we weren't the only ones doing things in the house. So we wanted you to know we were responsible for the mice—" She hesitated. "And gluing the windows."

"That would be me," Gabrielle admitted with a wave of her hand.

Jason shook his head hard. "For the love of God, *why?*"

Gabrielle and Amber glanced at each other

before Gabrielle answered. "I'm not really sure. We tossed around ideas to keep Jason working for Lauren that didn't amount to more than a nuisance. We didn't touch the wiring or the fuse box or anything dangerous!"

"The mice worked and Jason started staying over," Amber said. "And that should have been enough, but I felt since I'd done the mice, it was only fair Gabrielle dirty her hands, too. So I pushed her into doing the gluing." Amber lowered her eyes, embarrassed.

"We are so sorry," they said at the same time.

Gabrielle walked over and put a hand on Lauren's shoulder. "I realize how ridiculous it all seems now but I assure you that at the time—"

"And over drinks—" Amber added.

"It all seemed rational," Gabrielle concluded.

Derek pinched the bridge of his nose. "I swear these two shouldn't get together," he muttered.

"It's okay," Lauren said. "As crazy as it sounds, with everything going on in my life, I needed a laugh and you've given me one."

"So you're not mad?" Amber asked.

Lauren shook her head. "I'm not."

"Jason?" Gabrielle asked.

He glanced heavenward. "I'm stupefied."

Mike grinned. "It's a state I've become used to."

"So you forgive us?" Gabrielle looked unconvinced.

Jason slowly nodded. "If Lauren's not mad, then neither am I."

Gabrielle's shoulders slumped in relief.

"Thank you! We'll make it up to you," Amber promised.

Lauren grinned. She knew exactly what she wanted in return. "How about you tell me where you got those gorgeous boots!"

"Bloomingdale's," the other woman said. "Do you want to plan a shopping trip?"

"Thursdays are my day off," Amber said. "So if not today, next week?"

Lauren shook her head, wishing she could take them up on their offer. Not only did she love clothes and shopping, but a girls' day out sounded like a treat. One she couldn't afford, not in time or in cash.

"I'd love to but I need to spend my free time here." She gestured around the house. "It's got to be finished by December first."

Amber perched her hands on her hips and surveyed her surroundings. "Can we help?"

Lauren shook her head. She'd never impose. "No, thank you, but I really appreciate the offer."

"How *are* things going?" Derek asked.

"Other than the fire damage? It's coming along

slowly but surely," Jason said. "I'm tackling things room by room so at least there'll be finished components by the deadline."

"Where did the fire start?" Mike asked.

"The fire department said the wires in the electrical panel were tampered with," Lauren said.

Mike let out a slow whistle. "Any suspects?"

"Plenty of people with access. Nobody with motive."

"If you need any help, don't hesitate to give me a call," his cop cousin offered.

"Now that you mention it," Jason said, "if I give you a list of people, can you run simple checks for me? See if anyone had any connections to Lauren's grandmother or sister? I'm looking for a motive. A reason for someone to want to sabotage this house."

"Anything I can do," Mike promised.

Jason slapped his cousin on the back. "Thanks."

"Same for us," Amber reminded Lauren. "If you change your mind and decide you need any help cleaning out the house, give us a ring."

Goodbyes said, Mike and Derek ushered their wives out of the house, leaving Lauren with the impression they weren't finished lecturing the two women. But despite the anger, there was plenty of love between these couples, as well.

Lauren envied them.

LAUREN HAD BEEN RIGHT about the police confiscating her grandmother's papers for evidence, and since her sister had taken many of the notes, they'd kept things for a potential trial. Even the small cabinet in her grandmother's closet had been emptied. Just when she'd given up finding anything helpful, Lauren had remembered that her grandmother's night table drawer had a secret compartment. When she was a little girl, Mary used to leave surprise gifts for Lauren and Beth there. So many bad memories had taken place in recent years, she'd almost forgotten there had been any good ones.

Inside the secret compartment, Lauren found an old diary. The book was small, bound in tan leather with dog-eared pages. Since she probably wouldn't find anything recent or relevant to her problems inside, Lauren placed the diary on her pillow to look through after she'd finished her work for the day.

Hours later, she finally curled up in bed with the diary. Jason eased in beside her. "Anything interesting in it?" he asked.

She flipped through, taking care with the thin, often cracked pages. "I'm not sure. I don't even recognize the writing."

He propped himself against the pillows and

headboard and she scooted backward, curling into him so they could look together. As she scanned the pages, she realized that something liquid had spilled on the old pages. Although the paper had long since dried, it was yellowed and the writing had smudged.

What was clear, however, was that the entries had been made by one of Lauren's ancestors.

"It looks like it's written by *another* Mary Perkins," Lauren said, excited. "Not my grand-mother, but an earlier one."

"Interesting," he said, nuzzling her neck in a blatant attempt to distract her with sex.

And oh how she wanted to be distracted. In a few minutes. After she examined the diary a little longer.

He ran his tongue up and down her throat, but receiving no response, groaned, "I'll wait."

"Thanks. I'll make it up to you." And she had every intention of keeping her word.

She turned her attention back to the small book in her hand. The more she read, the more she wondered if the book belonged to *the* Mary Perkins, the woman who had placed the original curse on Jason's family. Unfortunately the entries weren't dated.

Lauren's heart beat rapidly in her chest as she

studied the fragile pages. The beginning was like a window into a woman's thoughts and longings, making Lauren uncomfortable. She didn't appreciate feeling like a voyeur, but before she could turn the page, something caught her eye.

The word *curse* had been written in capital letters at the end of the entry. "Jason, look!"

He leaned over her shoulder, his breath warm against her skin. "What does it say?"

"Before the smudging, the entry mentions an offering of some kind. After that the only clear word is *curse*. I think this book belonged to *that* Mary Perkins!"

He glanced at the diary warily. "If it did, I'm not sure I want to know." He shuddered, then met her gaze, his turning heated. "Besides, do we really want to revisit our family history when the present is so much more interesting?" He slipped his hand under her nightshirt and settled his palm flat on her belly.

So much for his willingness to wait.

"But—"

"No buts. We can't figure this out ourselves. Talk to Clara tomorrow. I'm sure she'll know how to help you decipher it." His gruff tone indicated his mind was on anything but ancient history.

"Hmm. That's a good idea. And while she's at

it, maybe she can exorcise the demons from this place and make the whole project run smoother."

He shook his head. "Whatever floats your boat."

She grinned. "That would be you."

He lifted the book out of her hand and placed it on the nightstand, effectively ending the conversation. Then he turned to her, pulling her into his arms and sealing his lips against hers. His mouth was as hard as his body, his kiss every bit as compelling. He kissed her, making love with her, swirling his tongue inside her and drinking her up.

Every inch of her body tingled in anticipation, needing more and wanting it now. "Wait."

She left him only long enough to undress, tossing her underwear and shirt onto the floor. He took her cue and stripped quickly, meeting her naked on the center of the bed. Every time they came together like this, she wanted to stop and look at him, savor every inch of his skin. But the urge to join with him won out.

She rolled toward him, and when his bare skin touched hers, the world seemed to stop spinning. Nothing existed except them. He urged her back against the mattress. With his knee, he parted her legs and positioned himself over her, his sexy gaze boring into hers.

She already knew she was ready for him, but

he surprised her by not reaching for the condoms they'd placed in the nightstand drawer. Instead, he propped himself up on one arm and stared into her eyes.

She glimpsed a wealth of emotion as he lowered his lips back to hers, kissing her more gently this time. But he didn't stop with her lips. He moved over the curve of her cheek, across her jaw, then down her neck and shoulder, pausing at what she thought of as his favorite spot. He nuzzled the sensitive area between her neck and shoulder, alternating soft love bites with longer laps of his tongue.

She shivered in delight and moaned aloud, her skin growing more sensitive. The rest of her body reacted, her nipples puckering tight against the cooler air.

The need for him to touch her there, to pull her breast into his mouth and ease the building ache, was strong. She also had an overwhelming urge to reach out to him, but he stopped her, placing her hands back on either side of her body.

"You can have your turn later. Right now you're mine." His eyes darkened at the prospect of having her at his mercy.

"You're a tease," she told him.

"And you'll love every second," he promised.

Then, as if he'd read her mind and discovered her deepest desire, he dipped his head, catching one turgid nipple in his mouth.

She sucked in a sharp breath, exhaling slowly as he focused all of his attention on that single breast. But the wicked man wasn't happy with just one. With his hand he cupped her other breast and simultaneously worked on them both, intensely sucking and teasing one nipple, while plumping and kneading the other.

Sensations built and collided inside her. Nothing mattered but Jason and the deliberate attention he paid to her breasts until she writhed on the mattress, her lower body bucking upward and begging for relief.

"Is this what you want?" he asked in a gruff voice, firmly cupping her mound.

Lauren leaned her head back and groaned, thrusting her pelvis against his hand.

"I'll take that as a yes?" he asked, chuckling.

She forced her heavy lids open to find him staring at her, his own eyes dark with desire.

"You can take that as, it's nowhere near enough." She needed him to thrust hard inside her and fill the growing emptiness.

"All you had to do was say so." He dipped one finger inside her. "So wet," he murmured. Using her own moisture, he glided his fingertips over the delicate flesh, up one side, down the other, until finally he took pity on her and thrust his finger deep inside once more.

Lauren lifted her knees and squeezed her flesh around him, contracting and seeking relief from the unrelenting waves pushing at her body but never offering her real release. She knew she was close, just as she knew he was intentionally prolonging the combination of pleasure and agony. Watching her as she moaned, writhed, even begged him for more.

In the far recesses of her mind, she knew he must be sacrificing his own pleasure for hers, but she couldn't focus. Didn't want to.

Jason had never been more turned-on in his life. All his energy and thought went into pleasing her, and it was the most incredible high, watching her face contort with pleasure, viewing her body craving his and listening to the heavy, breathy moans as she came closer and closer to release.

"I need you," Lauren pleaded with him, and he nearly came right then.

"What is it you need?" He wanted to hear her say it.

"Inside me. I need you inside me."

He groaned and dove for the nightstand, pulling

a condom out with shaking hands. He yanked it on and moved over her, drawing her hands above her head, and sealing his lips to hers.

He broke the kiss only to look at her face as she spread her legs and he thrust deep. Her body shuddered around him and she exhaled hard, her breath warm against his neck.

He felt her. Every dewy moist part of her surrounded him. Jason wanted to draw the sensation out, make love to her for hours, but the minute he felt her wet heat, he knew he wouldn't last.

Especially when she pulled her legs back, urging him deeper. Jason lost control, pumping in and out as Lauren met him thrust for thrust. Her soft sighs punctuated the sound of their bodies joining, grinding, *making love.*

The thought came to him suddenly in a blinding burst of light, as clear as any finish line. He pulled out and thrust back deep. *He loved her,* he thought, as the most intense orgasm of his life washed over him.

Jason collapsed on top of her. Their heavy breathing intermingled with what should have been satisfied silence. Except he was far from satisfied.

The sex had been incredible. Fantastic. Beyond anything he'd ever experienced. He now understood the difference between having sex and making love. Because until now, sex had always been about him. His wants. His needs. His satisfaction. Of course he'd always made sure his partner had been pleased, too, but his heart had never been engaged in the act.

This had been all about the woman lying beside him. She'd fallen asleep already and he got out of bed, pulling the covers over her to keep her warm. A quick trip to the bathroom and he returned, climbing back in beside her.

She woke long enough to snuggle in the crook of his arm, mutter something unintelligible and fall back to sleep. He pulled her close, toying with her long hair.

He appreciated everything about Lauren. She'd taken on the huge burden of this house all alone. She never complained as things went wrong and expenses piled up. She dug in and worked hard without expecting others to do it for her. She was beautiful inside and out. Sexy in ways that went beyond things he could see.

In Lauren he'd found everything he hadn't known he was looking for. Unfortunately he faced losing it soon. All he could do was make the most of their time together instead of counting down the days until the end.

THOMAS HAD PLANNED on visiting Clara in her shop. He saw it as his duty to guide Edward in the right direction—into Clara's arms—and he still was convinced his plan had merit. If he could persuade her to date him, or at least get her to pretend an interest in him, Thomas believed jealousy would force Edward to confront his feelings. Yet instead of driving to Crescent Moon, Thomas found himself pulling into Edward's isolated street.

Thomas knew why he'd driven here instead. He'd been unable to shake the look in Jason's eyes when he and Hank had refused Lauren Perkins's invitation to come in for coffee. Thomas had allowed the past to affect the present, much as his brother Edward had been doing his whole life. As a result, he'd hurt his son badly. Thomas didn't like what he'd done, but his actions forced him to admit he wasn't as immune to the curse and the Perkins family as he'd like to believe. Which led him to a deeper understanding of Edward's troubles.

Judging by the way Jason looked at Lauren, he wanted her around for a long time to come. Which meant Thomas needed to get his act together and deal with the past.

There was no better place to start than by reaching out to his brother. He should have done it sooner. And he shouldn't have tried to put Clara between them as a buffer because he was a coward. Afraid of having to have a real conversation with his brother for the first time in way too many years. Having driven by Crescent Moon first, Thomas knew his brother would be here alone.

He headed down the long driveway, pleased to see the jujus that used to hang from the trees and line the road as a form of spiritual protection against the curse were gone. Surely that had to be a sign Edward was moving in a more positive direction. That his medication and psychiatric sessions were working.

Thomas parked the car and stepped into the cool air, heading for his brother's front door. Before he could reach out and ring the bell, Edward greeted him, walking out onto the porch, skunk in hand.

"Go away," Edward said, dangling the skunk in front of him like a shield.

Edward used Stinky Pete, as he called the animal, to scare away unwanted visitors, but Thomas wouldn't be deterred. "Put that descented excuse of a pet down and let me inside."

"Hell no." Edward met his gaze with more clarity than Thomas had expected. His hair, recently cut, was neatly combed and he was clean shaven.

That Edward felt he needed to use the skunk against his own brother pained Thomas greatly. But he wouldn't allow Edward to win this battle.

"I have something to tell you and I'm not leaving until I have my say." Thomas folded his arms across his navy overcoat. "So we can stand out here all day or you can let me in and hear me out."

Edward frowned.

"The quicker you agree, the quicker I'll be gone," Thomas said, grabbing for the only bargaining chip he could think of.

"Come in," Edward said gruffly. Turning his back on Thomas, he strode inside. He let go of the skunk, who darted out the door, much to Thomas's relief.

Before Edward could change his mind, Thomas followed him in.

Order. That was the first thing that struck Thomas about his brother's house. Though Thomas hadn't been inside often, the clutter of the past had always surrounded him. It had been there as recently as June, when Jason had come home. Not even Clara's cleaning had cleared up the mess inside. Until now.

"Place looks good," Thomas said carefully.

"Clara enjoys puttin' the candles and scented crap around the house," Edward said.

Thomas nodded. "And cleaning?"

"Some of that was me. You know what they say. Out with the old." Edward swept his arm around, gesturing to neat, almost empty shelves and tables.

"You didn't come here to talk about my house-keepin'. What do you want?"

Obviously Edward wasn't going to offer to take Thomas's coat. "I want to tell you…I'm sorry. For a lot of things."

"Can't change the past," Edward said gruffly.

Thomas inclined his head, once again struck by his brother's newfound focus.

A kernel of hope grew inside him that maybe he and his brother could come to an understanding. "I agree. But I'd like to change the future."

"How? By going after Clara this time?" Edward, shoulders stiff, turned away and walked into the family room, placing distance between them.

"No, that's not what I want," Thomas said.

"Then what? You want to drive me insane by pretending you still want her?" Edward thrust his hands in his front pockets.

Thomas couldn't believe the irony of his brother's question. "I wanted just the opposite. You live with Clara. She cares for you and it's obvious to me you care about her. You act jealous, but when it comes to admitting you two have a future, you run for the hills."

Edward shrugged. "That's my choice. It's my life."

"Well, I just wanted to push you in the right direction, that's all. The other day, when you thought I was interested in Clara, you got all worked up. So I thought if I could get her to go out with me, I'd push you right into her arms."

Edward turned to face him, disbelief on his face. "Are you sayin' you aren't interested in her?"

Thomas knew this moment was critical. Only the truth would win his brother's trust.

Or turn him away forever.

Thomas couldn't lie. So he opted for honesty. "I'm saying I won't ever make a move on her."

Edward narrowed his gaze. "You're admitting you're interested?"

Thomas drew a deep breath. "Only a dead man wouldn't be interested. I'm saying she's off-limits to me."

A sudden flash of confusion crossed Edward's face. "I don't understand. Why are you here now?"

A lump rose to Thomas's throat. His brother was so close to returning to full sanity, but the distrust he'd built up over the years was painful to watch.

To feel.

"I'm here because we're getting older, Edward, and I don't want to waste what time I have left estranged from my family, running from an ancient curse." He drew a deep breath. "Do you?"

"I'm not running from the damn curse anymore.

I'm on medication and getting healthy!" Edward spoke too loudly, too forcefully.

"Then why are you running from the one woman who loves you and could make you happy?" Thomas asked, raising his voice to match his brother's.

Edward grew red in the face. "I'm not takin' advice from you. I still don't know if I can trust you."

Those words took some of the bluster and certainty out of Thomas. "No, you don't," he agreed. "You'd have to take my word for it. And my word's all I've got to give."

Knowing he'd worn out his welcome, Thomas turned toward the door. "But if you don't trust me, at least trust Clara. You deserve some happiness," he said to Edward before letting himself out.

Only after he shut his brother's door behind him did Thomas allow a lone tear to fall. Brushing it aside, he headed for his car, determined to take his own advice. For his son's sake if not his own, he would try to make peace with the idea of Lauren Perkins and let go of the damned Corwin Curse.

## CHAPTER TWELVE

LAUREN ENJOYED watching Jason work. Not just working with his hands, which of course was a sight to behold. But when he was mentally processing something and deep in thought, she could watch him for hours. His brows furrowed, his full lips pulled together, he alternated between tapping a pencil against the kitchen table and his right temple.

"What's got you so frustrated?" she asked, almost afraid to break his concentration.

"I'm just going over the fire department's report. Trying to figure out who was behind this. The local police are investigating, but it bothers me to wait for them. If you'd been in the house, you could have been seriously hurt. I want this bastard found." Jason spoke through a clenched jaw.

His protectiveness warmed her.

"Anything interesting in the report?" she asked.

"The wiring was tampered with in a way that no

one would know when sparks would catch. Just that at some point, they would."

"So we can't narrow down time, other than after the electrician signed off, right?" Lauren asked.

"Exactly." He leaned back in the chair, kicking his legs out in front of him. "Which brings us back to my list of people with access to the house. It just doesn't make sense to me that one of my guys would do this. What would they have to gain?" His frustration was obvious.

She lowered herself into a chair beside him. "Maybe it's not one of your guys. Like you said, you hired other people who have been in and out of the house." She rubbed her hands up and down her arms, chilled again by the thought of someone plotting against her.

"According to Mike's quick check, none of my crew had any specific dealings with your grandmother or sister. Neither did their families, which in my mind clears them."

Lauren nodded. "Agreed. Plus I trust your judgment. If you hired them, they must be good guys."

He treated her to a wry smile. "Thanks for that."

She shrugged, not wanting to make too much of her feelings for him. She was barely hanging on to her promise to keep him at an emotional distance. She'd already seen firsthand how impossible it would be to join their families in any way. And of course, once she sold this house, her life and career were in New York.

Lauren cleared her throat. "I called Sharon and ran the names on the list by her, too. She spoke to Richard, who as mayor definitely knows most families in town."

He glanced at her. "Did she offer any insight?"

"Just that Richard plays poker with Gary Willet, the drywaller, and swears he's a decent guy, a family man, and in poker his tells are always obvious. She said he couldn't hide a thing if he wanted to."

"Okay, that leaves the plumber. I'm still waiting for J.R. to call me back with information on him. And I've got Mike running a background check."

As if on cue, Jason's cell phone rang. He glanced down and grinned. "Bingo. It's J.R."

While Jason took the call, Lauren fed the cat and cleaned the coffeemaker, keeping busy until she heard him say goodbye.

"Well?"

"Not sure what we've got. Brody Pittman is a new employee. He also worked on Mrs. Hawley's corroding pipes last week. He doesn't know much about him. Oddly he hasn't been able to get in touch with him since the fire here."

Lauren frowned, unsure what to make of that. "He isn't finished with the pipe restoration, is he?"

"No. So his sudden disappearance is odd considering the guy is usually chomping at the bit to get to work."

"I guess we have to wait and see if Mike comes up with anything on the guy. In the meantime, I am going to see Clara and talk to her about the journal. Want to come?"

He shook his head. "I'd rather keep working."

Lauren took one look at his tense expression and decided he needed a break. She rose and walked behind him, placing her hands on his shoulders.

"Your crew is working," she said, massaging his stiff muscles, working her fingertips into the tight knots. "You can take a break and come with me. It'll do you good to get out of here for a little while."

He groaned and tilted his head forward, giving her better access to his neck and shoulders. She pressed into his muscles, then released, taking her cues from the appreciative noises coming from the back of his throat.

"So you'll tag along with me to Clara's?" Lauren asked once she had him more relaxed. "And maybe grab a quick lunch at The Diner before coming home to deal with this place?"

"I'll do anything you ask as long as you don't stop touching me."

She wrapped her arms around his neck and leaned down, pressing a kiss against his cheek. "Much as I'd like that, there are workmen in rooms all over the house." Straightening, she walked around to face him. "Let's go talk to Clara. I bet she'll have some insight into the diary."

"Oh joy," he said sarcastically. But a smile tugged at his lips.

She'd obviously relaxed him, but she doubted it would last long. Not once he discovered that instead of accepting his offer of a loan, she'd made arrangements with a friend in New York, a model with a good income, to buy her Porsche for cash.

BELLS TINKLED, announcing Crescent Moon had visitors. Clara sensed these people were important even before she looked beyond the long strings of beads that partitioned the back end from the rest of her store.

When she stepped out, she caught sight of Lauren Perkins and Jason Corwin browsing through her wares, waiting for her. "If it isn't two of my favorite people!" Clara said as she strode out to greet them.

"It's good to see you, too." Lauren smiled, but

as always, Clara sensed the hesitancy behind the mask. The young woman was never quite certain of her welcome.

Hoping to change that, Clara wrapped her arms around Lauren first, enveloping her in the bright blue of her caftan.

She then turned to Jason, hugging him the same way.

"I was so worried when I heard about the fire. But I knew in here you were both fine." She clasped her hand against her chest, feeling her beating heart, which had indeed informed her that the fire hadn't touched them.

"More likely the town gossips let you know there were no injuries," Jason said, laughing as he discounted her sixth sense.

Clara stared at him—through him—before she broke eye contact.

As there were no other customers, she could give them her full attention. She sensed they needed it. "Lauren, what can I do for you?" she asked.

"Are you so certain we're not here for Jason?" Lauren grinned.

Clearly she understood Jason well.

Clara smiled. "You'd think after my tarot reading he'd become a believer." She liked Jason too much to fault him for being a skeptic.

"Ah, yes, the tarot reading," Lauren said. "He mentioned something about that."

"What did he say?"

"Something about a fortune-teller predicting he'd meet me." Her eyes danced with laughter at his description.

"Did he tell you I predicted a lady in red would rock his world?"

"Not in so many words," Lauren murmured.

"And if I recall, he suggested you might be wearing a red mask."

Startled, Lauren glanced at Jason. "I don't believe he mentioned that."

"I love your outfit." Clara pointedly glanced at Lauren's red fringed boots and matching scarf before nodding knowingly. "There's still time for him to come around."

Lauren and Jason glanced at each other, unsure of what to say.

"Come sit." Clara gestured to a small table where she consulted with customers. "I just brewed some tea. Let me get some for you both." They obviously needed to relax.

A few minutes later, she joined them, placing small teacups in front of them. "So. What brings you here?"

Lauren reached into her purse and pulled out a

small book. "I found this in my grandmother's house. It was written by one of my ancestors and we're hoping you can shed light on some things."

She handed it to Clara, but the negative energy emanating from it was so strong, Clara let it drop to the table.

"What's wrong?" Lauren asked.

"Evil spirits?" Jason asked, laughing.

Clara shot him a quelling look. "Disturbing auras," she explained, using delicate words to avoid upsetting Lauren. "Did it belong to your grandmother?"

"I don't think so. It's not in her handwriting. But I think it might have belonged to the Mary Perkins who set the actual curse."

Thankfully Jason kept quiet.

"How do you know?" Clara asked, intrigued despite the book's negative energy.

"The references." Lauren gently flipped through the pages. "A lot of these pages are worn with age and it looks like they've been ruined by water, but there are legible words."

"Like what?" Clara leaned over to get a better look.

"*Curse* and *offering*," Jason said, his tone cool and slightly sarcastic. "I told Lauren you'd probably be able to give her some insight."

Jason's wariness stemmed from the fact that the diary mentioned the Corwin Curse. He obviously didn't take the words seriously.

Lauren did.

As she should, Clara thought. "Sit tight." Clara rose and retrieved a book from her personal library. "This has a chapter that explains the origins of curses, how to set them, break them, things like that. I don't like to deal with negativity, so I'm more than happy to help you understand the offering involved with this curse."

"That would be great," Lauren said, her tone eager.

Clara perused the book until she came to the chapter she remembered, then she skimmed the pages to refresh her memory. "Well, here's what I can tell you. Offerings are used in different ways. They can be for worship or devotion," she said, reading from the book. "Or to be more specific in the case of the Corwin Curse, the diary could indicate that something was offered as a gift in return for placing the curse."

"This is ridiculous." Jason sounded annoyed. "Even if some crazy witch thought she placed a curse on my family, who's to say things like curses and spells even exist?"

"Who is to say they don't?" Clara asked, staring at him pointedly.

He frowned but said nothing.

Lauren had winced at his use of the term *crazy witch*.

"Does it say what the offering was?" Clara was reluctant to touch the diary again.

Lauren had no such concerns and began to flip through it. They sat in silence as she thumbed through page after page, slowly scanning each one before moving on.

She shook her head. "It's really hard to read, but it talks about an offering and then—" she turned some pages, squinting as she looked for writing that was more legible "—something hidden *in the heart of the house.*" She frowned. "How odd."

"Nobody ever mentioned an item important to the family? Something that might be missing?" Clara studied the young woman's serious face.

Lauren shook her head. "Not to me. I wonder if my sister knows anything. Not that she could tell me if she did." At the mention of her sister, Lauren's shoulders slumped down.

She obviously loved her family despite everything.

Jason reached for Lauren's hand. "We could go

see her and you could talk to her. Even if she doesn't answer, it might make you feel better."

"You'd do that for me?" she asked, surprised.

Jason nodded.

"Thank you," she said. "We'll talk about it later."

Interesting, Clara thought, observing the dynamic between them. Jason mocked the curse. He didn't want to deal with the journal. But when it came to Lauren's feelings, he was right there for her. Though her distress had been caused by people who'd deliberately hurt his family, Jason wanted to ease Lauren's burdens. Even more clearly, she accepted his comfort and relaxed when he offered it.

Just as Clara thought, they were meant to be.

"You two hold the power to break the curse," Clara said, closing her own book.

"How?" Lauren asked.

"Curses are traditionally broken by returning the offering."

"But we don't know what that is!" Lauren's frustration was clear.

"If fate wants you to find out, then you will," Clara assured her.

Jason scowled. "Can't you offer her better advice than relying on fate?"

Clara shook her head, wishing she could. "Some things need to be figured out without influence. I can tell you that you seem closer to discovery rather than farther."

"I'm confused," Lauren admitted.

"That's because Clara's being deliberately cryptic," Jason said, his frustration clear.

"Trust yourselves. Your instincts." Clara leaned closer. "Your *feelings*."

Lauren smiled. "Thank you. I really appreciate your time." She drank from her cup for the first time. "Mmm. This tea is delicious."

Clara smiled. "Let me send you home with some. It will help relax you."

"That would be nice." Lauren gathered her coat and stood.

Rising, Jason helped her put it on before shrugging his own jacket over his shoulders. "Thanks, Clara. I appreciate it, too."

"My pleasure. You're family to me. If you'd like, I can put some items together for you that will lure good spirits to the house." She'd have to give some thought to what would help the most.

Lauren's cheeks flushed with excitement and interest. "I'd love that."

"Good. I'll drop them off with the tea later this afternoon." She walked them to the door.

"You don't mind coming over?" Lauren asked, suddenly hesitant.

Clara paused at the shop entrance. "Why would I?"

Lauren glanced at Jason, as if unsure whether she should speak.

"My father and Uncle Hank refused an invitation to come in," he explained. "Nice and neighborly, huh?" Embarrassed, he shoved his hands into the pockets of his leather jacket.

"Don't be too hard on them. It's difficult to overcome years of ingrained fear. Give them time." Clara's voice was gentle.

Jason shook his head. "Why bother when some things never change?"

Clara gently tapped his cheek with her hand. "You're too skeptical for your own good."

He grinned. "What can I say? At least I'm here."

"Which I take as a very good omen. And speaking of good omens, did you know your father paid a visit to Edward?"

Jason's shock rippled through the air around them. Clara could feel it.

"What for? Did he threaten to steal you away if Uncle Edward didn't step up?" Jason exuded anger.

The poor man had mixed feelings toward his parent. Not that Clara blamed him. His father's generation of Corwins were a confusing, complex lot.

She hoped she could soften his attitude. "Actually

he apologized and said he wanted to reconcile. He told Edward about his original plan to make him jealous by pursuing me." Clara shifted uncomfortably at the thought. "Then he changed his mind and opted for honesty with his brother instead."

"Really?" Lauren asked. "That's such a positive step. Jason?" She nudged him with her arm. "It sounds like you got through to your father."

Jason nodded slowly. "Maybe. Did Uncle Edward accept the olive branch?"

Clara sighed. "Not yet. But he did relay the story to me clearly, without anger, without ranting and raving. And *that* is progress of another kind. Who knows what will happen next."

Lauren wrapped her arm around him. "It's a step, Jason."

He didn't reply.

How big a step remained to be seen, Clara thought. Not just for his uncle but for himself, Lauren and the fate of their families.

Because what they didn't know yet, what they couldn't know, was that Jason and Lauren held more power together than alone. A Perkins and a Corwin in love would go a long way to defeating the centuries-old spell. Fate would dictate the outcome…and there was no predicting the ways of the heart.

IN THE WEEK since their visit to Clara's shop, Lauren hadn't mentioned going to see her sister. Jason wondered if she still wanted to keep him separate from her family or whether they'd just been too damn busy to focus on anything but the house.

In the week since the fire, they'd gone to work with a determination that impressed him. From his crew, who pulled extra hours, to Amber and Gabrielle, who'd come in when they could to help, everyone had stepped up. Of course until the already delayed insurance adjuster showed up tomorrow, nobody could touch the fire-ravaged area, but there had been progress with the rest of the house.

Lauren hadn't told the buyers about the fire, hoping the repair would be under control by closing on December first. She intended to disclose the truth but she wanted to finish the job before she did. Jason suggested she level with the buyers now. After all, when they'd gone to contract and agreed on the renovation prior to sale, nobody had anticipated a fire destroying a part of the house. He thought maybe the buyers would close regardless of whether they could fix the fire damage in time as long as they agreed on a new completion date. But Lauren was determined to stick to the terms of the contract. *Move-in condi-*

*tion.* Unless she had no choice, she intended to live up to that clause.

Jason respected her spirit and determination, and he'd been doing everything he could to help her meet her goals, pushing aside the niggling thought that at least one of them had something meaningful to work toward. He buried his personal frustration and headed into town to run errands.

Lauren had asked him to pick up food for Trouble and some other items at both the grocery and pharmacy. On a whim, he also found himself buying an oversize kitty condo for the cat and flowers for Lauren, spontaneous purchases he hadn't been able to resist.

He'd also purchased a cleaner for his car, since Trouble tended to leave paw marks on the hood every time he slept there, which tended to be most of the day. At night he ended up in their bed, snoring.

Jason wondered if they made nose plugs to prevent the godawful noises they heard each night. He was even tempted to take Trouble to the vet to make sure there wasn't anything seriously wrong with a cat who sounded like a running freight train. Even more unbelievable, Jason was contemplating keeping the cat after Lauren was gone. But he refused to let his mind go there until he had to.

When he pulled his car into the driveway, he immediately noticed something was off. Lauren's Porsche wasn't in its usual spot. He figured she must have gone to town to run errands, when a different thought struck him: Why wouldn't she have just called him and asked him to pick up whatever it was she needed?

He checked his cell, but Lauren hadn't called. He hoped her sister hadn't had another incident, sending her running for the prison. Though she'd been visiting that place alone for a long time, Jason hated the idea of her being on her own. He'd been kicking himself for not accompanying her on her last visit.

His family's reaction would be explosive and he had no real desire to make the trip, but he *did* want to be there for her. Maybe that was why she'd sent him on the cat food run. So she could leave without him pushing to join her.

He hoped like hell that hadn't been her plan. He grabbed the shopping bag and the flowers in one hand, put the kitty condo under his other arm, and headed for the house.

He was braced to find a note. Instead he found Lauren curled up in the den with a box of tissues by her side.

Jason dropped his gifts onto the couch and sat down beside her. "What's wrong?" he asked, wrapping an arm around her.

Her eyes were damp. "I thought I could do this and not look back, but I can't." She blew her nose and tossed the tissue into a wastebasket beside her.

A distinct sense of unease crawled up his spine. "You thought you could do what?"

She straightened her shoulders and stiffened her posture, definitely a bad sign. "I sold my car," she said as she pulled out a fresh tissue. "I needed a minute but now I'm fine. Ready to get back to work." She started to head past him.

As if he'd just let this go. "You sold your car," he repeated, needing to say the words in order to make them real.

She raised her chin. "Yep."

"The Porsche."

She nodded.

"Your symbol of success."

She drew a deep breath. "Exactly. It's just a symbol. Success will still come. Or not. Either way, I'm okay. It was silly to cry over a car." She walked back to the couch where he'd deposited his purchases. "What is all this?"

"Don't change the subject." He grasped her arm, turning her back around. "You aren't crying over the car, you're crying over resentment. Understandable resentment at your sister and your parents for putting you in this position to begin with."

And if he could get any one of them in front of him for five minutes, he'd give them a good piece of his mind. None of them would ever forget what Lauren had done for them or how grateful they should be.

"You're dead wrong. I was crying because I had some stupid sentimental moment. As for my family, I do not resent them! I'm doing what has to be done because that's what family members do for each other!" she yelled at him, as if trying to convince herself more than him.

He knew better than to point that out. Instead he asked her a question. "Would any of them do the same for you?"

## CHAPTER THIRTEEN

*WOULD ANY OF THEM do the same for you?* It was a low blow but Jason had to ask.

Lauren sucked in a ragged breath, one he felt in his own gut.

"Are you kidding?" she asked him.

He shook his head, determined to see this through. "Your parents have already proved they wouldn't," he said gently.

She speared him with a deadly glare. "This isn't about my parents."

Okay, so she did truly accept that she wasn't at the top of their priority list. "So it's about your sister."

Lauren folded her arms over her chest, already defensive. "Of course she'd do the same for me if I were sick. It just so happens, the situation has always been reversed."

He wasn't so sure her sister would look out for anyone except number one. But Lauren wasn't going to see that particular truth. Jason's point went beyond whether or not her sister would be there for her in her time of need. It went beyond the money she was spending on her sister's appeal. And surprising even to him, it went beyond the fact that she'd sold her beloved convertible instead of taking his money.

His real concern was for Lauren's state of denial when it came to her sister. "What if Beth isn't sick?"

Lauren's expression turned from outraged to incredulous. "What are you suggesting?"

That your sister is as crazy as your grandmother was, Jason thought, and immediately realized he'd boxed himself into a corner. At first he'd been upset she'd sold her car instead of taking his money. His initial reaction had been all male ego. He could admit that much.

But when he stepped back, he knew that there was more to it. He'd wanted Lauren to see the truth. That unlike the house, which would bring her a return, investing money in her crazy sister was the equivalent of throwing it away. But he couldn't say that without hurting her and putting a wedge between them.

"Well? Are you going to explain?" She tapped her foot impatiently.

This was what he got for reacting to her news without thinking things through. Big mistake. Now he owed her an answer that wouldn't set her off.

"I'm just saying that the doctors are treating Beth's mental breakdown, but the fact remains that the things she did were…criminal. Just like your grandmother." He tried not to wince at his own description, which was painfully accurate.

"And you don't think I realize that?" Lauren's voice cracked as she spoke. "But she's my *sister*. My baby sister, and she's not as strong as she looks. She was weak enough to be manipulated by my grandmother, and *I'm* responsible for that."

He hadn't seen that one coming. "How do you figure?" he asked, and braced himself for her reply.

She walked over to the mahogany bookshelves and picked up a small framed photograph he'd never noticed before. This was one room she hadn't tackled yet because she liked spending time in here and he realized why. It was the most personal of all the rooms, with the fewest reminders of her grandmother's position as mayor and her abuses of power.

Lauren handed him the photograph.

Two adorable young girls stared up at him. Lauren, the taller older sister, had her arm protectively around her younger sister's shoulder.

"How old were you here?" Jason asked.

She glanced at the picture. "I was eleven and Beth was six. We were always close, until the summer I turned eighteen and took off. She never really forgave me for abandoning her, and when she came to live with my grandmother, she turned to her completely." She drew in a ragged breath. "That's why it's my fault. Because I left her to be manipulated by my grandmother."

He grasped her shoulders. "So you could live your life! You aren't her mother, you're her sister. You had every right to break away when you did!"

Lauren pulled out of his grasp. "I abandoned her to a crazy woman." Her eyes filled with tears. "Which makes me equally responsible for the choices Beth made."

Jason shook his head in frustration, disagreeing with her words. He desperately wanted to hold her, but her shoulders were so stiff he was afraid she'd break if he touched her again.

"I still say it wasn't your responsibility. And even if you feel it was, how could you know what your grandmother was capable of?"

Her eyes were sad. "It doesn't matter. She relied on me and I let her down. So whether or not she's sick or as crazy as my grandmother, I need to be here for her now, in any way I can. If that means selling my car for cash to pay her lawyer, so be it."

Jason realized there was no arguing with her. She was bound and determined to see this situation through distorted lenses. He was equally determined to get her to see she wasn't responsible for her sister's choices.

"You don't understand, do you?" Lauren said "Well, I'll show you in person. Let's go."

"Where?"

"You said you wanted to go with me to visit my sister. Now's your chance. Oh. If it isn't obvious, I need you to drive, so let's move it."

She started to walk out of the room, then paused and turned back. "Why aren't you coming?"

He closed the distance between them. "You took me by surprise, that's all. After our conversation, I didn't expect you to suggest a visit."

She shrugged. "You know what they say. Be careful what you wish for."

As he followed her out of the room, a serious foreboding shook him. Hard.

THEY MADE the hour's trip to the Bricksville Correctional Institution in near silence. By the time Jason found himself standing outside Beth's door, he had a newfound understanding of what Lauren had to endure each time she visited. And a growing respect for her for doing it without complaint.

"Hi, Beth," Lauren said as they entered the room, her voice high-pitched and deliberately cheery.

Beth Perkins lay in bed staring straight ahead. As Lauren had described, she appeared fragile against the white sheets.

Jason hadn't known Beth well. Like Lauren, he'd been gone by the time Beth had come to live with her grandmother in Perkins, and he had only a vague recollection of her from the summer he'd met Lauren. Her crimes, however, were as much town lore as the curse, and he was well versed in those. According to rumors, beneath the fragile surface was a core of steel and no heart. Because he loved Lauren, he wished he could believe differently. Because he was a Corwin, he found it incredibly hard.

"Beth, I brought a visitor." Lauren eased herself into a chair beside the bed and took her sister's hand. "This is my friend Jason."

Lauren had insisted that they wouldn't introduce Jason by his full name to avoid upsetting Beth.

For Lauren's sake, he'd agreed.

Jason watched Beth carefully.

She had no reaction to the introduction. She stared straight ahead at an invisible point in front of her, something he'd expected. Lauren told him Beth never did more than blink and she was right.

He couldn't help but be curious about this woman who was capable of setting fire to a building full of innocent people in order to further her own personal goals.

Jason had personal experience with a woman who had her own agenda. Katrina wanted her lover to win gold and she'd manipulated Jason so he could do it. The only reason Jason hadn't seen through Katrina's act earlier was that he'd been thinking with his dick and not his brain. She was a former gymnast, and the tricks she'd done in bed defied description. He'd confused sex with love and that mistake had led him to this point. He was a contractor—a decent enough occupation—but since losing his Olympic dreams, he looked into the future and didn't like the emptiness he saw.

He pushed those thoughts aside and concentrated on Lauren, who lovingly stroked her sister's hand. Lauren had wanted him to come here and see the fragile woman Beth had become. Jason acknowledged that fragility.

But if she came out of her state, would she change?

He leaned against the wall, watching as Lauren updated Beth on the progress they'd made in the house.

"We're so close," Lauren said. "The walls are patched and painted, thanks to Jason. The floors need buffing, but that will come last, after all the

work is done. It was all coming together except…"
Lauren's voice trailed off and she turned to Jason.

He nodded, encouraging her to continue. There
was no reason not to tell Beth about the fire. It was
in a contained area and the damage would hopefully be fixed soon.

"We had a little incident." Lauren drew a visible
breath. "A fire. But no one was hurt," she said
quickly. "We…I mean, I wasn't even home when
it happened. The fire started in the electrical box,
but the fire department came quickly and only one
small area was damaged. Luckily there wasn't
much smoke damage. As soon as the insurance
adjuster shows up, hopefully tomorrow or the next
day, I can start fixing the area, so the fire shouldn't
hold up the sale." Lauren's voice was forcefully
optimistic.

Jason knew she was determined to finish in time
but he was nowhere near convinced they'd meet
the deadline.

"Oh! I have interesting news," she went on. "In
my cleaning, I found an old diary. At first I thought
it was Grandma's, but it wasn't in her handwriting
and it was too old."

A muscle twitched in Beth's jaw.

Jason wondered if he'd imagined it. He glanced
at Lauren, but she wasn't looking at her sister's

face as she continued talking. "I think the diary belonged to one of our ancestors." She held on to her sister's hand. "You'd be fascinated. It talks about all sorts of history, like the curse…" Her voice trailed off and she stared down at the bed. "I shouldn't have mentioned that," she said softly.

"Don't worry." Jason sought to reassure her. "I'm sure she's not processing."

Lauren glanced at Beth, then jumped up. Her eyes flamed with disbelief. "Hey! Quiet with that kind of talk. I've been talking to her for the past year because the doctors said she might eventually respond to something I said." Her voice cracked with emotion.

Jason groaned. Stepping closer, he wrapped his hand around her shoulder and pulled her against him, whispering in her ear. He tried not to allow his body to react to her familiar, fragrant scent.

"I'm sorry," he said. "That came out wrong. And you're right. I don't know anything about this…situation. Go on." He jerked his head toward the woman in the bed. "If this is a subject she'd enjoy, keep talking."

Appeased, Lauren nodded and sat down beside her sister again, picking up where she'd left off. "The diary mentions an offering. A woman I know—she's Wiccan—she read from a book and explained how offerings are something people use to place a curse." Lauren glanced down as if to gather her thoughts. "If only you were able to talk to me, I'm sure you'd have some great theory about what it could be."

To Jason's shock, Beth's eyes began to move rapidly. Almost as if in response to Lauren's words. *But it can't be possible,* Jason thought.

He remained silent, deciding to observe more.

"The diary also mentioned the heart of the house," Lauren continued. "I keep wondering where that could be?"

Beth gripped the bedrail harder, her knuckles turning white.

Uneasy, Jason glanced at Lauren, but she was still staring down at the floor. She must have long grown used to talking to herself.

"I really need to look into our family history," Lauren said, surprising Jason. "I know our family founded the town. The original Perkinses were shipping magnates, right? So what could they have had of value to use as an offering? Unless it wasn't of monetary value but emotional?" She swiveled in her chair until she faced him. "Maybe I'll research curses, too. Or at least I can ask Clara what she thinks."

Jason enjoyed how her cheeks flushed pink whenever she was excited about a topic. Or when she was excited about *him,* he thought wryly at a completely inappropriate moment.

A sudden gurgling noise interrupted them and Jason redirected his gaze. Beth's eyelids were fluttering like crazy, her jaw twitching.

"Beth?" Lauren looked up and began stroking her sister's cheek.

Her sister calmed down, silent once more.

"The doctors said there can be periods where she'll act like she's coming out of it, but it's just the body responding to stimuli," Lauren said sadly.

Jason frowned. He didn't see it quite the same way. From no reaction to boring topics to an extreme reaction at mention of the curse. Coincidence?

Very odd, Jason thought.

And extremely curious.

HOW COULD HER SISTER be with *him,* Beth wondered.

And how stupid did Lauren think Beth was?

She'd introduced him as Jason. No last name. As if Beth wouldn't know everything about the current generation of Corwins. Beth recognized the snowboarder from his photographs. The ones in the portfolio she and her grandmother had compiled.

It was obvious from the way Lauren and Jason Corwin looked at each other that their relationship was more than just business.

Again.

Apparently Lauren thought she could tempt fate twice. Beth had looked out for her sister the first time, turning Lauren's personal diary over to their grandmother when she'd made the mistake of sneaking around with Jason Corwin when she was only seventeen. But now that she was locked in here, there was nothing Beth could do to protect her sister this go-round. Beth barely remembered not to shake her head in disgust and frustration. Some people never learned.

Jason Corwin and his failed Olympic bid were living, breathing proof that the curse was still in effect, striking any Corwin man who fell in love. And wasn't that what the first Mary Perkins had intended when she'd used diamonds as an offering? So why would Lauren want to be the woman on the receiving end?

Nothing in the curse protected a Perkins. Because no Perkins worth their name would get involved with a Corwin man. Perkins women chose their men carefully, used them and kept or disposed of them depending on need. Like Beth's current lover.

She still hadn't heard from him, but now that she knew there'd been a fire in the house, she was certain he'd received her message and targeted the electrical box. Unfortunately he hadn't been smart enough to use a decent accelerant. At least she'd chosen gasoline to set fire to The Wave. Unfortunately she'd been so beside herself worrying about her grandmother losing the election, she'd had a breakdown, causing her to get caught red-handed.

Beth clenched her teeth so hard her jaw ached. She still couldn't believe she hadn't been able to hold it together, but that was the past. In the lucid months she'd spent in here, she'd realized she was the sole remaining Perkins who *believed.* It was a huge responsibility. One she'd live up to. She'd never make such a foolish mistake again.

Success depended on planning. And Beth had a plan. With the construction on the new wing complete, she couldn't count on seeing her lover again. She had to get in touch with him one last time. Because he had to get her out of here.

She was reaching her breaking point and she didn't know how much longer she could keep up the catatonic charade. She thought she'd covered her shock over seeing Jason Corwin. She wasn't so certain about her reaction to Lauren's news about the hidden diary.

Why hadn't her grandmother told her about the journal? Grandma had made sure Beth knew about the diamonds, so if she ever needed a safety net, she had only to find the valuable family jewels.

Oh well. Beth couldn't figure out the mind of a dead woman, but that journal might contain more of a clue than Lauren realized as to where the diamonds were hidden.

*The heart of the house.*

What the hell did that mean? Beth had to figure it out, and to do that she needed to get her hands on that journal. She didn't know where Lauren was keeping it, but it had to be in the house.

She definitely didn't trust *him* to find the diary for her. She needed to read it herself, to see if she could make sense of the words. And she needed to solve the mystery and find the diamonds first. Before her too-curious sister got herself involved in something she couldn't possibly handle.

LAUREN THOUGHT she knew what exhaustion was, but not even the manual labor on the house could compare to the mental drain from visiting her sister with Jason by her side. Her cheeriness had been even more forced than usual. Her stories more intense.

And all the while his focus hadn't been on Lauren. He'd been eyeing her sister, watching her intently. The pressure of wanting Jason to accept Beth, weaknesses and all, had worn on Lauren in unexpected ways.

Why did she care what he thought?

She was afraid to explore the reasons too deeply. Because she already knew. In the end, that reason played to her deepest fear.

Rejection.

Lack of acceptance.

By now she should be an expert at letting such things roll off her shoulders. Mother, father, sister, grandmother. All had turned their backs on her in one way or another. Which was why Jason's earlier question had hit her where it hurt most. In the heart she no longer let anyone get close enough to touch.

He was right. No one in her family would do for her what she'd done for Beth.

Lauren wished like hell the truth changed her perspective but it didn't. She still felt responsible for pushing Beth into her grandmother's clutches and she'd do whatever she had to in order to make up for that. She already had.

And she'd survive her time in this town, her time with Jason, by regrouping. Wrapping her independence around her like a shield. If that meant distancing herself from him, so be it.

When he pulled into the driveway, she turned to him, wondering how to tell him.

"I appreciate you taking me with you." He stretched his arm over the back of her seat and leaned in close.

The sympathy in his eyes unnerved her, making it more difficult to find that distance she needed. "I just wanted you to see for yourself."

He inclined his head. "I'm glad I did."

Without warning, a thud sounded and they both jerked their bodies in the direction of the sound.

Trouble had landed on the hood of the car and curled up in a ball.

"Silly cat. Look how he glares at us." Lauren watched the feline, who stared back through golden eyes.

Jason cut the engine. "Speaking of staring, I watched your sister carefully today."

Lauren bit the inside of her cheek. "I noticed."

"But when you talk to Beth, you don't look at her."

He'd caught that? "Because it hurts too much. Can you blame me?"

His expression softened. "Of course not." He brushed her hair off her shoulder, toying with a few strands. "But maybe there are things you've been missing."

Wariness crept through her. "Such as?"

"She does have reactions."

"I know. And I told you what the doctors said. It's her body's normal response."

His hand grazed her shoulder and remained there. "What if it's more than that?"

"I don't know what you're getting at, so can you stop beating around the bush and get to the point?" She already sensed she wouldn't like what he had to say.

"It seemed to me that Beth responded to specific things you said. They weren't just random movements."

"Such as?"

He drew a breath. "It started when you brought up the diary. Facial tics and gestures. It got worse when you started to talk about looking into what kind of offerings were used to place the curse."

Lauren's throat swelled with emotion as his words proved what her heart feared. "I'm really disappointed in you, Jason. You only saw what you wanted to see. A crazy woman reacting to that damn curse." Her arms suddenly felt as if they weighed a ton and it was hard to lift them. Her entire body hurt, she realized.

"I didn't mean to upset you."

Lauren shook her head. "That's okay. You're

entitled to your feelings. Besides, you just reaffirmed what I was about to tell you."

He drew back his shoulders, stiffening in preparation. "Go on."

"I'm tired. I want to go inside and take a nap."

Relief crossed his handsome face. "You want to take the afternoon off? That's fine." He checked his watch. "There's not much left of the day anyway. Let me send my guys home. We can relax and order in dinner and pick up work tomorrow when you're feeling better. I'll even give you a massage," he promised in a suggestive, teasing voice.

She shook her head before she could take him up on his tempting offer. "I can't. I'd rather…I mean, I need to be alone."

He raised his eyebrows, surprise etching his expression. "Okay, I'll finish work while you rest. Then—"

She jerked her head back and forth once more. "Please, just go home for the night. We'll get back to work tomorrow." She had to force out the words.

He reared back as if she'd slapped him. "Don't do this. Don't pull away. We can work through this together."

Lauren clenched her fists, letting her nails dig into her palms, drawing courage from the pain.

"Why are you so sure Beth is reacting to specific things? To the curse?"

"Because I saw her with my own two eyes?"

He reached for her hand but Lauren refused to let him touch her. "Beyond that. Why would Beth react to mention of the curse?" she asked, rephrasing.

Jason rolled his eyes. "Don't make me go there," he said in a firm voice.

"I have to. Answer the question. Why do you think that my sister Beth, my grandmother Mary's granddaughter and assistant, would react to recent news of the curse and offerings?" Lauren pushed him.

She wanted to hear him say it.

"Fine." He leaned in close. "Because she believes in that curse with every fiber of her being. Because she hates my family and wants the legacy of the curse to continue."

*"Why?"*

"Because she's a damned Perkins, that's why," he said, his voice raised. "Are you happy now?"

Lauren's eyes filled with tears. No, she wasn't happy. But she was right. He'd never truly be able to accept Beth. Which meant he'd never truly be able to accept Lauren, either.

LAUREN HAD BAITED HIM, Jason thought. And even knowing she was setting him up so she could push him away, he'd allowed her to manipulate him anyway.

"Idiot!" he said, stamping his foot.

Fred lifted his head and let out a lazy howl before laying his head back on the floor. As soon as his uncle saw Jason's car pull into the pathway to the barn, Hank walked The Fat Man over.

Jason knew he was in trouble the moment he realized the old barn felt less like his home than the Perkins house. Things only went downhill from there. Sleeping with gas-producing Fred wasn't the same as sleeping with Lauren and her snoring cat, and Jason woke up in a pissed-off mood.

When his doorbell rang, he answered without looking to see who was there. The freezing November air hit him as soon as he cracked open the door.

"Hey, cousin," Mike said, walking inside.

Jason slammed the door shut behind him.

"I stopped by the house but Lauren said I'd find you here. So I left Amber there to help out and here I am."

"What are you guys doing out here so early?" Jason asked, knowing Mike and Amber lived an hour away in Boston. Even Amber didn't normally arrive until eleven on her day off.

"I have news," Mike said. "I wanted to run that

check for you earlier but I've been on a case and haven't been able to breathe until now."

Jason waved away the apology. "It's fine. What have you got?"

"I didn't want to tell Amber without you there." Mike reached into his back jeans pocket and pulled out a sheet of paper. "Your plumber has an interesting background."

Jason grabbed the paper, scanning the page. He didn't have to look far. "Last job before JR Plumbing was at the Bricksville Correctional Institution." Jason's hands began to shake. "Are you kidding me?"

Mike shook his head. "He worked on the crew building the new wing. To do that he had to be prescreened. I ran a criminal check anyway and he's clean. But—"

"I already know the *but*," Jason said. "Bricksville is the facility where Mary Beth Perkins is currently being held."

"Bingo. And the construction, which was recently completed, bordered the psychiatric wing of the prison," Mike said.

Jason drew a deep breath. "I saw the wing yesterday when I went with Lauren to visit her sister."

Mike let out a low whistle. "Visiting relatives? That's something you only do for love."

Jason shot his cousin a warning glare. "Let's not discuss it, okay?"

Lauren had already decided her sister provided one very convenient barrier to any serious relationship. And now he had to go tell her their plumber friend, Brody Pittman, had ties to the same prison ward where her sister was being held. The same *unresponsive* sister Jason could swear had reacted to the subject of the Corwin Curse.

Coincidence?

After testing positive for drugs he knew he'd never taken, Jason no longer believed in the word.

## CHAPTER FOURTEEN

CLARA FELT the evil before she reached the house. Poor Lauren. No wonder she'd looked so stressed and uptight. Her special herbal blend of tea would work wonders to help her relax, Clara thought. A cleansing ceremony might also fix what ailed both Lauren and the house. She'd have to judge once she stepped inside.

Lauren met Clara at the door with a warm greeting. As they entered the house, a black cat skirted past her. Clara watched him go, unfazed by superstition.

"That's Trouble," Lauren said, gesturing to the furry feline.

"I take it he's earned his name?" Clara asked.

"And then some." Lauren smiled but it didn't reach her eyes. Clara wondered if there was more than the stress of the house wearing on her. If Lauren wanted to confide, Clara would provide an opening and then a shoulder to lean on.

"I'm sorry I couldn't get over here last week like I promised but the shop got busy." Clara shrugged off her coat and Lauren hung it in a nearby closet.

"That's okay. We took an unexpected trip and we weren't here. But I'm glad you're here now." Lauren shut the closet door. "Let's go into the kitchen. Follow me."

Clara did and found herself in a cheery room that defied the negative energy in the house. Yellow curtains hung on the windows, dark cherry cabinets and hunter-green granite countertops indicated the room had been recently redone. "I love cooking and this is a beautiful place to work," she marveled.

Lauren nodded. "My grandmother didn't spend much time in here but this was one of the few rooms she kept up. I think it was because she enjoyed having a cook prepare her meals."

The fact that Mary Perkins hadn't used this room much herself explained the sunny energy Clara felt in here. She'd love to spread the aura to the rest of the house.

"As promised, I brought you tea." She pulled the canister of tea leaves from a shopping bag. "And I labeled how much to use and how long to let it steep." She reached into the bag once more, removing one of her favorite items. "And this is an easy-to-use individual tea maker."

The young woman's eyes opened wide. "Clara, this is amazing. Thank you! How much do I owe you for all this?"

Clara waved away the question. "This is a gift. My idea, my pleasure." Before Lauren could argue, Clara stood. "Let me show you how it works."

Lauren hesitated, uncomfortable accepting gifts. She finally relented. "Thank you. I'll heat some hot water." She checked the kettle on the stove and turned on one burner while Clara got to work, measuring tea leaves.

"I'll make one cup for you and one for me. Where is Jason? I think he can use some of this, as well."

The temperature changed in the room. Warm to chilly, Clara thought, certain she hadn't imagined the drop.

"He should be here soon." Lauren turned her back and pulled two mugs from a cabinet.

"Problems between you two?" Clara asked, deciding she couldn't help if she didn't pry at least a little.

"Fundamental disagreement is more like it." Lauren leaned against the counter, hands braced on either side.

She carried her burdens like heavy baggage,

Clara thought sadly. "No two families are alike. At their core, all people are different." She offered the only words of wisdom she could.

"Especially our two families."

The teakettle signaled the water had boiled and Clara took control, preparing two cups and setting them down on the table.

Clara lowered herself into a chair across from Lauren, whose tension hadn't eased. "Relationships aren't simple. They take work."

"What Jason and I have isn't a relationship," she said without looking up.

In an attempt to soften the words to come, Clara placed her hand over Lauren's. "Who are you lying to? Me or yourself?"

Lauren shook her head, no anger showing in her expression. "I'm not lying, just facing reality."

A reality that could be changed, if the young woman wanted to make the effort. "Take a sip of tea. It will help you relax," Clara urged, nodding at the mug.

Lauren took a long sip of tea and a genuine smile eased over her face. "This is delicious."

"Thank you. Now let me ask you something. What about the power of positive thinking?"

Skepticism crossed Lauren's face. "What about it?" she asked warily.

"I believe it's life changing. Life affirming. Look what it did for Edward and me." Clara's belief was born of experience. All she could do was impart her wisdom and hope Lauren understood.

POSITIVE THINKING, Lauren thought. The concept wasn't a new one. It had brought her to the precipice of something big in her career. But reality dictated there were too many burdens for it to succeed between Lauren *Perkins* and Jason *Corwin.*

But Clara's excitement was tangible and Lauren looked up, really seeing the other woman for the first time. Her eyes sparkled. Her cheeks flushed pink. And her skin glowed.

Lauren had been so preoccupied with her own problems she hadn't noticed the changes in the other woman.

"What's going on?" Lauren wasn't just curious— she genuinely liked Clara and cared about her.

"Edward asked me on a date!" Clara exclaimed, her joy obvious.

Lauren smiled. "That's great news! It's a huge step for him, isn't it?" She vividly recalled the distraught man Jason had led to the car after Edward had discovered a Perkins and a Corwin were working together. The same man who'd hidden in his house for years, driven away from human contact by fear of the curse her ancestors had placed.

Clara held Lauren's gaze as she spoke. "His medications are finally working. He's seeing the world more clearly and it's a beautiful thing! I waited years to see this happen."

Lauren's heart filled. "I'm so happy for you, Clara. I understand how long it's been and what a difficult road."

"But I never gave up on him. I never lost hope even when we were apart. I just waited for a sign that the time was right for us." Clara wrapped her hand around the warm mug.

Lauren took another sip of the tea. As Clara said, the brew was working to relax her. "I'm not trying to burst your bubble or be a downer, but even hope has its limitations. I don't mean for you and Edward, but for others."

Clara shook her head. "Only if you allow it to." She reached for the Crescent Moon shopping bag. "I have a few more items for you. There are candles to put around the house and a dream catcher to place over your bed. And *this* is something new." She handed Lauren what looked like a sterno log.

"What is it?"

"It's for the fireplace. When burned, it releases

positive energy into the room. Used in this house, it will be cleansing," Clara explained.

Lauren didn't know how much she believed Clara's claims, but a little good energy certainly couldn't hurt. "Thank you. I'll give it a try."

The older woman nodded. "While you're at it, try thinking more positively about your own life. About Jason and the things you want. Whatever you put out in the universe, you will get back." Clara rose from her seat. "And now I have to get back to the shop."

Lauren smiled. "Thanks for everything, and I'm so glad we had time to talk." She hugged the other woman, grateful for her thoughtfulness, generosity and time. She'd try to hold on to a more positive outlook—and hoped Jason would do the same.

WHEN JASON ARRIVED at Lauren's, she was busy in the parlor, a room he'd already completed work in. He assumed her choice was intended to send him a message. She didn't want to deal with him at all.

Tough.

He walked into the room filled with wall-to-wall bookshelves. Lauren was packing old hard-covers into a box, pausing every so often to study the covers or contents.

He cleared his throat.

She jumped, startled. "Jason!" Before she had a chance to think, a clear welcome lit her gaze, but just as quickly her eyes turned wary. "I didn't hear you come in."

"You were wrapped up in those books."

She nodded. "I'm trying to decide which books the library could use and which to give away to Goodwill. Sharon is coming over later to help me. So what's on your agenda today?"

Businesslike. And yet her tone was light. He had the sense she was as unsure of where things stood between them as he was. He'd just have to wing it and see what happened.

"Until the adjuster comes, we'll keep to the room-by-room schedule we set up." He stepped farther inside. "So how come you're not doing the same? I thought you'd be working with me in the living room."

"Since finding the diary, I'm curious about what else is hidden in this house. I thought maybe there'd be another one buried in here."

He wanted to believe her, but she slid her gaze from his too quickly. He wasn't buying her story for a minute. "You can't avoid me by switching rooms."

"I'm not lying," she said through clenched teeth.

Maybe she was telling the truth. But since changing their routine coincided with her decision he should sleep at home, he doubted it. Not that there was anything he could do about it.

"I have some news you're going to want to hear." He changed the subject.

"What's wrong?" she asked, concerned. She'd accurately judged his somber tone.

"Let's sit." He gestured to one of the wing chairs.

He thought she'd argue. Instead she walked over and sat down, crossing her long legs in front of her, waiting for him to join her.

He chose the closest chair and settled in. "Mike called. His check on Brody Pittman turned up some interesting results."

Her attention caught and she leaned closer, resting her elbows on the arm of the chair.

There was no easy way to break the news so he dove right in. "Brody Pittman's last job was at the Bricksville Correctional Institution, working on the new wing."

Surprise then disbelief colored her expression but she remained silent, obviously digesting the information and trying to decide how to react.

"I'm sorry," he said when the quiet became overwhelming.

"Why? Because our plumber also worked at the prison?"

He didn't think she'd be deliberately dense, yet

he also knew she was too smart not to have covered all possibilities.

He struggled to control his growing frustration. "The new wing is right next to the psychiatric hospital where your sister is." Instead of connecting the dots, he highlighted the important points, hoping she'd draw the correct conclusion.

"So? My sister isn't responsive. Brody couldn't have run into her. And even if he did, what motivation could that possibly give him for tampering with the electrical system in this house?" she asked.

"I haven't figured that out yet," he admitted. But not for lack of trying. The connection was clear. Just not the motive.

"I thought so," she said, her voice all too satisfied. "So all you've got is distrust of my sister because her last name is Perkins. Isn't that perfect?" She turned her back, staring out the window.

He set his jaw. "Lauren?"

"Yes?" Her hands were clenched tight.

"I'm not having this argument again." He refused to give her the satisfaction. "I have work to do. You know where to find me if you decide to be rational. Not just about the obvious, but about *us*." With that, he rose and walked out of the room, leaving her to stew in silence.

He hoped.

SO MUCH FOR POSITIVE thinking and keeping an open mind. Lauren blew out an exasperated breath. How had she lost control of her life so quickly?

When she'd sold her designs to Galliano, she'd known she'd be taking a break from work until after the Paris shows. The timing had been perfect, since she'd needed to fix and sell this house. She just hadn't counted on Jason Corwin blowing into her life and digging at old wounds. Some he'd caused when they were young and others her parents and sister had inflicted. When she'd approached him at the festival, she'd been thinking about fun, not feelings. Who knew he could still affect her so deeply?

She admitted to herself that she'd baited him into saying those things about her sister the other day, grasping at any excuse to throw him out before he could abandon her. She'd acted in anger, forgetting that his leaving meant she'd be living with the mice infestation without Jason's comforting body beside her at night.

Somehow she'd managed to get some sleep and walk around the house, proving to herself she was braver than she'd realized. But her insides still churned at the thought of the little visitors and Trouble didn't do nearly enough to catch them.

Still, she'd proved she could manage, if not conquer, that particular fear.

Then Clara had challenged her to think positively. To put her deepest wishes into the universe and hope they came back to her. So she'd greeted Jason without harboring anger from their visit to her sister. And what had she received in return?

He basically accused her of lying about her motives for working in this room and then he dropped the bomb about Brody Pittman being at the prison. *How could that be anything but a co-incidence?* Day after day, her sister sat in bed or a chair and stared into space. How could she have any interaction with the man? And even if by some bizarre fluke they had met, what could that have to do with this house and the fire in the electrical system?

Lauren pressed her palms against her pounding head. She wasn't looking for a fight with Jason, nor was she trying to be blind to her sister's faults. She just looked at the facts, and for the life of her, Lauren couldn't reach the same conclusions as Jason. He insisted on thinking the worst without proof.

They made love in such perfect unison, but when it came to the important things in life, they couldn't even agree to disagree.

THOMAS SAT ACROSS from his brother Hank in a booth at the far end of a restaurant two towns over from Stewart—far enough away that there were no familiar faces. Thomas faced the back wall and slunk down in his seat, embarrassed he'd let Hank talk him into spying on Clara and Edward's date.

"Here they come now." Hank, who faced out, pulled his Red Sox baseball cap lower on his head and slipped on a pair of sunglasses.

"Like that's going to help," Thomas muttered. "It's nighttime and you look like an ass."

Hank snorted. "I'll take another beer," he said to a waitress passing by.

"Would you like anything?" she asked Thomas.

He shook his head. "Unless you can make him disappear, I'm good." He lifted his still full glass of club soda.

Hank leaned forward, elbows on the table, staring toward the center of the restaurant. "What do you know! Edward held the chair for Clara," he said in a hushed yet still loud whisper. "I'm surprised he remembered that's the right thing to do on a date."

"Maybe he read Emily Post." Thomas shifted uncomfortably in his seat. "Listen, we can still go out the back door and they'll never know we were here."

Thomas didn't want to get caught. Though

Edward wasn't speaking to him, his brother had taken his advice and started to move forward in his relationship with Clara. Thomas believed his brother would forgive him next. At the very least he still held out hope. But if Edward discovered Thomas and Hank lurking here, he would probably pile another wrong onto the list of grudges he already held against him.

Hank shook his head. "If you're going to be such a downer you should've stayed home."

"You've got a point, but someone had to make sure you behaved." Thomas had had visions of Hank crawling on his hands and knees, ending up beneath Clara and Edward's table in order to hear their conversation.

"I don't buy that excuse. You wanted to see how things worked out between them for yourself." As Hank spoke, he leaned around the booth once more. "They're talking like civilized people!"

Thomas wouldn't let Hank get sidetracked. "If I'm so interested in Clara and Thomas, why are you the only one spying?"

"Because someone has to, and I fill you in as soon as I see something worth reporting! Come on. Admit you're as interested in these two getting together as I am."

Thomas hated it when he couldn't argue with

his brother's reasoning. Thank goodness, it wasn't often that Hank was right.

Thomas leaned back in his seat, arms folded across his chest. "Of course I'm interested. I want Edward healthy so we can be a family again, and these baby steps he's taking with Clara will help lead him back to us, too."

"Aha!" Hank picked up a fork and waved it at him.

"But that doesn't mean I'd invade their privacy to do it."

"Stick-in-the-mud." His lips turned down in a classic Hank-pout.

Thomas shook his head, suppressing a grin. He'd already decided not to respond.

Suddenly the ringing of Hank's cell phone broke the silence. The loud song called attention to their booth, and as Hank fumbled to find his phone, the song continued its seemingly never-ending chorus.

"Why didn't you put that thing on silent?" Thomas hissed.

"Because I don't know how." Hank finally found the phone and flipped it open, ending the serenade. "Talk to me," he said, again in a too loud whisper.

"Who is it?" Thomas asked.

Hank put up a hand, telling Thomas to wait, his

concentration on the call. He listened, nodding until he finally said, "Holy cow!"

"What?"

Hank ignored him. "Yep, he's with me. I'll let him know and we'll call you when we get home." He disconnected and placed the phone on the table. "I knew I shoulda brought my shotgun."

"For the last time, what is wrong?" Thomas asked.

"That was Derek and you'll never believe why he called." Hank met Thomas's gaze. "That lunatic Elizabeth Perkins escaped!"

Thomas blinked, certain he'd heard wrong. And if he hadn't, how was such a thing possible?

He leaned closer to Hank. "Do you think we should tell Edward, so he hears it from family first and not from some stranger?"

"No need to tell me anything, I overheard everything," a deep, familiar male voice said.

Thomas cringed.

Edward stood by their table, Clara beside him. "Odd choice in restaurants for you two, isn't it?"

"When did you notice us?" Thomas asked, mortified.

"When 'Old McDonald' rang on the phone."

Thomas shot Hank a deadly look before turning his attention back to Edward. His brother looked *neat.* He was dressed in a pair of pressed pants and a clean button-down shirt. No tie. Hair freshly trimmed and combed, the same as his beard. He looked fantastic. Like the brother he'd almost forgotten he'd ever had, Thomas thought, and barely refrained from complimenting him. He didn't want to embarrass Edward, especially in front of Clara, who stood patiently while the three men talked.

"I just wanted to be close by in case you needed me," Hank said in an attempt to defend his actions. "Isn't that right, Thomas?"

Thomas clenched his jaw tight. Hank was covering, but Thomas had promised himself he wouldn't deceive his brother. Not by omission or by lying to himself, either.

He gripped the napkin in his lap. "I came to keep an eye on him." Thomas jerked his thumb toward Hank. "But to be even more truthful, I also feel like I have a vested interest in whether you two end up together." The admission didn't come easily, but Thomas was pleased with himself for making it.

"Why?" Clara asked, clearly appalled. "I wouldn't date you even if Edward were foolish enough to end things between us." She placed her hand on Edward's shoulder. "Not ever."

Thomas admired her spunk and unnecessary defense of his brother. He should have realized the potential for misunderstanding. "What I meant was that if Edward could work toward a resolution with you, maybe you will make peace with me next." He steeled himself for his brother's verbal punch, but to Thomas's shock and relief, Edward's face seemed to soften.

"Why is nobody dealing with the fact that that crazy Perkins lady escaped?" Hank blurted out.

"Oh, Goddess, help us," Clara said, turning her attention heavenward. "Some men just don't have the sense she gave a goat."

Clara was right and Thomas groaned. Leave it to Hank to break a potential peace by mentioning the Perkins family.

Hank raised his hands in a gesture of defeat. "Don't everyone get your knickers in a twist. It's an honest question, but I realize I shouldn't have asked."

Thomas turned his gaze to Edward, awaiting his volatile reaction.

Edward drew a deep breath. "It's fine. The Perkins lady has nothing to do with me."

Thomas had never been so relieved.

"Are you nuts?" Hank blurted out.

"He means, are…" Thomas started to rephrase Hank's words, then realized he couldn't. "I don't know what he means. But…are you sure that's how you feel?" he asked Edward.

After all, his reaction was quite a turnaround from the past.

"No," he admitted. "No, I'm not sure. But it's what I'm working toward feeling. And repeating that mantra day and night is keeping me calm. So I'd appreciate it if you would help me on that mission. And if you can't, then stay away." Edward squared his shoulders, challenging his brothers.

Thomas wanted to applaud.

Clara smiled. In fact, she beamed, radiating pride and happiness in Edward.

Thomas didn't blame her.

"Now if you don't mind, we'd like to get back to our date," Edward said.

Thomas nodded.

Hank did the same.

Thomas waited until after Clara and Edward were out of hearing distance.

"Amazing," Hank said before Thomas could speak.

"Agreed." He looked around for the waitress and signaled for a check. "Now do you want to go find out what happened with Elizabeth Perkins and how Lauren and Jason are holding up?"

Hank nodded, a big smile on his face. "I thought you'd never ask!"

# CHAPTER FIFTEEN

LAUREN STARED OUT the window overlooking the lawn in the front of the house. The sun had set a long time ago but the police car parked out front kept vigil.

In case her sister showed up.

And Jason had insisted on staying over for protection. In case her sister showed up.

As if Lauren needed protection from her own sister. She may have misjudged Beth's deviousness and mental state, but she'd never accept the fact that her sister could hurt her.

But Lauren knew better than to argue with the men who insisted she needed watchdogs. The little lady needed protection, the old cop had said. Lauren bristled at the memory.

"Are you going to watch the police car all night?" Jason asked, coming up behind her.

"It's not like I'm going to get any sleep." She

continued to stare out into the dark night. The car was barely visible, but she knew it was there.

"I'm sure we could find something more interesting on TV."

She shook her head.

"Do you want to talk?" Jason placed a hand on her shoulder, his strong touch meant to reassure her.

But how could anything calm her now? His musky scent aroused her, but she wasn't in the mood for sex or conversation. She still needed to process her sister's escape. The charade. The lies.

She exhaled, her warm breath fogging the window in front of her. "No. I just need time to think." About how she'd been so easily deceived.

She tried to reassure herself that she wasn't alone. The doctors had been fooled, as well.

Jason removed his hand and, despite not wanting the attachment to him, she felt the loss.

"I just want you to know, I am sorry. I didn't want to be right about your sister."

She inclined her head. "I know. And you've been a gracious winner." She couldn't bring herself to look him in the eyes and see the pity there.

"There are no winners in this situation." Without warning, he gripped her arm and turned her around. "And I don't take any pleasure in your pain."

She believed his words. She just couldn't deal

with anything beyond the fact that her sister, the sister she'd sold her car to protect, was an escaped felon.

"Did the prison say when Beth's doctor would call you?" Jason asked.

They'd heard about the escape from the institution but not any details about how she'd managed the feat. Lauren only knew it involved fire. Her sister's weapon of choice.

"Lauren?"

Jason's voice brought her back to the present and she shook her head. "The prison says he's tied up with the police."

A loud knock sounded at the front door. Since receiving the news, they'd locked the doors.

Lauren wasn't in the mood to answer. "Would you mind?" She waved toward the entryway.

"Of course not." He headed for the front door.

No sooner had the creaky hinges sounded, indicating he'd opened the door for their visitors, than she heard familiar male voices.

"We came as soon as we heard the news," Jason's father said, his tone kind and concerned.

"I can't believe the loony-toon arsonist escaped!" Hank wasn't as compassionate.

Lauren cringed at the description. But she was forced to admit it was on target. Her crazy sister had set fire to The Wave last year and apparently she'd set another one today to facilitate her escape.

Nausea rose in Lauren's throat.

"Uncle Hank, if you're going to talk like that in this house, I'm going to have to ask you to leave." Jason defended her honor.

At this point, Lauren wasn't sure she deserved to be defended. She'd talked to her sister for hours and never once detected something was off.

She straightened her shoulders and headed to the entryway to greet the men. "Jason, he has every right to be upset. Everyone does."

Jason shot her a grateful look. "Lauren's being generous. Now you do the same for her."

Lauren smiled. "Well. I see you decided to come into this house after all. What changed?"

Thomas flushed, his cheeks turning red.

Nothing seemed to embarrass Hank. "We wanted to see how Jason was doing. Imagine if your crazy sister came here and realized you and my nephew were a *thing*. News like that might send her over the edge. If she's not there already."

At his words, Lauren's blood chilled. "Oh my God. What if she recognized you? What if she already knows?"

"Recognized him how?" Thomas asked.

Jason placed a calming hand on Lauren's

shoulder. This time she *did* take comfort from his touch.

"Lauren and I visited her sister in prison," he said.

Hank's eyes opened wide, and without warning, he reached over and smacked Jason on the side of the head.

"Hey! What was that for?" Jason raised a hand to his head, rubbing the spot.

"For being an idiot! You went to see a Perkins in prison?" Hank yelled.

Lauren's temples began to throb. "Look, we didn't tell Beth Jason's last name, so there's a chance—"

"There's no chance!" Hank insisted. "I heard when the police raided this house last year they confiscated files on almost every citizen. Especially us Corwins. Trust me, she knows."

Lauren's gut told her he was right.

"Could it be that the visit upset her enough to precipitate the breakout?" Thomas asked, always the polite, rational brother.

Lauren shrugged. "I don't think it matters what precipitated it. She's out. She has an agenda and I can't begin to guess what it is. It's not like she confided in me." She paused, thinking about what she did know about Beth. "I can tell you two things for certain."

All three men stared at her intently.

"One." Lauren held up a finger. "Beth wouldn't hurt me, and two, she's not stupid enough to show up here." She raised a second finger.

"That's a lot of faith in a—"

"Don't say it, Uncle Hank." Jason grabbed his uncle's elbow and started nudging him to the door. "We appreciate you stopping by to check on us, but as you can see we're fine. And we have police protection." He pointed to the street through the side windows near the front door. "So you two can go home and rest easy."

"But—"

"No buts. I'll call you in the morning and check in," Jason said, his tone firm.

Thomas nodded. "He's right. Let's go." The two men had started for the door when Jason's father suddenly turned. "Ms. Perkins?"

Surprised, Lauren met his gaze. "Yes?"

"Try to rest easy. You can trust Jason to make the right decisions. You're in good hands." Thomas Corwin nodded at his son. Then he led his brother out the door.

Once the men were gone, Lauren retreated to the den once more. Jason followed, settling into a seat on the couch.

She eased down beside him, her mind on Thomas Corwin's words and the love in his expression. She'd never known such unconditional love and acceptance from her own parents and never would. But she was glad Jason had found it with his dad.

Lauren smiled. "Your father is proud of you."

Jason glanced away. "I don't know why he would be."

Lauren blinked, stunned at his words. "Why would you think that? You're a son anyone would be proud of."

He cocked his head to one side, struggling to find the right words. All it had taken was his father's comment about Jason making the right decisions to bring his frustration and insecurity roaring back.

Not that he didn't think of his failings every day, but since Lauren's return, he'd been able to put them to the back of his mind.

Until now. "What's there to be proud of? What *decisions* did I make that were so sound that you'd trust me to make the right ones for you? I blew the one thing I went after in life. I let myself be duped by a woman. I spent half my life training for my one big moment and never made it because I allowed myself to be led around by my— Never mind." He rose from the couch and walked to the window she'd been looking out earlier.

"Now who's unfairly blaming himself? Did you do drugs? Ingest them? Cheat? No, you did not. So I won't have you trash-talking yourself!" Lauren was obviously appalled on his behalf. "Just where did this negativity come from?"

"It's always been there. Ever since the committee refused my appeal…when I realized that nobody would ever believe in me again. I just never let you see it." He stared out the window into the dark night. "Hell, I try not to see it myself."

Lauren stood and crossed the room, raising her hand to his face. "Jason, you have always been the most honest, determined, goal-oriented man I've ever met. I'd trust you with my life. How can you not believe in yourself?"

Instead of comforting him, her words only served to remind him of his failures. His current lack of a goal, a dream.

"I don't believe in myself because I allowed my goals to be taken away from me. And I haven't replaced them with anything meaningful since." He turned and walked out of the room.

TWO DAYS of tense silence passed. Two days of nonstop work on the house to fill the time while waiting for news on Beth. The insurance adjuster came and went. He took photographs to submit to the company and promised to get back to them. Meanwhile, Lauren felt brittle, yet somehow she kept moving, thoughts of Paris keeping her going. She had to focus on her upcoming debut, because nothing here in Perkins made sense.

Since their conversation the day of her sister's escape, Jason had withdrawn. They slept in the same bed but he made no overtures toward her, and when she rolled on top of him in her sleep, he pulled away. She ought to be grateful he was giving her the distance she'd been asking for.

She wasn't.

He'd become a man filled with his own demons. Demons she believed he'd suppressed beneath a brave facade until his father's comment shattered the illusion he'd created for himself.

She ached for him, surprised he couldn't see that his father's perception of him was dead-on.

And she was angry at herself for being so emotionally invested in Jason, since it was going to be that much harder to leave him behind.

EARLY THE NEXT MORNING, Jason placed Trouble's food bowl on the kitchen floor and the cat dove for his meal. The feline devoured the canned food while Jason wondered how even a cat could eat such foul-smelling stuff. "Better you than me," he muttered.

He called his crew together and gave them assignments for the day while he could look forward to haggling with the insurance adjuster. The sooner they agreed on a settlement, the sooner he could begin work on the area damaged in the fire. If they finished in time for closing, Lauren would accomplish her goal, sell the house and walk out of his life. The end was near.

He was finished deluding himself and he had his father and Lauren to thank for opening his eyes. "You're in good hands," his father had told her.

"He's proud of you," Lauren had said.

They'd inadvertently brought him face-to-face with the past he'd been trying to outrun. He wasn't over it yet, much as he'd tried to lose himself in Lauren and pretend otherwise. And when she was gone, he'd have plenty of time on his hands to figure it all out.

In the meantime, he'd been giving her what she wanted—the emotional distance that would make it easier to leave later. He'd taken a lesson from Lauren and put up his own walls to protect himself, even though he knew it wouldn't make losing her hurt any less.

"Jason!" Lauren called from across the house. "Jason!" He started for the bedroom but she came running, meeting him in the kitchen.

"What's wrong?"

"Beth's doctor just called on my cell and you'll never guess who came to the prison not long before the fire and Beth's escape?" Her cheeks were pink, her words rushed.

Only one name came to mind. "Brody Pittman?"

She nodded. "He said he left his tools, and because he'd had clearance before, they let him in. But nobody had turned in any tools after the construction work finished. And within half an hour, my sister had escaped."

"So there *is* some connection between them."

"Looks that way. The police have an APB out on them both."

Jason tried to follow the logic in his brain and couldn't. "Let's talk this through. So your sister and Brody meet up at the prison. We don't know how long ago. In the meantime, you come to the house and find it's been vandalized, right?"

Eyes wide, Lauren nodded. "Go on."

"Then one day, Pittman gets himself hired at JR Plumbing, the only plumber in town, so he can end up *here* when your hot water heater breaks."

"Or was tampered with?" she asked.

"I knew you were smart." He grinned. "Okay, what reason would your sister have for sending Brody Pittman here to screw with the house?"

Lauren hazarded a guess. "She didn't want me to sell it?"

He leaned against the counter. "But why would she go to such lengths to hold on to this old place? Sentimental reasons? Or something else?"

Lauren shrugged. "I don't know."

She sounded frustrated and he didn't blame her. "Let's backtrack. What else did the doctor say?"

She closed her eyes, trying to remember. "He said Beth had been agitated ever since our visit."

Just as Jason thought, her sister had reacted to their conversation. "And we discussed the Corwin Curse and the journal," he said, naming the two things Beth had responded to. "And then she escaped. Because…"

"She wanted something."

"The journal?"

Lauren sighed. "That might have been the impetus for her escape, but what about before? What was she sending Brody Pittman here to find?"

They stared at each other blankly, until something else niggled at the back of his mind. "Um, Lauren?"

"Yes?"

"If Beth is looking for something in this house, she *will* come back here."

Lauren shivered. "The police aren't sitting in their car anymore. They're doing drive-bys."

"I know." Another reason Jason refused to go home.

Lauren shifted uncomfortably. "I still don't think my sister would hurt me," she said at last.

Jason, on the other hand, wasn't so sure.

GABRIELLE HAD an impromptu book-signing and speaking engagement in Boston. She'd invited Amber and Mike and Jason and Lauren. Despite the awkwardness between Jason and Lauren, they'd agreed to go. For Gabrielle's sake.

Lauren was excited. A night away from the house. A night on the town. An evening when she could wear fun, funky clothing, put her troubles behind her and just have a good time.

She'd even taken the morning off from working on the house to head over to the nearest mall for a quick shopping trip. She couldn't drive to New York for her clothes, but she could afford a few purchases on her credit card, or so she told herself as justification.

No sooner had she walked into the house and placed her bags on the floor than the doorbell rang. She shrugged off her jacket, placing it on the coat stand, then looked through the peephole before opening the door to one of the local cops she'd met before.

"Ms. Perkins, may I come in?" the officer asked.

A chill rushed through Lauren as she nodded and stepped back to let him inside.

"What's wrong? Did you find my sister?" she asked, visions of a shoot-out running through her mind.

"What's going on?" Jason asked, striding up to her side.

He acknowledged the cop with a nod of his head.

"He was just about to tell me." Lauren swallowed hard, unable to keep the tremor from her voice.

Jason placed his hand on her shoulder and she appreciated the support.

The officer took off his hat and tucked the cap beneath his arm. "No, ma'am. We haven't located your sister but we did have a report of a sighting."

Lauren's heart pounded hard in her chest.

"Where?" Jason asked.

"There was a convenience store robbery across state lines in Rhode Island. The suspects fit the description of your sister and her accomplice. Witnesses claim they took off in a southwesterly direction. Away from here."

"Robbery?" Lauren could barely speak through her dry mouth.

The officer nodded. "I'm sorry to have to add to your burdens, but that's the most recent update."

"We appreciate it," Jason said. "Is the search focused in Rhode Island now?"

"It's as good a lead as we've got, so the Rhode Island authorities are following up. Of course we'll still be vigilant here. This is her home, and if she panics and needs help, she might come to you." He studied Lauren intently, as if sizing her up.

"What?" she asked, uncomfortable under the scrutiny.

"If you hear from her, you *will* let us know?"

"Of course! And I don't appreciate you thinking otherwise."

Jason's grip on her shoulder tightened. "He's just doing his job."

She nodded. Antagonizing the police wasn't a smart strategy.

"If there's anything else you can tell us that you think might help find her, call. I'll let myself out. Lock the door behind me." He tipped his head and started for the door.

Then he was gone.

"Robbery?" Lauren asked.

"You can't even pretend to know what's in her mind anymore," he said.

She nodded. "You're right about that. If she's in Rhode Island and heading away from here, do you think she's given up on whatever it is she wants from this house?"

Jason spread his hands in front of him, apparently as confused as Lauren was. "Like I said…"

"I can't begin to guess at what's going on in her mind." She sighed then met Jason's gaze. "Hey. Why didn't you tell the police there might be something here she'd come back for?" Lauren bit the inside of her cheek.

It hadn't been easy for her to remain silent. She'd been surprised Jason had kept quiet, too.

He shoved his hands into the front pockets of his jeans, staring at her. "I did it for you. We have no solid proof she wants anything here, just a series of coincidences like you said. I figured I'd give you the benefit of the doubt."

"Even if you are certain she's behind the vandalism, the tampering and the arson?"

He nodded, not denying his belief. "Even then. She escaped. She'll be caught eventually and the truth will come out." His expression filled with compassion and, despite the emotional distance between them, something that looked suspiciously like love.

Lauren's heart beat more rapidly in her chest, her emotions a rioting mix she didn't know how to deal with. And as long as he kept his feelings inside, as long as he kept sending out mixed signals instead of overt ones, she didn't have to.

She ran her tongue over suddenly dry lips. "I don't know what to say except thank you."

She might not have anticipated her sister would fake mental illness, but she had to believe that whatever Beth's motives had been, she was far away from here by now.

"THEY HAVE TO LEAVE the house sooner or later," Brody said in the whiny voice Beth had come to hate. She cringed every time he opened his mouth.

Still, she'd needed him and he'd come through. She'd managed to contact him with the nurse's cell phone and leave a message. He'd gotten into the prison by telling them he'd left his tools behind, and a little fire had distracted people, enabling him to sneak her out amid the chaos. Minimum security and paying close attention to who was stationed where had helped.

But now that she was out, she didn't need Brody anymore. Only he didn't take a hint. Why would he when he knew about the diamonds, Beth thought, frustrated.

"Beth? Can't you figure something out?" he asked.

"We need to have patience." She glanced around

the hiding place she'd chosen, a detached garage in a neighbor's house next to her old home. It wasn't comfortable but it was safe.

These neighbors spent winters in Florida, and like most people in town, they didn't use burglar alarms. In this old garage, they'd had no reason. Even better, this particular neighbor had had a property line dispute with her grandmother. They'd lost in court, naturally. It had been so easy for her grandmother as mayor to switch old land surveys on file. Beth figured it was smart of her to pick a house where there was no love lost between the owners and the Perkinses. Less chance of the police thinking Beth would be hiding out there.

"I'm hungry," Brody said.

Another whine.

Beth gritted her teeth. "Then you should have chosen a convenience store with more cash in the register because we need to ration what little we have."

After leaving the prison, they'd ditched the car in a busy parking lot and walked until they found an unlocked car Brody could hot-wire. Another thing he'd been good for besides sex.

There wasn't much else. He'd forgotten to bring cash for their road trip, leaving them no choice but to knock over a convenience store. It had been her idea to drive to Rhode Island for the job, keeping far from home. And in case anyone watched them leave afterward, she made sure Brody drove in the opposite direction from home. They'd waited a day in a motel, where she'd cut and dyed her hair, after which they'd doubled back on side roads to end up here.

"Can't we go in when they're asleep to get the diary?" Brody asked for what seemed like the hundredth time.

"No! I'm not risking having to hurt my sister." Considering she had no idea where Lauren had put the damned thing, they'd need time to search.

They'd just have to wait until both Lauren and her Corwin boyfriend decided to leave the house together.

## CHAPTER SIXTEEN

LAUREN CLOSETED HERSELF in the bedroom to dress for Gabrielle's book signing. All the workmen were gone for the day except for J.R., the plumber, and she didn't want company while she was changing.

Since the news that Brody Pittman was her sister's accomplice, J.R. had insisted on coming by the house to check the boiler work and replace some of the pipes. He said he'd also check everything out as all Pittman's work was now suspect. Lauren appreciated J.R.'s diligence and she hoped Brody Pittman hadn't cost her extra money she didn't have to spend on this house.

To work on the boiler, he'd had to turn off the heat and it hadn't taken long for the cold weather outside to seep inside and turn the house into a virtual freezer. Earlier in the day, she'd made a fire in the bedroom fireplace, a nice feature in this old New England home. Lauren had decided to toss

Clara's log in for good measure and she wondered if any of the positive energy had taken hold. She could use some, if such a thing was possible. Time would tell. A small flame still crackled and burned, but clearly it was almost out.

She freshened her makeup and dressed in tapered black slacks, a bright multicolored silk blouse belted at the waist and, of course, her favorite red fringed boots. One last look in the mirror, a quick fix of her bangs, and she was ready to go.

She found Jason in the kitchen talking with J.R. and she took a moment to savor the sight of him. He wore a cream-colored sweater, black denim jeans and loafers, and looked so sexy she wished things between them were back the way they had been a few short weeks ago. She hoped he'd lower his defenses for the night at least, so they could enjoy the signing.

And each other.

Besides, she didn't need his cousins noticing tension and trying to play matchmaker when there was clearly nothing left to bring them together.

A knot the size of a walnut wedged in Lauren's stomach. Ridiculous, since she hadn't wanted any ties to this town when she left for good.

She didn't miss the irony in her life. She'd driven in on a high in her beloved red convertible. She'd be leaving in a rental car, feeling depressed and blue.

J.R. GAVE JASON a rundown of what he'd found during his inspection of the plumbing. The good news was that the work Brody Pittman did in the house was sound. It also appeared that the man had lied about some of the other items that needed replacement and repair—obviously in a bid to buy himself more time in the house. More positive news for Lauren's checkbook.

"Hi," she said, announcing her presence.

"Hey." Jason glanced up and the breath was sucked out of his lungs.

She'd chosen a soft, flowing blouse with a deep vee, showing more than a generous hint of cleavage while covering everywhere else. Completely appropriate yet seductively sexy, he thought. And her long hair fell over her shoulders, thick and shiny, begging for him to run his hands through it. Better yet, he wanted to feel those silky strands over his naked body. Jason swallowed a groan.

"Hey there," J.R. said. A decade older than Jason and happily married, the other man couldn't tear his gaze away from Lauren, either. "Don't tell my wife I said so, but you look beautiful tonight."

A flush stained her cheeks. "Thank you!" Her gaze slid to Jason.

"Perfect," he agreed. "Are you ready?"

"I sure am." Her eyes sparkled with an excitement that was contagious.

"Have fun, you two. And don't worry about the plumbing. Everything looks good. Better than we could have hoped."

Relief flashed over Lauren's face. "Thank you. That's wonderful."

"My pleasure."

The three of them walked out of the house together. A few minutes later, J.R. pulled out of the driveway and his truck disappeared down the street.

Jason and Lauren settled in his car and buckled their seat belts. He started the engine, but before putting the gears in reverse, he stretched his arm over the top of the seat and turned to Lauren.

"You look beautiful," he said, unable to hold back the honest words.

She treated him to the first wide smile he'd seen in too long. "Thanks. You look pretty handsome yourself."

"Thanks." He accepted the compliment with a grin. "I appreciate you coming tonight. Especially with everything going on. It means a lot to Derek and Gabrielle. And to me."

She nodded. "I'm honestly looking forward to it!"

"Great. Then let's get going." He backed out of the long driveway.

They drove past the residential neighborhood and reached the turn into town. He was halfway down Main Street when Lauren started to frantically paw through her purse and mutter softly.

"What's wrong?" he asked.

"I forgot my cell phone."

He slowed the car. "Want to go back?"

She nodded. "I'm sorry, but in case there's news about my sister, I need to have my phone."

He glanced at the clock on the dashboard. "No problem. It's still early." He managed a three-point turn and was about to drive off when someone waved at them.

"It's Uncle Hank," Jason said, rolling down his window.

"Where are you two off to? Oh, I know. Gabrielle's book signing." He barely paused for a breath. "Even your father is going, but am I allowed? Oh no."

"Why not?" Lauren asked.

"I've been banned!" Hank rolled his eyes. "Isn't that the most ridiculous thing you've ever heard?"

Jason grinned. "Not really. Remember the signing at the local library a few months ago?" Jason hadn't been in town but he'd heard all about it.

"Extenuating circumstances," his uncle muttered.

"Ever since, Derek hasn't trusted him to behave," Jason explained to Lauren.

"My own son. Isn't that an insult?" his uncle asked. "Besides, I had my reason. She was disputin' the Corwin Curse when everyone in this town knows how we Corwins suffered because of those dang Perkins!"

Jason stiffened and hit the window button as Hank began his familiar rant. "Goodbye, Uncle Hank," he said, cutting off the older man's words.

Jason glanced at Lauren.

"I'm fine," she assured him before he could ask.

But her set jaw told another story.

"I should be used to it by now," she said.

But it was clearly a blow. And he knew better than to start any conversation that would lead to an argument, so he let the subject go.

Heading home, he pulled into the driveway. "Want me to go in for you?"

She shook her head. "I think I know where I left the phone. I'll be right back."

She jumped out of the car.

Jason settled in to wait.

LAUREN RAN BACK into the house. She normally wasn't scatterbrained. In fact, she was pretty organized by anyone's standards, but her sister's escape had distracted her.

She checked the kitchen first, thinking maybe she'd left her phone on the counter.

No luck.

However, she felt a cool breeze from the far side of the room and slowly walked to the back hall. Jason had long since fixed the broken locks and windows and nobody used this part of the house. An unsettling feeling overtook her. She flicked on the hall light, and sure enough, the glass panes above the outside door had been smashed. Someone had probably stuck their hand inside to open the door, which now swung in the wind.

A shiver that had nothing to do with the cold raced over her skin. She knew exactly who'd broken into the house.

"Beth." Lauren shook her head in a combination of dismay and frustration. She hadn't thought her sister would come back here. Once again, Lauren had underestimated her devious sibling.

Suddenly, and Lauren hoped irrationally, she was afraid. She needed to get out of here. She couldn't walk over the broken glass without making noise or hurting herself. Her only option was to sneak out the front door as quietly as she'd come in. Then get Jason and figure out what to do.

Plan formulated, she took two steps back, hit a solid body and screamed.

A firm hand clamped over her mouth. "Be quiet."

She considered biting him, but his grip was too tight. Her eyes teared at the painful pressure.

"I'm going to let go and you aren't going to scream. Understand?"

She recognized Brody Pittman's voice and nodded.

He slowly eased his grip.

She turned to face him, rubbing her sore cheeks at the same time. "Where's my sister?"

"Bedroom." He nudged her in the side, pushing her closer to the door. "Just in case you get any funny ideas about trying to run—" He poked a sharp object into her back.

He had a gun.

Bile rose in her throat, but she remained calm. Her sister was a few feet away and Beth wouldn't hurt her.

*How do you know that,* a little voice in her head asked. How could she assume anything about her sister now?

They approached the bedroom and Brody gave Lauren a rough shove into the room. "Look who I found."

Lauren stumbled in and came face-to-face with her now red-haired sister. "Beth!"

"Lauren, why couldn't you have just stayed away?" Beth asked, sounding annoyed.

"I forgot my phone—" Lauren glanced around her room and realized Beth had been going through the drawers, tossing things onto the floor in search of— "What are you looking for?"

"The diary," Beth said. "Just give me the diary you were talking about and go away. Forget you ever saw me here."

Lauren blinked in surprise. "I can't do that!"

"Of course you can. And you will."

"First tell me what is in the diary that's so important?" Lauren asked, needing to understand all the unanswered questions. "Why did it freak you out so much that I found it? And what are you looking for in the house?"

Brody groaned. "I'm tired of all this yapping. Her boyfriend's waiting out in the car. Just give us the diary!" He waved the gun at her, his frustration and intent clear.

Shaking, Lauren glanced at her sister.

"Put that away, you imbecile!" Beth's tone allowed for no argument.

Brody lowered the gun but he remained vigilant.

Beth met Lauren's gaze. "Look, I know you're upset…"

Lauren couldn't control the shrill laugh that escaped her throat. "You don't know anything about me or you wouldn't have put me through the hell of visiting you month after month in that psych ward, thinking you were lost forever!" Lauren wiped the tears in her eyes with her jacket sleeve.

Beth shrugged almost apologetically. "If it's any consolation, I *was* out of it until two months ago. But once I came to, I had to look out for myself, just like I've always looked out for you!"

Lauren's head began to pound, and with every bizarre word her sister uttered, the pain grew worse. "You think you looked out for *me?*"

"Of course! Look at the mistakes you made. Going out with Jason Corwin when you were seventeen. If I hadn't shown Grandmother your diary, who knows where you'd be today! Not on your way to Paris, that's for sure." Beth folded her arms across her chest, proud of herself.

Lauren couldn't believe what she was hearing. "You showed Grandma my diary? How could you?"

Beth waved away Lauren's question. "You don't have to thank me. I'd do the same today if I could, but I have more important things to do.

You're going to have to come to your senses and get rid of Jason Corwin on your own this time."

"Beth, listen. I have your lawyer working hard on getting you transferred to a good private psychiatric hospital. I sold my car to add to his retainer. Turn yourself in and this will all be okay." She reached for her sister, but Beth stepped away.

"The diary. Where is it?" Beth asked harshly.

Startled at the change in her sister, Lauren merely pointed to the nightstand.

"Liar! We already looked there." Without warning, Brody slapped her across the face, sending Lauren sprawling backward.

She righted herself before she fell to the floor. Hand on her cheek, she glared at him, choking back tears. She wouldn't give him the satisfaction.

"Don't you ever touch her again." Beth glared at him, then turned back to Lauren, who didn't have the time to sort through her sister's oddly protective behavior.

"You were never like Grandmother or me," Beth said. "We're the ones who understand what it means to be a Perkins. We know we have to protect the legacy. Keep the curse going. I need the diary," she said, her tone too calm. But her eyes were growing more vacant, reminding Lauren of the day she'd set the fire at The Wave.

Frightened she'd go off the deep end and leave Lauren alone with a gun-wielding Brody, Lauren started for the nightstand. All the while, she hoped enough time had passed that Jason would begin to wonder where she was and come inside to look.

"She'd better not be wasting our time," Brody said, pacing on the other side of the room.

"I'm not. There's a fake drawer in here." Somehow Lauren maintained her composure. "What's so important about the diary?" she asked her sister while she struggled to release the compartment with unsteady hands. Maybe if she kept asking questions, she'd kill more time.

"Diamonds. There are diamonds buried somewhere in this house and I think the diary holds the key to where they're located," Beth said. "Hurry."

"That's why you sent Brody to vandalize this place and knock holes in the walls?" The pieces of the puzzle finally made sense, Lauren thought.

"Exactly."

Lauren rose, diary in hand. "I've read it from cover to cover. Most of it's not legible, and what is won't reveal anything."

"That's for me to judge. I'm Mary. I'm one of the chosen," her sister explained to Lauren as if she were talking to a child. "Now hand it over."

Brody waved the gun in a silent threat.

Knowing she had no choice, Lauren extended her hand, intending to give the book to her sister….

JASON HAD GIVEN HER enough time. He'd even dialed her cell, hoping the ring—if she had it on loud and not silent or vibrate—would help her find the lost phone. She hadn't answered.

He yawned just as Trouble appeared, leaping onto the warm hood of the car and staring at Jason intently. Damn cat unnerved him sometimes.

The cat. Jason clearly remembered he and Lauren had left the cat *inside* the house when they'd left the first time. He'd watched Lauren go in for her keys and Trouble had not run out the front door.

Yet here he was now.

Watching.

Staring.

Yawning.

His gut churned uncomfortably, and he didn't know why. So he was going inside.

LAUREN KNEW Jason would show up soon. All she had to do was bide her time. And hope that Brody didn't turn the gun on Jason when he arrived.

She shuddered at the thought and kept her focus shifting between Brody, who stood near the bedroom door, and Beth, who was immersed in reading the diary.

"Well?" Brody voiced the question on Lauren's mind. "Anything in there that'll lead us to the diamonds? We have to get the hell out of here fast."

Beth shook her head in frustration. "So much of it is ruined, but on the same page it mentions the curse it mentions an offering—in the *heart* of the house."

Lauren knew better than to remind her sister she'd already told her as much.

Beth glanced up, a dazed look in her eyes. "Think, *think*," she said, pounding her hand against her head.

"I say we take whatever money she's got on her and get away while the getting's good." Brody leveled his gun at Lauren's heart.

Panic washed over Lauren. She looked beyond Brody toward the door and caught sight of Jason standing there. His eyes locked with hers, conveying all his strength in that one look before he backed out of view once more.

"Well? She's no good to us anyway," Brody muttered.

Suddenly, Beth shrieked at Brody. "You won't threaten my sister again!" She dropped the diary and grabbed the poker beside the fireplace, stunning both Lauren and Brody.

Before either could react, Beth brought the metal down on Brody's head, the poker connecting with his skull. A sickening crack reverberated through the room and Brody fell to the floor.

Nauseated and stunned, Lauren stared at her sister. A stranger she didn't know and probably never had.

"I warned him to leave you alone," Beth said in a monotone voice.

Lauren swallowed hard. If this was how Beth looked after her, Lauren wanted none of it. She spotted the gun lying next to Brody and started for the weapon.

"No!"

Beth barked out her command and Lauren froze.

Slowly, Lauren straightened, her hands spread out in front of her. "Relax," she said to her sister. "See? I'm not moving."

"But I am." Taking advantage of the chaos, Jason chose that moment to silently make his entrance. He couldn't get near the gun, but he bolted across the room and grabbed the diary, the one thing Beth desperately wanted.

With a shriek, Beth raised the poker over her head, her gaze narrowed on Jason, who visibly braced himself.

For the blow?

Or to take Beth down?

Lauren knew he could probably handle Beth. He outweighed and outmuscled her, but Lauren didn't want either one of them hurt.

"Beth, don't!"

At the sound of Lauren's voice, Beth paused. "Why not?" she asked, as if it were a reasonable question. "He's standing in the way of everything. And besides, he's a *Corwin*."

"Because I love him!" Lauren yelled without thinking, her sole focus on stopping her sister.

Her words had the opposite effect. Beth screamed as if she'd been attacked and ran for Jason, poker in hand.

Acting on instinct, Lauren dove for her sister's legs, knocking her down. The poker fell to the floor at the same time Jason took the diary and tossed it into the barely burning embers in the fireplace.

"No!" Beth scrambled to her knees, grabbed the poker and managed to drag the book out, but it was too late.

The journal had caught fire and Beth had jerked her arm back too hard. The book went flying at the old draperies.

Lauren watched in horror as the entire valance and hanging drapes went up in flames.

"The diary!" Beth wailed, and started crawling toward the fire.

"Don't move!" Jason said, approaching Beth, gun in hand.

Lauren had been so consumed by the scene in front of her, she hadn't seen him go for the weapon. Neither had Beth, apparently, and even now, her focus was on the diary, which had already burned.

"Let's get out of here," Jason said, warily watching the flames and Beth. "Lauren, go!"

She hesitated, not wanting to leave them, then ran for the doorway. At the same time sirens sounded. She paused and glanced back.

"I called the police," Jason said. "Get going!" He wrapped his hand around Beth's arm and began to drag her out of the room, kicking and screaming about losing the diary and the diamonds.

She was so hysterical, he needed all his strength to remove her from the burning room.

The one thing he didn't need was the gun.

## CHAPTER SEVENTEEN

*DÉJÀ VU,* Jason thought as the fire department worked to put out the quickly spreading fire inside the house. Outside, the police had taken over. Lauren and Jason were led to the ambulance to be checked by paramedics, for which Jason was grateful. He didn't want Lauren to have to watch her sister's ravings any longer than necessary.

They cleared him first and asked him to leave while they checked Lauren. He started to argue, but she waved him away. "I'll be fine."

From the pained look in her eyes, he doubted *fine* would happen anytime soon, but he gave her the space she needed because he could use some, too.

When he'd seen Lauren with a gun held to her chest, he thought he'd pass out right there. Fury had ripped through him along with frustrating impotence because there was nothing he could do. Any impulsive move could have cost her life. Since he'd already called the police, he'd waited for his opportunity.

Lauren had obviously waited for hers, as well. He couldn't be more proud of her. She'd stunned him on many levels, not the least of which was her strength—of character, of body and of heart.

It was her heart that scared him most of all. A classic case of be careful what you wish for—the woman he loved also loved him back. And she'd gone on to prove it, tackling her sister in an effort to save him.

Love.

At one time he'd thought it was enough. The Perkins-Corwin differences hadn't bothered him. His family's negative feelings about Lauren and her sister had never mattered to him. Not even the Corwin Curse had been an issue. Lauren wasn't her sister or her grandmother. They might share the same genes but she was her own unique person—giving, warm and special.

And therein lay the problem. She deserved a man who was her equal. Once upon a time he would have believed he was that man. Now when he looked in the mirror, he saw a man adrift and without goals. After the highs of competitive snowboarding, merely earning a living in his contracting business wasn't enough. Neither was living off Lauren's money and future successes.

He needed to redefine his own goals and dreams. Only then could he give Lauren what she deserved.

LAUREN PUSHED DOWN her sleeve and reached for her coat. Her blood pressure was fine considering the ordeal she'd just been through. She didn't need oxygen. They'd escaped the fire in time. And though her cheek was sore from where Brody had slapped her, she had no other physical scars.

The emotional ones were another story.

Her sister was certifiably insane. Crazy. Why hadn't Lauren seen it before? Why had she insisted on believing the best of a woman who had already demonstrated violent tendencies? At least she knew the answer. Because they were related by blood and someone had to believe in Beth if she were going to get better.

But what had Lauren's Pollyanna attitude gotten her? She had no money left in her bank account, her beloved car belonged to a beautiful model in New York, and she had been finally and irrevocably disillusioned by the remaining family member she'd tried to have faith in.

She took little consolation in the notion that in Beth's twisted mind, she'd believed she was protecting Lauren. They were family. But when she looked at the devastating consequences, it didn't seem enough anymore.

"You're good to go, Ms. Perkins," the paramedic said.

Lauren nodded. "Thanks."

She stepped to the edge of the ambulance. Outside, reality awaited her. The burning house, police interrogation and prying eyes.

She drew a deep breath and stepped into the cold night air. It had been too much to hope she wouldn't have to face anyone. The entire Corwin clan had gathered around Jason.

With her house surrounded by police and firemen, she had nowhere to go in order to escape.

"Lauren, there you are!" Clara's voice sounded first as she broke through the crowd and headed Lauren's way.

Her red wool coat stood out from the rest of the group in dark jackets and she ran to Lauren, pulling her into a warm embrace.

At the motherly hug, tears Lauren hadn't known she was holding back began to flow.

"There, there," Clara said, sensing the extent of her turmoil. Clara patted Lauren on the back, comforting her in a way she'd never experienced.

She couldn't even remember her own parents hugging her when she was upset. They subscribed to the *pick yourself up and get back on the horse* theory. At the memory, Lauren's tears fell harder as the events of the night came back to her all over again.

"Honey, do you want to come back to my house?" Clara asked.

Lauren stepped back, dabbing her damp eyes on her sleeve and probably smearing what was left of her makeup. "Thanks for the offer but I don't think Edward would appreciate my company." She forced a smile.

"You might have a point, but he's getting there," Clara said, reassuring her.

Lauren glanced around. "Is he here with the rest of the family?"

Clara shook her head. To the other woman's credit, she didn't try to explain away or excuse his absence.

Lauren didn't want Clara to feel badly so she pulled herself together, standing up straighter.

Amber and Gabrielle swarmed her next, greeting Lauren with warm hugs.

"I'm so glad you're okay," Gabrielle said, looking her over.

"Why aren't you at your book signing?" Lauren asked.

Gabrielle shook her head. "We heard about

the fire and turned right around! Family's more important."

"She's right," Amber said. "We came to make sure you and Jason were okay." She peered at Lauren. "You *are* okay, right?"

"Other than the smeared makeup, I'm fine. Just a little shaky." Lauren forced another smile, comforted by the outpouring of support offered by these women.

The men joined their wives, checking on Lauren's welfare and expressing their sympathy about the house before stepping away, leaving her with breathing room and time to think.

"Did you happen to hear what happened to… the accomplice?" Lauren asked them.

She hadn't had a chance to find out if Brody Pittman had survived the fire.

"I heard the firemen rescued a man who was unconscious but breathing—they took him to the hospital," Amber said.

"And they think he'll survive," Derek added.

"Don't stress yourself out about it, okay?" This from Mike, the cop cousin.

Lauren nodded. "Thanks."

To her relief, they'd let her avoid the subject of her sister and her role in the fire, and for that Lauren was grateful. She'd never accept or understand her sister's actions. Nothing was worth hurting other people, especially not money or power. Or diamonds. All she could see in her sister's eyes was greed. And that made Lauren sad.

She glanced at Jason's family, grateful they'd let the topic go. She lacked the will to defend Beth, and she definitely didn't have any reserve energy to cope with Perkins bashing.

Which was too bad, since Thomas started to walk toward them. Lauren looked around for Jason. He stood at the end of the driveway talking to the police who'd remained after her sister had been taken away.

She steeled herself to face the older Corwin man alone.

"Lauren, I'm so glad you're okay," Thomas said.

"Thank you," she said to Jason's father.

"I heard it was quite an ordeal," he said diplomatically.

She nodded. "At least no one was badly hurt."

Reaching out, he pulled her into a brief hug and released her just as quickly, leaving her speechless.

Pleased, but speechless.

"Thomas!" Hank Corwin rushed up to them. "I heard the cops say that they'll push for maximum security for the Perkins broad this time!" There was glee in his voice.

Nausea rose in Lauren's throat. Before she could stand up for herself and inform Hank of how inappropriate and thoughtless his comments were, the rest of his family surrounded him.

Gabrielle and Derek, Amber and Mike, and Thomas faced him. "Shut up!" they all said at the same time.

Hank looked confused. "I was just telling you what I heard."

"Just think before you speak," Thomas said. "She may be simply a Perkins to you, but she's Lauren's sister and you're hurting her every time you open that big mouth!"

Lauren's own mouth opened but she couldn't manage a word. She wanted to thank Jason's father, but she was stunned and suddenly too exhausted to even stand.

Almost miraculously Jason appeared. He came up behind her and wrapped his arm around her waist, supporting her at a time when she needed it most.

JASON TUCKED Lauren into his bed back home, in the barn behind his uncle's house. She'd managed to shrug off her coat, kick off her shoes, and shed her pants and top before crawling into bed and passing out.

He undressed and climbed in beside her, pulling

her warm body close to his. Cocooned like this, he could almost forget the rest of the world existed. And for the remainder of the night, that's exactly what he did. Attuned to her every movement, he slept when Lauren slept, awoke when she tossed and turned, and basically kept an eye on her all night long.

The next morning arrived too soon. To Jason, sunrise brought with it the beginning of the end.

As the sun peeked between the blinds, Lauren rolled over, propped on one arm. "Hi."

"Hi, yourself." He reached over and brushed a few strands of hair from her cheek, revealing a crease mark in her skin. "Sleep well?" he asked.

"All things considered, I guess so." She seemed to pause in thought and he waited, letting her take the lead. She'd talk about whatever subject she was ready to tackle. He wouldn't push.

"It's over," she said at last.

His stomach plummeted. Even knowing what was to come didn't make the blow any easier.

"I don't have anything left to put into the house," she said, elaborating further.

Obviously his mind had been elsewhere and he scrambled to catch up with her conversation and ignore his rapidly beating heart.

"Before you jump to any big decisions, we

don't know the extent of last night's damage or whether insurance would cover another incident. You might get lucky."

Lauren drew a deep breath and shook her head. "You don't understand. I'm finished. Done. I can't deal with the house anymore and frankly I don't want to. Besides, at this point the chances of me completing the project to buyer's specifications on time are slim to none."

He wanted to argue, if for no other reason than to lift her mood and give her hope, but in his heart he knew she was right. "What will you do?"

"I haven't had time to think, but my gut tells me to just cut my losses and sell it as is. Hopefully someone will want a fixer-upper," she said.

"Smart."

She'd come to the only conclusion she could. From a business and monetary standpoint, the damage from the first fire had been extensive enough to put her deadline in jeopardy. Last night's fire had merely compounded the cost and time involved, bringing her to the breaking point. And most importantly, from an emotional perspective, Lauren was obviously drained.

"Despite everything, I meant what I said last night." Lauren's voice softened as she changed the subject. Her beautiful eyes focused on him.

There was no mistaking what she meant.

"I love you, Jason." She said the words anyway.

His heart swelled and broke at the same time.

They were the words he'd wanted to hear and she deserved to know he felt the same. "I love you, too."

She reached for him and he came over her, his lips settling on hers, kissing her deeply, knowing in his heart they'd never have this moment again.

He paused only to grab a condom in the nightstand. Then they connected and he savored every moment, holding her, joining his body with hers.

They loved each other. And for this brief time, it was enough.

AN HOUR LATER, Lauren had showered and met Jason in his kitchen for breakfast. He'd run out for coffee and doughnuts. Since they'd never eaten dinner last night, she was starving.

Although she was emotionally drained, her body still tingled from making love with Jason. And that's what they'd done. For the first time they'd made love with no emotional barriers between them. She'd felt it in every fiber of her being. Felt *him*.

Just as she felt his regard on her now. "What?" she asked, focusing on his steady stare.

"I was just wondering what's got you so distracted?"

While showering, she'd been thinking about where they could go from here, and she spoke before she could chicken out. "Come with me," she said to him.

"What?"

"Come with me to Paris," she said, her excitement building now that she'd let herself say the words aloud.

Stunned, he slowly lowered his cup to the table. "And then what?" he asked, his enthusiasm nowhere in sight.

Panic enveloped her, hammering away at the heart she'd just given to him so openly. "Well, you could be with me when my designs debut. We could see Paris together. And then…" Her voice trailed off.

He reached out and placed his warm, strong hands over hers. "And then I come to New York and do what while you soar to the top of *your* profession and achieve *your* dreams?" he asked gently.

"We'll figure it out together." But even as she spoke, she saw the light in his eyes dim.

"I know what it's like to have goals and a dream. And without those things now, I'm lost." He spread his hands in front of him. "Before you showed up, I was grumpy and nobody wanted to be near me. I thought I'd pushed past it, but lately I've been forced to admit…I don't know who I am or what I want. But I do know I can't live off your money and your success. I need to define my own." His tone implored her to understand.

"I get it. And I respect what you're saying, but—"

She'd learned at a young age not to push people for more than they were able to give.

Bracing her hands on the table, she rose to her feet. "I feel sorry for you, because you don't know what you're missing." She wrapped her pride tightly around her and strode from the room.

It was so ironic. There had been too many people in her life who'd found her lacking, and now here was Jason, the love of her life, telling her she was too much for him. She couldn't take it. Because though his reasons were different from her sister's and her parents', he was still doing the same thing. Rejecting her, who she was and what she offered him.

To hell with all of them. She couldn't get out of this town fast enough.

LAUREN SPENT the rest of the day in a frenzy of activity. She called Sharon, who picked her up at Jason's. Together they ran errands in town while Jason headed to the house to meet up with his crew.

First Lauren called on the real estate agent who'd arranged the original sale. The woman agreed to contact the buyers, explain the situation and ultimately refund their escrow money. Then once the insurance company inspected the new damage, Lauren arranged to relist the house—as is. On Sharon's recommendation, Lauren hired a service to clean out the house, box the remainder of her grandmother and sister's items, and give them to the Salvation Army.

A whirlwind morning and she'd accomplished more than she'd thought possible. In fact, she could get away from this town and its memories by nightfall.

Sharon accompanied her back to the house so she could fill Jason in.

"Are you sure you want to rush out of here?" Sharon asked, not for the first time this afternoon.

Lauren nodded as they walked up the front walk together. The acrid stench of smoke filled the air, reminding her of everything painful. "I'm sure. And I'm not rushing. If anything, I gave everything and everyone here plenty of chances. It's past time for me to leave."

Using her key, Lauren unlocked the front door and stepped back, letting Sharon precede her inside.

"Lauren, is that you?" Jason called out to her.

"Yes. I'm here with Sharon."

"You're never going to believe what I found."

Lauren glanced at Sharon.

"Any clue?" her friend asked.

Lauren shook her head. "Not one. Let's go find out."

Lauren hadn't been in the bedroom since last night and she wasn't thrilled about going in there now.

Turned out she didn't have to. Jason met her in the hall, the cat under one arm and what looked like a black velvet pouch in his other.

"What's going on?" Sharon asked.

"That's what I'd like to know!" Lauren said.

"Let's go somewhere where it doesn't smell so bad." Jason handed Trouble to her and they followed him back down the hall.

"I couldn't find the cat," Jason said as soon as they were in the kitchen. "Last time I saw him he was stalking mice, but he was nowhere to be found. Of course he was in the last place I checked."

"The bedroom." Lauren placed Trouble on the kitchen floor.

"Actually your grandmother's office. But he escaped on me again and I just recaptured him in the bedroom. Anyway, the mice had apparently been nesting in the office fireplace."

"Thank God we didn't light a fire in there!"

"You're telling me." Jason laughed. "Look what the mice had stashed in there." He held up the jewelry pouch. "Trouble here found it when he was sniffing after the rodents."

Lauren shuddered. She might have spent one night alone with the mice but she hadn't grown to like them.

Jason opened the threadbare pouch and poured a handful of diamonds onto the kitchen table.

"Are they real?" Sharon asked, leaning closer for a better look.

"They'd have to be appraised to know for sure," Jason said.

Lauren couldn't tear her gaze from the diamonds. "Tell me where you found them again?" she asked.

"Inside the fireplace," Jason said. "What's wrong?"

"In the *hearth!* Of the house!" Lauren cried, pieces of an old family puzzle suddenly coming together.

"I'm confused," Sharon said.

"Hang on and you won't be." Lauren's heart pumped in excitement. "I found an old diary in my grandmother's night table. We think that's what my sister was looking for when she came back here." She glanced at Jason. "Remember the diary mentioned an offering. And then it said something about the *heart* of the house. Maybe it really read the *hearth* of the house! Don't you see? Those diamonds are the offering my ancestors used to place the curse!"

## CHAPTER EIGHTEEN

LOUD BANGING woke Jason. He tumbled out of bed, his head pounding as if a freight train was rolling through it. Why did he have a hangover the likes of which he never wanted to experience again?

Another loud, banging knock sounded at his door. "I'm coming!"

He swung his door open wide to find his entire family standing outside. With a groan, the reasons for his hangover came flooding back.

Two days ago, he'd found the diamonds. Then Lauren had made the connection between the jewels and the Corwin Curse and she'd immediately called Clara to come over. Clara, with her otherworldly wisdom, had revealed that the offering—in this case the diamonds—was the key to breaking the curse. It was up to Lauren Perkins to figure out how.

Lauren had figured it out immediately. She'd turned the jewels over to the Corwin family, giving the offering to the cursed family and thereby breaking the curse forever, at least according to Clara.

All good news until in the midst of the chaos, Lauren had snuck out, leaving his family to celebrate and Jason with a note. *I hope you find what you're searching for. Love, Lauren.* To add insult to injury, she'd asked Sharon to look after her cat while she was in Paris. Not Jason.

Which brought him back to his current hangover.

And his family who'd followed him inside his house.

"Tell me why I can't get any peace in my own home?" Jason asked.

"It's not your home, it's mine. You just live here," Hank said, stepping forward.

"Nice, Uncle Hank." Jason glanced around, waiting for his father or another relative to step up and support him.

The way they'd done for Lauren.

But his entire family stood by and let Hank abuse him.

Jason groaned. "Okay, why are you all here?"

Thomas straightened his tie and grinned. "To tell you those diamonds were worth a fortune. Split among the three families, we're not broke anymore!"

"We weren't broke before," Jason reminded him. And Lauren needed the money a lot more than he did.

"Neither were we," Derek said, glancing lovingly at his wife, whose books sold well.

"The point is, we have a nest egg now," Thomas said. "Jason, you'll get your share, too."

Jason would make sure his share went to Lauren.

"Even Edward said he would accept the money," his father added.

"Because his medication and therapy are working." Gabrielle turned to Jason. "Maybe we could put you on the same regimen and you'll come to your senses, too." Her pregnant belly protruding from beneath her jacket, she poked Jason in the shoulder.

"Hey, what was that for?" he asked.

"After all our hard work getting you two together, you let Lauren just pick up and leave!" Amber said, obviously upset.

The two women were like a tag team. "I'd call it meddling, not work," Jason muttered.

"He does have a point," Mike said.

Amber hit her husband in the arm.

"Let's not forget, if it wasn't for the mice we brought over, you wouldn't have found the diamonds, so I'd quit complaining about our so-called meddling." Gabrielle eyed Jason with frustration.

"Leave it to the women to twist things," Derek said, stepping out of his own wife's reach.

Jason rubbed his burning eyes. "They happen to have a point about the mice and the diamonds." Even Jason knew when it was smart to concede defeat. "As for Lauren, it's more complicated than it seems." And he didn't intend to discuss this with his entire family. "Can everyone go home and let me deal with my own life?"

Gabrielle frowned. "Fine. Amber and I will go with Hank and Thomas back to their house. I'll let your cousins knock some sense into you."

Amber ushered the older men out the door and Gabrielle followed.

Mike waited until they were alone before turning to Jason. "You look like shit. We both know it's because Lauren's gone, so cut to the chase. What will it take to get her back?"

Jason decided to suck it up and admit the truth. Who better than his cousins to understand? "She asked me to go with her and I said no."

Derek shook his head. "Have you learned nothing from all the years I lost with Gabrielle? So tell me why the hell you're sitting here hungover instead of being with the woman you love?"

Wasn't it obvious? "What the hell kind of life do I have to offer her?"

"If this is about the bogus drug test—"

Jason scowled at Mike. "Hell no. It's about life. I've lived my whole life going after the gold, then one day it's gone. I'm home running a contracting business that's boring as shit and I don't recognize the guy I see in the mirror each day."

"So do something about it!"

"I have. Before I got stinking drunk, I called a couple of snowboard companies—Venue, Flow and Sapient to start—and offered my services for testing. I'd kill to get back on the mountain again." And though testing wasn't the same as sponsorship, Jason would start somewhere and work toward proving himself. If he could get a company to ignore his jaded past.

"Are you waiting for me to applaud?" Mike asked, his tone laced with sarcasm. He paced the den before turning back to stare at Jason. "Do things your way and you'll have a career and no one to share it with. Is that what you want for yourself?"

No. "Hell, no."

Jason's head suddenly cleared. Not just from the hangover but from the idiocy that he'd been hanging on to.

Mike and Derek were right. What good would it do him to carve out a new set of goals without Lauren to share them with? Hadn't he gone that route once before, when he'd been too young and stupid to understand what he was giving up?

Did he really want to tackle that slope again?

No.

Jason needed a shower. Then he had to look up flights to New York. Or Paris. Or wherever he could find Lauren right now.

Without a word, he turned and headed for the stairs.

"I think he caught on," Jason heard Mike say.

Derek laughed. "It's about damned time."

Jason wasn't as amused as his cousins. Because, unlike them, he understood Lauren's insecurities, where they stemmed from and why she couldn't let them go. By rejecting her, he'd hit on each and every one. It didn't matter that he'd basically told her she was too good for him. She'd never see it as a compliment. He'd refused to accept her for who and what she was. In Lauren's book, he'd committed a huge sin.

He only hoped it wasn't an unforgivable one.

LAUREN MOVED UP her trip to Paris. She'd been back in New York for a few days, but after so much time away, it felt like she'd been gone for a year. After living in the large house with Jason, she found being alone in her tiny apartment claustrophobic and lonely. She truly hoped a change of continent would help her find herself again.

Because she wasn't the same person who'd left Manhattan for Massachusetts. Back then she'd wanted only to finish the job and get on with her life. Yet now the life she'd been so eager to return to seemed less fulfilling than she'd remembered and she resented Jason for doing that to her. She wanted to rediscover the driven professional consumed with her goals and getting to the top of her field.

It had been too long since she'd sketched or even thought about what she wanted to create after the show in Paris. She'd put her designs on hold to help her family, and for what?

Whoa. Lauren gave herself a mental shake. She'd promised herself she would not second-guess the choices she'd made. She'd done right by her family and she could live with her decisions. Nothing else mattered.

Time to turn the page and move forward. She'd packed her sketch pads, certain France would provide fresh new inspiration for her designs. She'd clear her head, meet people and expand her horizons. And hopefully she'd also get over having her heart broken by Jason Corwin.

She pressed her palms against her temples. Okay, so it was going to be more difficult to stop thinking about her time with Jason than she'd hoped. But she'd promised herself she wouldn't dwell there, if only because she couldn't change the past. Especially since in this case, she *should* have known better than to hand Jason her heart.

She glanced at her watch. She had about half an hour before she had to leave her apartment and catch a taxi to the airport. She pulled a soda from her refrigerator and settled onto a couch to watch TV. Unable to find anything on regular television, she turned to the cable news channels in time to catch a sports recap. From football, the newscaster moved on to the upcoming winter Olympics in February 2010, Lauren's least favorite subject, and one that wouldn't aid her quest not to think about Jason Corwin.

She had picked up the remote to change the channel when she caught sight of the name below the photo on the screen. Rusty Small, Jason's nemesis. The snowboarder who, along with a woman named Kristina, had set Jason up to test positive for banned substances.

Instead of channel surfing, Lauren raised the volume.

"Rusty Small became the United States's hope for snowboarding gold after leading contender Jason Corwin tested positive for drugs and was banned from competition. Small's status and even his ability to compete in Vancouver are now in doubt following his own positive drug test."

"What in the world?" Lauren leaned forward in her seat.

"The IOC is still investigating. However, there is one common element between Small and Corwin testing positive. Both men were involved with the same woman at the time their tests proved positive. Kristina Marino is currently missing and authorities are searching for her. More information as it becomes available."

Lauren checked her watch again, then shut off the television. She had to leave for the airport, but the story stayed with her. It was unlikely Rusty Small's problems would lead to Jason being cleared, but it did show Karma hard at work.

Impulse had her reaching for her cell to call Jason, but hard-earned lessons made her put the phone away. Focus forward, she reminded herself.

"Paris awaits," she said aloud.

Too bad Paris was the city of love, and she'd be visiting alone.

INTERNATIONAL FLIGHTS MEANT long wait times in the airport. Lauren remembered waiting with her parents for hours at a time while traveling abroad.

She and Beth would play word games to keep themselves busy. One of the few good memories she had of Beth.

Lauren had taken a few days to calm down before calling the prison to check on her sister. They had her in some form of psychiatric solitary confinement. For her protection and for the safety of others, they'd said. Lauren completely understood their rationale. She also hadn't been surprised when Beth's lawyer had informed her that Beth would be charged with additional crimes.

Although it pained Lauren to do it, she'd told the lawyer she had no more money to spend on her sister's case. If that meant Beth would be at the mercy of a court-appointed public defender, then so be it. Lauren hadn't washed her hands of her sister. They were still siblings and Lauren loved her—or maybe she loved the sister she remembered. Lauren wasn't sure about anything except the fact that Beth was criminally insane. All beyond the scope of Lauren's comprehension. Or her responsibility. She was only sorry it had taken her so long to accept the truth.

Annoyed with her train of thought—yet again—Lauren decided to break up the airport monotony and head to the sundry shop. She bought herself a bottle of water and some magazines for the long flight. Then, returning to her seat, she stuck her earbuds in her ears and began to page through the most recent issue of *Vogue*. But for the first time in memory she was unable to get lost in the world of fashion. Her thoughts kept drifting to recent events: the fire, her sister and, yes, even Jason.

Especially Jason.

Yet when someone tapped her on the shoulder, the unexpected touch nearly made her jump out of her seat.

She yanked on the wires, pulling the buds out of her ears, and looked up—into Jason's eyes. "What are you doing here?" she asked over her rapidly beating heart.

"I thought you invited me to Paris?" He sounded out of breath.

She frowned. "I recall you turning me down. Flat."

He treated her to a cocky smile that would have had her blind with anger had she not caught the uncertainty in his eyes. But just because he doubted his welcome didn't mean she'd let him off the hook easily.

She still didn't know why he was here. Or what he really wanted.

She wrapped the white headphone cord around her iPod and shoved it into her travel bag, taking her time before leaning back into the chair.

Jason eased himself into the seat beside her and reached for her hand. "I'm an idiot," he said at last.

Lauren folded her arms across her chest and glared at him. "You don't hear me arguing."

"And I didn't expect you to make this easy." He laughed, the sound brittle. "Look, I deserve your anger and suspicion and any other emotion you want to throw my way."

"Still not arguing." But her heart pounded in anticipation and her throat swelled with unexpected emotion as she waited for him to explain.

Instead, he first brushed away a tear she hadn't realized she'd shed.

"Before you arrived, I'd lost everything that ever mattered to me. I was working a job that passed time but wasn't fulfilling, and I was just going through the motions of living." He leaned closer. "Then you showed up, and suddenly there was everything I didn't know I was looking for. Life suddenly *mattered* again."

It was time to call him on his behavior. To hold him accountable. "So you pursued me. You manipulated the situation so you'd get my job, and then you went about making me feel things." She glanced down at their intertwined hands. "Things I didn't want to feel for you again."

"Guilty," he admitted.

She nodded. "Meanwhile, all I wanted was a fling while I was in town. I'd planned to leave without any regrets or emotional ties, but that wasn't enough for you, was it?" In the end he'd stolen her heart.

"How could it be enough?" he asked. "I wanted you. All of you. And I wanted you to give yourself to me freely." His deep eyes bored into hers.

"Yet when I finally did, you tossed it back in my face. Just like—"

"Just like your parents. Just like your sister. I made you feel like everything you offered wasn't enough." His voice was gruff as he admitted to understanding her heart and her soul.

In his eyes, she viewed the warmth and love she'd been searching for all her life. "Why are you here now? What changed? Other than the fact that you realize you're an idiot?" she asked, tears finally flowing. "Why did you push me away?"

He cupped her cheek in his hand. "Because I thought you deserved someone better. Someone who hadn't lost everything and who was happy with his life. Who could be your equal."

"So what changed your mind?" she asked, because if she didn't understand, she'd never trust him not to do a one-eighty again and abandon her.

"That's easy." A wry smile twisted his lips.

"You left me. And I discovered what it meant to really be alone. Then Mike and Derek asked me what getting back into snowboarding would mean if I'd lost you, and that's when I knew. Nothing has any meaning without you."

His voice cracked and Lauren leaned forward and kissed him, sealing her lips over his, savoring his taste and his warmth. His familiar scent wrapped around her, giving her comfort and arousing her at the same time. Suddenly life had color again.

She never wanted to let him go.

"Flight six thirty-nine to Paris, France, is ready to board." The announcement penetrated the cocoon they'd wrapped themselves in, but she still didn't want to release him.

Jason had dug out his passport, packed quickly, flown to New York and finally tracked Lauren down. He didn't want to break this long-awaited kiss, but he had no choice. "They're boarding." He unwrapped her arms from his neck, separating them with difficulty.

Lauren groaned. "Do you really think I'm getting on that flight without you?"

He reached into his back pocket and pulled out his ticket. "Why do you think I was so out of breath? I got to your apartment only to have your neighbor tell me you'd left an hour before. Luckily for me, you'd given her your flight information and she believed I wasn't a stalker. I had to hightail it to the airport, buy my ticket and make it to the gate in time."

"And I'm glad you did. But you still haven't told me what happens *after* Paris."

He drew a deep breath, still in shock himself by everything that had happened in the short time since she'd been gone. "Well, I'd put a call into some snowboard companies, asking if they'd be interested in having me test their boards. I saw it as a way to get back into the sport in some small way." Just the thought had given him a renewed sense of purpose.

"And?"

"When they finally called back, not only did they agree, but apparently my notoriety doesn't bother them anymore. Get this. They're currently bidding against one another to get me to endorse their product."

"That's fantastic!" she said, genuinely pleased for him.

"My former agent's on top of things while I'm out of the country. And my family is convinced they have you to thank."

"For God's sake, why?"

"They think you broke the curse when you gave them the diamonds."

"Come on." She raised an eyebrow, obviously not a believer.

"I'm serious! Look at the evidence, at least from their perspective. First Rusty gets nailed doing steroids…"

"I just saw the news on television. How was he dumb enough to get caught, knowing what happened to you?" she asked.

"Ready for this? I got a call from Kristina. She sweet-talked Rusty into getting back together just so she could set him up. She used the same tricks he'd put her up to for me. Then she called the IOC and tipped them off." He shook his head. "She's now off sunbathing on a secluded island waiting for the scandal to blow over."

"I'm stunned."

"Never underestimate a woman scorned."

"Exactly." Lauren gave him a pointed look.

"So back to why they think I ended the curse?" she prompted.

"Right. There are plenty of other reasons. For one thing, Uncle Edward proposed to Clara—"

"He what!" Lauren blinked. "You've got to be kidding."

Jason shook his head. "Then the sponsorship

opportunities came up—this after I'd been banned from boarding and dropped by every company known to sports."

Lauren took one look at his pleased expression and couldn't help but smile herself. "I guess the tides *are* turning."

"Final boarding, flight six thirty-nine to Paris, France," a voice said over the intercom.

Somehow they'd missed the row-by-row boarding announcements.

Jason stood. "So, are we going?"

She rose to her feet beside him. "*I'm* going. As for you…"

Uncertain of what to expect, Jason held his breath.

"You still haven't told me your post-Paris plan." She tapped her foot on the floor, glancing back and forth between Jason and the boarding gate.

He knew it was the time to lay it all on the line. "I was hoping we could take *our* share from the sale of the diamonds and use it as a down payment on a house," he said, speaking quickly. "Somewhere close enough to the city so you can commute to Galliano or whatever smart label snatches you up." As he spoke, he grabbed her bag along with his and started walking to the gate. "But also someplace where we can hop a flight or drive to the nearest ski lodge," he said as he handed his ticket to the agent.

"Four C," the woman said, scanning his paper and handing it back to him.

Lauren blinked in surprise, then slid her ticket across the counter.

"Four B," the attendant said. "Have a nice flight."

They started down the gateway and she turned to him. "How did you manage adjoining seats?"

He grinned. "I told you, ever since you handed over the diamonds, it's been one lucky break after another." And then he played his final hand.

Reaching into his pocket, he pulled out a velvet box. He bent down on one knee and opened the box to reveal an emerald-cut diamond ring. "Marry me," he said, rather than asked. "*That's* my post-Paris plan."

Lauren squealed and nodded, tears flowing. He placed the ring on her finger, grabbed her hand and together they made a mad dash for the plane.

ON TAKEOFF, Jason recalled Clara's tarot reading, back when he'd been skeptical of ever finding happiness again.

"Ace of Cups reversed," she'd said, telling him he had no hope of finding love. Informing him he feared being alone forever. She'd been right. She'd gone on to explain that he needed to stop hiding from his past. She'd been more right than she knew. He grasped Lauren's hand, knowing that he now had everything Clara had dangled in front of him—the white picket fence and the happily ever after. With the woman he'd always loved.

Talk about a lucky break, he thought, happier than he'd ever been.

## EPILOGUE

In the early twenty-first century, in the small village of Stewart, Massachusetts, 1.5 miles west of Salem, site of the now infamous Witch Trials, a brave, smart Perkins female broke the infamous Corwin Curse. And in case anyone dared to suggest otherwise, for good measure, she married the remaining young single Corwin man, uniting their families in blood and in love.

THE CURSE NOW LIFTED, even the older Corwin generation found love, including the starched, stuffy Thomas and the more cantankerous Hank. They married sisters, who happily moved into their joint home. Across town, Clara and Edward also married and lived happily, their home shared with Edward's descented skunk.

For the younger generation of Corwin men, babies abounded, beginning with a girl for Derek and Gabrielle, followed by another girl for Mike and Amber. Jason and Lauren became the proud parents of triplet boys, destined to carry on the Corwin name.

And so it was that the Corwins, who had once lost everything, invested the money from the diamonds, and prospered.

Broken curse?

Coincidence?

Or was luck blessing them at last?

\* \* \* \* \*

*The Corwin cousins have finally beaten the family curse and found their happily-ever-afters. But there are still a lot of men in this country that could use a push in the right direction.*
*Especially in a big place like Manhattan...*

*Who better than* New York Times *bestselling author Carly Phillips to give them the nudge they need?*
*Don't miss the start of The Bachelor Blogs Available in June 2010 wherever Harlequin books are sold.*
*Visit www.carlyphillips.com for titles when they become available.*

# REQUEST YOUR FREE BOOKS!

## 2 FREE NOVELS
## FROM THE ROMANCE/SUSPENSE
## COLLECTION PLUS 2 FREE GIFTS!

**YES!** Please send me 2 FREE novels from the Romance/Suspense Collection and my 2 FREE gifts (gifts are worth about $10). After receiving them, if I don't wish to receive any more books, I can return the shipping statement marked "cancel." If I don't cancel, I will receive 4 brand-new novels every month and be billed just $5.74 per book in the U.S. or $6.24 per book in Canada. That's a savings of at least 28% off the cover price. It's quite a bargain! Shipping and handling is just 50¢ per book.* I understand that accepting the 2 free books and gifts places me under no obligation to buy anything. I can always return a shipment and cancel at any time. Even if I never buy another book from the Reader Service, the two free books and gifts are mine to keep forever.

185 MDN EYNQ  385 MDN EYN2

Name _____ (PLEASE PRINT) _____

Address _____ Apt. # _____

City _____ State/Prov. _____ Zip/Postal Code _____

Signature (if under 18, a parent or guardian must sign)

### Mail to **The Reader Service:**
**IN U.S.A.:** P.O. Box 1867, Buffalo, NY 14240-1867
**IN CANADA:** P.O. Box 609, Fort Erie, Ontario L2A 5X3

Not valid to current subscribers of the Romance Collection,
the Suspense Collection or the Romance/Suspense Collection.

**Want to try two free books from another line?**
**Call 1-800-873-8635 or visit www.morefreebooks.com.**

\* Terms and prices subject to change without notice. Prices do not include applicable taxes. Sales tax applicable in N.Y. Canadian residents will be charged applicable provincial taxes and GST. Offer not valid in Quebec. This offer is limited to one order per household. All orders subject to approval. Credit or debit balances in a customer's account(s) may be offset by any other outstanding balance owed by or to the customer. Please allow 4 to 6 weeks for delivery. Offer available while quantities last.

**Your Privacy:** Harlequin is committed to protecting your privacy. Our Privacy Policy is available online at www.eHarlequin.com or upon request from the Reader Service. From time to time we make our lists of customers available to reputable third parties who may have a product or service of interest to you. If you would prefer we not share your name and address, please check here. ☐

BOB09

# HARLEQUIN® *Blaze*™

*It all started
with a few naughty books....*

As a member of the Red Tote Book Club,
Carol Snow has been studying works of
classic erotic literature…but Carol doesn't
believe in love…or marriage. It's going to take
another kind of classic—Charles Dickens's
*A Christmas Carol*—and a little otherworldly
persuasion to convince her to go after her
own sexily ever after.

### Cuddle up with

# Her Sexy Valentine

## by STEPHANIE BOND

*Available February 2010*

---

# red-hot reads

# carly phillips

| | | | |
|---|---|---|---|
| 77375 | LUCKY STREAK | ___ $7.99 U.S. | ___ $8.99 CAN. |
| 77331 | LUCKY CHARM | ___ $7.99 U.S. | ___ $7.99 CAN. |
| 77351 | SECRET FANTASY | ___ $7.99 U.S. | ___ $7.99 CAN. |
| 77326 | SEDUCE ME | ___ $7.99 U.S. | ___ $9.50 CAN. |
| 77239 | SEALED WITH A KISS | ___ $7.99 U.S. | ___ $9.50 CAN. |
| 77110 | SUMMER LOVIN' | ___ $7.99 U.S. | ___ $9.50 CAN. |

*(limited quantities available)*

| | |
|---|---|
| TOTAL AMOUNT | $ _____ |
| POSTAGE & HANDLING | $ _____ |
| ($1.00 FOR 1 BOOK, 50¢ for each additional) | |
| APPLICABLE TAXES* | $ _____ |
| TOTAL PAYABLE | $ _____ |

*(check or money order—please do not send cash)*

To order, complete this form and send it, along with a check or money order for the total above, payable to HQN Books, to: **In the U.S.:** 3010 Walden Avenue, P.O. Box 9077, Buffalo, NY 14269-9077; **In Canada:** P.O. Box 636, Fort Erie, Ontario, L2A 5X3.

Name: _____

Address: _____ City: _____

State/Prov.: _____ Zip/Postal Code: _____

Account Number (if applicable): _____

075 CSAS

*New York residents remit applicable sales taxes.
*Canadian residents remit applicable GST and provincial taxes.

# HQN™
We *are* romance™

**www.HQNBooks.com**